D1172728

MOSCOW REQUIEM

MOSCOW REQUIEM

John Simpson

St. Martin's Press
New York

For information, write: St. Martin's Press,
175 Fifth Avenue, New York, N.Y. 10010
Manufactured in the United States of America

Library of Congress Cataloging in Publication Data
Simpson, John.
Moscow requiem.

I. Title.
PR6069.I424M6 1982 823'.914 81-16716
ISBN 0-312-54902-4 AACR2

To Roy F. Simpson
1914–1980

Author's Note

Ten years of reporting the affairs of many different countries, and of talking to innumerable officials and political leaders and real people as well, have gone into the writing of this book. Each of the characters in it is based firmly on a real person, though I have been obliged to make changes in both behaviour and circumstance in order to fit the demands of the action, and to avoid the more obvious legal pitfalls. As a result, this is not a *roman à clef*; but it wouldn't be truthful to say, in the standard terms of the publisher's waiver, that any resemblance to actual persons, living or dead, is altogether coincidental.

J. S.

Hereby it is manifest, that during the time men live without a common power to keep them all in awe, they are in that condition which is called war; and such a war, as is of every man, against every man. For WAR consisteth not in battle only, or the act of fighting ... but in the known disposition thereto, during all the time there is no assurance to the contrary.

Thomas Hobbes, *Leviathan.*

Part One

July Days

CHAPTER 1

Unfortunately there are, among our population of 240 millions, certain morally unstable people – they come singly – who have swallowed the bait of bourgeois propaganda. They are not only wrong headed, but also disseminate deliberately false fabrications, and commit serious crimes. *Prosecutor V. E. Drel, trial of Pavel M. Litvinov and others, Moscow, 1968.*

Moscow: Monday 15 July

The Moscow Metro was Stalin's supreme gift to the city; a great deal more useful than the extraordinary near-Gothic office blocks and hotels which he built, or even than the poplar trees which he planted in their thousands and which, in June and July, fill the air with great clumps of floating pollen like thistle-down, to be churned up by the passing cars as if there were a light fall of snow.

P. D. Abramov walked through the poplar-down along the main road to the Metro station at Yougo-Zapadnaya, shifting his plastic hold-all with the old Moscow Olympics sign on it from hand to hand every twenty yards or so. He tried to carry it in the same hand from one lamp-post to the next, but usually he found it was too heavy for that. On his right as he walked stood peeling blocks of flats, twenty storeys high, each indistinguishable from the one he himself lived in, each exuding the same smell of tomcat and boiled cabbage, each served by a door that slammed in the wind and a lift that rattled interminably up and down. To his left was a copse of birch trees and a straggling row of wooden houses that had been built before the Revolution. They were even worse to live in than the flats, though there was more room in them. Between them and the road was a belt of waste ground, which the builders of the flats had used as a rubbish tip twenty years before and never cleared.

Behind Abramov as he walked came two other men: low-ranking KGB men in plain clothes, each wearing a hat and jacket in spite of the heat. They had followed Abramov before, and they were familiar with the courtyard of his flats from hours of sitting in unmarked Volgas waiting for him to come out. Abramov wasn't difficult to follow, with his shuffling walk and his habit of ducking his head from time to time as he went along. At twenty-three, he looked as though he had decided to become an old man.

He went down the steps of the Metro station and put his five kopeks in the slot at the barrier, pulling the Olympics bag after him. At the foot of the moving staircase that led to the trains he turned left. A train came crashing noisily into the station and the KGB men had to jump down the last few steps of the escalator, cursing their luck at being the ones who had to do the following, while their third colleague drove the Volga back to headquarters. In the carriage, they sat by the doors at the far end. Abramov felt an impulse to go over and tell them where he was going, so that everyone could relax. But like them he had to play the game according to its rules; and besides, there were good reasons why they shouldn't know where he was going today.

Most of the other passengers were reading, or staring in front of them. He noted – as he always did – that no one crossed their legs. Was it from self-effacement, the desire to take up as little room as possible? he pondered. The train rattled out of the tunnel at the Lenin Hills, which overlook the centre of Moscow and the Moscow River. Abramov gazed affectionately at the Moscow River, and wondered if he would ever see it again. If everything goes well, he thought with some irony, I never shall. But he was conscious of no great anxiety. He settled the bag on his knees, and the KGB men busied themselves, pretending not to watch.

Abramov had no plans for getting away from them. He knew from experience that you didn't need to make plans; you just had to act instinctively when the moment came. The sun, which had been shining on the dingy yellow paint on the carriage walls, was blotted out by the tunnel again. Sportivnaya, Fruzenskaya, Park of Culture, Kropotkinskaya: the muffled voice from the loudspeaker called out the name of each station, and they waited the regulation thirty seconds for the doors to close again. Abramov's mind stayed obediently blank. And yet, as they pulled out of the Lenin Library station, he knew that the moment was about to come. The grey-green train, filled now with lunch-time passengers, picked up speed. Abramov stayed seated, in spite of the pressure of the standing passengers. They would shelter him for a second from the KGB men.

As the train stopped at the absurdly pompous Marx Prospect station, Abramov, keeping his head down, ducked in between the passengers who were getting out, pulling his Olympics hold-all behind him through the crush. The KGB men had spotted what was happening, and were already standing up. Together they pushed out of the door beside them, on to the platform. But the intervening crowd was thick. Abramov moved with the crowd through one of the pairs of grey-veined marble pillars, which separated the platform from the station concourse. The hats of the KGB men, above the crowd, showed him that they were still seven or eight teeming yards behind. As Abramov reached the far side of the pillars he slipped aside and took shelter.

The crowd, with the two homburg hats desperately turning from side to side visible above it, moved relentlessly on towards the escalators. Abramov turned back round the pillars and hid himself in the corresponding recess on the other side. The digital clock at the end of the platform showed that the next train was due in one minute fifteen seconds. Abramov smiled. He picked up the hold-all, and on an impulse unzipped it a little way. Inside he could feel the packages of leaflets. Pushing them aside, he closed his hand experimentally round the butt of a 9 mm pistol, wrapped in cloth.

Resentful, alienated, desperate, P. D. Abramov was part of an historical process: the slow collapse of the Soviet empire. Like a small antibody in the vast, decaying corpus of Soviet power, he was making his way towards the heart of Moscow.

Moscow: Monday 15 July

A succession of antiquated lorries crawled past, before David Wortham could at last head out into the road that ran along the embankment of the Moscow River. He was impatient, and when Janacek's First Quartet blared out at him from the speakers at knee-level, he wrestled irritably with the volume control while edging his way through one line of traffic and into another. Momentarily, he glimpsed the Venetian building of the Embassy in his rear-view mirror. No one seemed to be trailing him; perhaps they never did. It was, he reflected, probably only the Russians who followed anyone around nowadays; it was too expensive in manpower, especially when you could simply attach a gadget to your suspect, or to his car. Every few days, Wortham went carefully through everything he owned, checking for signs that someone might have planted a device in the heel of one of his shoes, or the lining of his briefcase. The security people at the Embassy were delighted with him – which was another reason for thinking that they were not keeping him under surveillance. Once they had put in a formal complaint about his lack of interest in security, but nowadays he seemed to take it more seriously, almost, than they did themselves.

Wortham went out of his way down the boulevard in order to make a legal U-turn. That too was new for him; in the old days he had boasted of the number of traffic policemen he had slipped a ten-rouble note to. The car represented a greater security problem for him. It was regularly checked by the people at the Embassy, but that only took care of things that the Russians might have planted on it. When it came to checking for plants by the British themselves, Wortham was on his own. He had taken all the courses, and he knew where to look. His instinct told him that everything was all right, but he couldn't, finally, be sure.

He scarcely thought about the route he was taking. The car seemed almost to steer of its own accord, making the necessary turns without the need for conscious effort on his part. The day was just beginning to turn to a warm, golden afternoon, and it should almost have been enough to blot out the sense of gloom and betrayal he always felt when he made this journey. If there was a way out of the mess, he wasn't interested in it. As he headed for the Lenin Hills, the houses and the blocks of flats thinned out, and there was more open ground. He had always loved Moscow, in an exasperated, slightly patronizing way, and he loved it still; but not as much as he had in the days when he was not obliged to watch everything that he said or did. Now he was alone, cut off from the days of innocence, with nothing much except this journey, twice or three times a week, to comfort him.

The Janacek quartet was almost over by the time he

reached the open parade where Moscow University faced the panorama of the city. Even on a sunny day like this, it wasn't hard to find somewhere discreet to park. His licence-plate, with the distinguishing 'D-01' which marked him out as a British diplomat, had to be left far enough away for him not to be associated with it. Wortham deliberately dressed like a Russian nowadays, though it was easier in the summer than in the winter, when you needed good-quality clothes to keep you warm: clothes of a kind most Russians couldn't afford. His open-necked shirt and dark trousers were more or less acceptable at the Embassy, as long as he kept a tie and a jacket handy for the occasional formal meeting. There had been a few complaints about the way he dressed, but no one sensible at the Embassy took any notice. If they had, they might have seen that it was the best clue to Wortham's changed patterns of behaviour.

Moscow: Monday 15 July

At the head of Dzerzhinsky Square is a solid, yellowish, turn of the century building which still looks like what it once was: the head office of a Tsarist insurance company. Muscovites tend to avoid it, rather in the way westerners avoid walking under ladders. No matter how big the crowds in the square, the pavement on that side is quiet. For the pre-Revolutionary insurance office became the Lubyanka: the headquarters of a rather different kind of insurance – the security police of the Soviet state. The successive organs of state security were based there: Cheka, GPU, OGPU, NKVD, NKGB, MGB and finally, the most successful, the largest and the costliest of all the permutations, the *Komitet Gosudarstvennoy Bezopasnosti*. Ever since the Seventies, the real work of the KGB had been done from a sprawling modern building on the edge of central Moscow, near the ring-road;

but the Lubyanka remained the administrative centre, the KGB's main prison, and the office of the KGB Chairman and the hierarchy. The prison occupied most of the newer half of the building, and prisoners who were allowed exercise were taken for half an hour a day on to the huge flat roof, hidden from the world by a fifteen foot wall. The rest spent their lives below ground, in cells underneath the Lubyanka and under the roadway at the back of the building. The camber of the road seemed steeper there than elsewhere.

Abramov was not superstitious about walking alongside the Lubyanka. As he made his way up the slight hill, with the building beside him, he heard a clock strike twelve. He walked on, across the street at the back of the Lubyanka, without looking at it, and without thinking of the cells that lay beneath his feet. He was making for the shelter of a doorway, out of sight of the militiamen who guarded the KGB headquarters.

He slumped down on the doorstep of a disused office block, and reached into the hold-all. A few sandwiches and a thermos flask gave him protective colouring, though he was very far from being hungry. He set out the sandwiches, absent-mindedly. Everything had been carefully planned and timed. On Tuesdays and Thursdays, after the Politburo had met, the Chairman of the KGB drove back to the Lubyanka for lunch. The time varied, but it was never before 12.15 and never after 12.55.

Abramov had not carried out the reconnaissance himself, leaving that to three comrades, fellow-members of the group they called Volya, in imitation of the nineteenth-century terrorist group, *Narodnaya Volya*, or People's Will. Abramov was a Jew, and a known dissident; that, too, was protective colouring of a kind, and would provide him with a motive when he was captured. The others in the Volya group were completely unknown to the authorities. So far the group's activities had been few but spectacular. They had robbed a post-office and the pay-roll for a Moscow factory; and with the proceeds they had obtained the explosives for an unsuccessful bomb attack on the headquarters of *Gosteleradio*, the State broadcasting authority. And they had bought the gun which Abramov now carried.

It was already loaded. Abramov unwrapped it inside the bag, and gripped it. He had practised with it, briefly, in some birchwoods not far from his home, though that had been dangerous. He felt a vague nervousness now, but also a sense of freedom. He was about to cast off all constraints, and be himself after years of dissembling. Anyone who looked at him would have seen only a shabbily-dressed young Jew hunched over his sandwiches, but Abramov had, for the first time in his life, a feeling of power and significance. It was the gun that did it; that, and the knowledge that what he was about to do would soon be known to everybody in the world. His name would be broadcast on the foreign radio stations, and on Soviet television itself. Already he was half an outlaw – merely possessing the gun made him that – and it was impossible to turn back. The thought was almost comforting.

He heard the whining of the first police siren from the direction of Red Square at 12.24. He packed his sandwiches away, but the siren headed off in another direction, and he settled down again. The second siren came three minutes later, and got louder and louder. He stood up. From his doorway he could see down the hill into Dzerzhinsky Square, and from there past the shops in the direction of the Kremlin and Red Square. The Chairman of the KGB was the only member of the Politburo who drove in this direction, and a group of three vehicles, two of them police cars, were coming at speed up the middle of the road towards Dzerzhinsky Square. Between the police cars was a big ungainly Zil limousine, black, long and curiously box-like. Abramov tried not to hurry as he moved out of his doorway. His friends had told him that he had enough time, walking at a reasonable pace, to be in position before the official Zil reached the corner. He sauntered down the side-street, watching the Zil as it came fast through Dzerzhinsky Square, its way cleared by the peremptory whistles of the police on traffic duty. He turned the corner. As he walked down the wide, quiet road, over the cells where he himself might well find himself soon, his pace quickened.

There were only two militiamen on duty there and they were more worried about the approaching police sirens than about security. Neither of them paid any attention to Abramov. Now he was back on the same side of the road as the Lubyanka itself, and the noise of the sirens was getting louder. He reached the high bronze gates that led to the Lubyanka garage at about the moment the three cars began to turn the corner. Abramov halted obediently at the impatient signal of the militiamen. As the sirens were switched off and the Zil slowed down for the turn into the garage gates, Abramov reached into the bag and curled his hand round the familiar cool handle of the pistol. The gates took a little time to open.

For the first time, Abramov allowed himself to look at the Zil, and for a fraction of a second he was horrified to see that the curtains were closed at the back of the car; his friends had told him that the KGB Chairman liked them open. But it was too late now. Abramov thrust his hand inside the bag and gripped the pistol without taking it out, so that the bag was held out in front of him. Aiming along the line of the back seat of the Zil, only inches away, he pumped four shots through the black metal of the door. The pistol, muffled by the bag, made remarkably little noise. For an instant neither the policemen nor the Zil's driver realized what was happening. Then, suddenly, there was shouting, and a wild revving of the engine, and the Zil jerked its way at speed through the now open doors to the underground garage, the screaming tyres leaving puffs of smoke in the air behind them.

Abramov stood there, holding the bag out still with the gun inside it. He had been as shocked, in a way, as everybody else. He might have escaped if his reactions had been quick enough. Even now, the militiamen did not seem to have understood what had gone on. But the KGB guards were faster. All three, in their grey and green uniforms, threw themselves through the gates and knocked Abramov to the ground. As he lay there, quite still, his hand inside the plastic bag, they got slowly to their feet and began kicking at his head and sides, while the militiamen watched dumbly. Under the sharp pain of the kicks, Abramov let go of the gun and curled both his arms over his head, until one of the KGB men jerked him to his feet and, crooking an arm round his neck, forced him through the bronze gates of the Lubyanka building.

The bag lay on the ground. The militiamen looked at it, but it was none of their business to interfere. Finally one of the KGB men bent down to look inside. He swore, and called his colleague over to look; but even they seemed reluctant to touch it.

Moscow: Monday 15 July

Anyuta was already there. Wortham saw her colourless fair hair fly up in a sudden puff of wind, to be controlled impatiently by a well-manicured hand. Even at twenty yards' range, he could make out the shape of the red-lacquered fingernails she was so proud of. She was, at thirty, an eccentric, dressing with a curious mixture of style and abandon that somehow annoyed Wortham even when he found it most attractive. She was vain and difficult and noisy; and yet capable of great depths of tenderness and insight.

By now she had seen him. He was always a little afraid

that one day she would be mad enough to shout out to him, or run and kiss him, but so far in that one way at least she had always been sensible. She sat there, watching his thin, slightly hunched figure, older than her by seven years, walking towards her, and moved a little along the bench, invitingly. Sometimes it seemed to him that she couldn't really be at all interested in him, that it must simply be what everyone at the Embassy would say the instant they found out about the relationship – that Wortham was being set up. Perhaps he was; but he had never yet found the strength to resist.

It was one of her strongest and most alarming idiosyncrasies to insist on speaking to him in English; a language which she spoke far less well than he spoke Russian. She had learned her English from a British teacher, and used various mannerisms which she believed to be typically English.

'Hello, my dear David,' she said as he settled down on the bench; and raised an eyebrow in self-parody. Wortham looked at her. He thought she probably had the most perfect features of any woman he had ever known: Slavic features, with high cheekbones and heavy-lidded eyes that were sometimes pale blue and sometimes darker. She recognized the look of melting happiness in his face, and chose to allow it to irritate her. She ran her fingers through her light hair again, and turned her head slightly. Wortham saw the signs, and switched deliberately to the humorous and sceptical tones he knew she preferred in him.

'How can people look like you, when all you eat is potatoes?' he teased.

'You westerners are always wrong to us,' responded Anyuta. 'You know we eat meat once each week nowadays, and one day we will get deodorant from the west as well.'

'Maybe,' said Wortham, 'but all you'll do with it is flavour the bortsch.' His reply was absent-minded; he was already wondering about a couple walking towards them, arm-in-arm. Anyuta was in high spirits, and chose to carry on the joke. Her father was a senior official in the Central Committee of the CPSU; they lived extremely well. It was, however, a dangerous liaison for her as well as for Wortham; unless, that is, she had been deliberately ordered to have an affair with him. Wortham often thought it likely; but there was something in the way that she always stopped short of giving him any information about her father or his job that made him unable to make his mind up finally.

'Why don't we move from here? I feel about as inconspicuous as Stalin at a bar-mitzvah.' That one he had to explain to her; she enjoyed it, creasing her face into a grimace of pain, and laughing noisily. Now the approaching couple were well and truly interested. 'Look,' he said, half angrily, 'we're going to be pulling a crowd soon. Why don't we just walk a little way down the slope?'

'That way you can get me out of view and rape me.'

'Me? I haven't laid a finger on you since I got here.'

'Only because you prefer your wife.'

It was a shrewd blow, and it stopped the bantering. They walked off towards the ski-slope in the direction of the stadia erected for the 1980 Olympic Games. Despite himself, Wortham thought of his wife. Irritable, thin, English, as irrational in her way as Anyuta, she found Moscow a difficult place to bring up young children, and stayed most of the time in the flat, reading. They rowed incessantly, even in public.

There was something about being away from other people's eyes that brought out the tenderness in Anyuta. Perhaps, too, she sensed how much the mention of his wife affected him. She took his arm, digging her fingers into it affectionately, and they wandered aimlessly along the steep track which the skiers took in winter. Scarcely anyone was walking on the grassy slope now. They talked about the course she was teaching at Moscow University, and about the trouble he'd had with his new secretary, and argued over whether 'different' took the preposition 'from' or 'to'. It was typical of Anyuta, thought Wortham, to lay down the law about other people's languages. As they talked of the next night they would spend together, and where it would be, Wortham felt that neither of the choices – a tiny flat belonging to one of Anyuta's colleagues, who was going away for a week, or a room in the not particularly strict Hotel Cosmos – offered any security whatever. But he also knew that, unless he agreed, he would lose her.

Anyuta was an appalling chance-taker, a free spirit, except when it came to talking about her father and what he did. Wortham for his part never spoke of anything at the Embassy, except the most banal details. It was an agreement which suited them both. He admired her carelessness, and often sought unsuccessfully to imitate it.

In joking, and in occasional more passionate moments, the hour they had together wore away. Anyuta sang *Waltzing Matilda* in Russian, while Wortham sat on the ground and laughed. Slowly, unwillingly, they worked their way up the steep slope to the terrace. Anyuta broke away from him at the top, and walked back quickly in the direction of the university buildings. Twenty yards from him, knowing that he must still be watching, she turned and waved both her arms in an arc at him, and blew him an exaggerated kiss. He felt sadder and more uncertain than ever as he walked back alone.

Chapter 2

Happy indeed is the politician, happy is the statesman who can always say what he really thinks, do what he really thinks necessary, and work for what he really believes in. *L. I. Brezhnev, 'Little Land'.*

Moscow: Monday 15 July

The Chairman of the KGB was a dead man before the door of his car was prised open. One shot, perhaps the first, had smashed his thigh bone. Then, as he had toppled over on the seat, his head towards the side Abramov was shooting from, another had struck the back of his skull. They were still deciding what to do about the body when the sound of sirens started up again in the distance. The other Politburo members, alerted by radio-telephone to what had happened, were hurrying back for an emergency meeting in the Kremlin.

In a fourth floor office in the Lubyanka, a flustered KGB colonel in uniform was already starting to interrogate Abramov. Had there been anyone with him? What were his motives? How had he got the gun? During the interrogation other senior officers came into the room including, eventually, a lieutenant-general. No one hit Abramov, or even threatened him particularly. They wanted any information that would give them an immediate lead, and harsher methods would come later. But Abramov would say nothing. He even refused to talk about the pamphlets that had been in the hold-all with the gun: pamphlets which spoke about Stalinism and Soviet imperialism, and seemed at a first glance to share some of the language of Trotskyist opposition groups. Twice there were calls from the First Deputy Chairman of the KGB, who was by this time in the Kremlin; but each time the colonel was forced to report that nothing had emerged of any value.

The voice at the other end of the telephone line was angry as well as nervous. The hastily summoned Politburo meeting, with everyone but the dead KGB chairman in precisely the places they had occupied less than an hour before, added a sense of unreality to the shock each of them was experiencing. The first fear – that the murder was part of a co-ordinated campaign – now seemed less likely. The First Deputy Chairman had little enough to report from his telephone contacts with the Lubyanka building, but he felt able to go as far as that, at least. The shooting had been an isolated act, carried out by one man who had made no attempt to escape. And, drawing more on his imagination than on the information the KGB colonel in the Lubyanka had given him, he told the meeting that the attacker seemed to be mentally deranged. The second call to the Lubyanka, half an hour later, revealed the existence of the leaflets which Abramov had been carrying; the colonel, flurried and nervous, had forgotten to mention them before.

The dead Chairman would be a serious loss; that realization was only now sinking in for the fourteen men around the oval table in the eighteenth-century gold and white salon where the Politburo held its meetings. In particular, his death would be a loss to the Party Secretary. As he sat at the head of the table, the Party Secretary's forebodings were considerable. All leaders of the Soviet

Union since Stalin had had to rule as the first among equals, free agents only inasmuch as they retained the support of their most powerful colleagues. The Chairman of the KGB was one of them, and the most feared. In recent months his support had been crucial in blunting the strong opposition of the Defence Minister and the Party bosses of the Ukraine and Byelorussia. The incisive intellect of the KGB Chairman had stamped itself on the Politburo, and he had played a major role in some of the Soviet Union's most recent strategic successes. He had been the most civilized member of the senior hierarchy, invariably well dressed, with a noted taste for music and painting. Canvases by well-known western artists hung in his flat in the Kutusovsky Prospect in Moscow. At Ilyinskoye, not far from Moscow, where most of the Party leaders had their *dachas*, his was distinguished by the number of Russian and western antiques it contained. His English had been nearly fluent, his French good. The man who had once been a movie projectionist in the provincial town of Rybinsk had risen to dominate the government of the strongest power in the world.

The First Deputy Chairman of the KGB left the room, to stay on call and report back if the situation changed in any way. There remained the vital question of how, and when, to announce the news of the assassination. The death of so senior a figure would, as everybody round the table knew, have a profound effect on the balance of power within the Politburo, and on the Soviet Union's relationship with the outside world – powerful arguments for delaying the announcement of the Chairman's death for as long as possible.

But the counter-arguments for making the news known quickly were strong as well. The body was not being taken to a hospital or a morgue for the time being, but it was always possible that some passer-by had seen what had happened. The silence of the militiamen and the KGB men who had been there could be guaranteed for a time; but there was no chance of preventing the rumour from spreading if there had been other witnesses. Rumour, in a closed society, is a profound force. And the Politburo members knew that, if once the rumour leaked out, the report would be in the hands of foreign journalists by the evening. The Party Secretary spoke briefly of his fear that the news of the assassination would be twisted and used as anti-Soviet propaganda by the western news media. There was a murmur of approval around the table, as he finished, 'Might it not then be preferable for us to make the announcement now, in our own way, and so ensure that our people hear it first from us, without distortion?'

There was silence round the table, as everyone waited for the Minister of Defence, the Party Secretary's main opponent, to give his opinion. He looked around at the other faces, savouring the silence as the evidence of his status among them. His craggy face, with its heavy, downward-brushed eyebrows, turned finally to the Party Secretary.

'Surely we shouldn't always have to be afraid of what the enemies of our country and our entire system say in their propaganda? We aren't as vulnerable as all that, are we, Comrade Party Secretary? Our dead comrade, the Chairman of the Committee of State Security, was an honoured and much-loved figure among our people. His death will cause great suffering and shock. Should we not, therefore, prepare the people more gently for the news? I suggest, and naturally it is only a suggestion, that we should announce simply that the comrade Chairman has entered hospital for an operation. It isn't necessary for people to know about this dreadful crime. It's the kind of thing which only disturbs them. If you want my opinion, we should announce later on that the Chairman has passed away during the operation.'

He looked challengingly at the others. Not everyone met his gaze. In a Politburo divided along the lines of personality as well as principle, the slightest issue could become a battle-ground between the contending parties. In this case the issue of the announcement began to take on the colours of a faction fight. The Party Secretary's great strength in the past had been that the others were afraid of his supporter, the Chairman of the KGB. But now that support had gone, and the fight would immediately begin to appoint a new KGB head. It was a fight which the Party Secretary had to win if he were to keep his authority. The question of how the murder was to be treated had become a preliminary skirmish in the much greater battle for control of the Politburo.

It was the turn of the Party Secretary to scan the faces of his colleagues. Votes were taken at Politburo meetings only on very rare occasions. Otherwise, it was a matter of sounding out opinions, of allowing a consensus to emerge; those who didn't accept it would have to bow to the decision of the majority. Forecasting the decision was a delicate matter, requiring considerable insight and experience. The Party Secretary had both; and, as he listened to the two or three remaining speakers, and watched the eyes of the others as they met his gaze or looked down at the table, he knew that the vote had gone against him. It was not by any means the first time; but it had almost never mattered before. This time it mattered very much indeed. Convention demanded, however, that he should sum up the result of the debate with apparent impartiality.

'I think, then, that we are agreed: it would be better if we did not announce the news of this tragedy immediately, except to say that the comrade Chairman of the Committee for State Security has had to enter hospital for an operation.'

There was a polite murmur of approval, and several men joined in even though they had in fact supported the Party Secretary. His own head-count had indicated a majority of one for the other side. Not an insuperable majority, certainly, but a difficult one to overturn in a short time. There was nothing else to be decided. Everybody stood up with a feeling of some relief, even those who had lost. The Minister of Defence smiled and became suddenly noisy and hearty, and the First Deputy Chairman of the KGB was called in to be told of the decision. Glancing round the table, he briefly jotted down the agreed announcement and left to telephone it through to the Chairman of *Gosteleradio*. He could guess perfectly well what it all meant.

Moscow: Monday 15 July

At nine o'clock that evening, David Wortham was sitting at the far end of the dining-table, opposite his wife, with six guests ranged on either side of the table. The Worthams' cook and housekeeper, appointed by a Soviet government agency, was famous for her *blinis*. The *solyanka* soup had been finished and the dishes cleared away, and Valya was just bringing the *blinis* in, when the phone rang in the hall.

Janet Wortham had already shown signs of irritability during the evening; now she stood up angrily, and as she walked out she called over her shoulder, 'It's more than likely to be one of your wretched people from the Embassy, David. I thought you might have told them not to call you tonight, at least.'

Wortham laughed it off; everyone at the table was a friend, and most of them had long guessed at the state of the Worthams' marriage. Half a minute later, Janet Wortham came back.

'It's for you,' she said, looking away from Wortham and across at the far wall instead. 'It's a girl, a Russian girl. She speaks English. Do you have some kind of Russian mistress, David?' Someone laughed politely.

Wortham walked slowly over to the door, saying with some deliberation, 'Of course, but which of them can it be?' There was more polite laughter, but he was both annoyed and rather frightened.

It could only be Anyuta. She had once taken one of the cards from his wallet and, when she refused to give it back, he had made her promise never to ring him either at home or at the office. He cursed her insane carelessness, and tried to work out what he would say. He shut the hall door and stood by the table, in the light from an old-fashioned converted street sign that he had rescued from a demolition gang. When he lifted the receiver, he could hear noises on the line that showed the call was coming from a public call-box. Determinedly, he spoke in Russian, which Janet had never bothered to learn.

'Who's that?

'You know who this is.' Anyuta's voice was strained, almost frightened, but she still replied in English.

'I'm sorry,' he said, 'but I have no idea who you are or what you want.'

Anyuta paused at the other end of the crackling line, then said, 'You're probably right. But I must see you.'

'How can I possibly see anyone at this time of the evening? Besides, I have people here to dinner.'

'Listen, it's a matter of life,' said Anyuta, her English becoming more fractured. 'Come to meet me in the place you know. Please do not stay away. Please.' There was something in her voice that Wortham couldn't resist: loneliness, as well as urgency. But he was still uncertain.

'Do you mean I must get in my car and ...'

'No, David, the other place.' She hung up.

Wortham was appalled. He worked on the assumption that his telephone was tapped, and that even if they hadn't known about her from the start, the authorities would know now that he had a Russian mistress, who could be found and interrogated and perhaps used against him. The old relationship between them was unsatisfactory enough; now, he might never see her again, for fear of being followed and discovered, and either blackmailed by the KGB or forced to leave Moscow by the Embassy. He stood at the hall table, and punched the wall once, angrily, barking the skin from his knuckles. Sucking the blood that was already starting to stand out on his hand, he knew that he would have to go – that no amount of self-interest or common sense could keep him away from an appeal like that. If it was the last time he would see her, he still had to see her. He forced a smile, and walked back into the dining-room. The faces turned, expectantly.

'Well, who was she?' asked Janet.

'I've no idea,' Wortham said. 'All I know is she says she has something of great importance to tell to the British. How she could have got our number here I just don't know.'

The ready lie seemed to soften Janet a little. 'I'm sorry if you think you've got to go out,' she said. 'Try not to be too long.'

One of the dinner guests, a journalist for the Associated Press, asked Wortham if he wanted someone to go with.

'No thanks,' he said. 'It's probably just some dissident who wants to get out.'

He knew precisely where Anyuta would be. The only other place he had ever met her, apart from the Lenin Hills, was at a cinema about ten minutes' walk from the block of flats where he lived. She was waiting near the end of the queue. No one paid any attention to that kind of meeting, and Wortham was still dressed as he had been at lunch-time. In the deepening dusk, with crowds of other people on the streets, he was completely inconspicuous. The only thing that drew attention to them was Anyuta's beauty, and the ardent, clinging way she kissed him. They didn't speak, and she put her arm through his and guided him purposefully to the darkened gardens which ran down the centre of the avenue. Since the film was about to start, most of the benches in the garden were free. They sat down as far away as possible from a few other couples, who looked as though they were there for the evening, escaping from the constraints of home.

'What the hell were you doing, ringing me up like that? Don't you know what damage a call like that could do?' Anyuta hung her head, in a way that melted him in a moment. 'I'm sorry,' he added, 'but you must have realized.'

'Oh, David,' she said, 'please forgive me, but it is very important. Something terrible has happened today, and my father wishes the people in the West to know about it. He says it is essential for the peace of the world.'

'You mean, he knows about the relationship between us?' Wortham was horrified, for the second time that night.

'No, no, he thinks I have a connexion with a British journalist, a man from Reuters news agency whom I met at a party once. But I thought that if it was important I should tell you, and not a journalist.'

Wortham was still angry, but he found that even being with her under these circumstances was something to be glad of.

'Listen, Anyuta, I'm not really sure what's going on, but one thing I do know is that no one is going to believe me in the office if I go back there and say a girl sat down beside me on a bench and told me something vital for world peace. If I didn't get thrown out for playing around with Russian women, they'd throw me out for naïvety beyond the call of duty.'

There was no answering smile. Anyuta sat beside him, the street-lamps marking out the contours of her nose and mouth. Her eyes stayed in shadow. 'My father says he'll speak to you.'

'Look, that's even more stupid than your telling me. If you think I'm going to telephone some anonymous number ...'

Anyuta interrupted him by pointing with her foot to a bench on the other side of the gardens, where a man was reading a copy of *Pravda* by the light of a street-lamp. His face was hidden by the paper. 'That is he,' she said.

'But he'll know I'm not the man from Reuters.'

'No, he won't look at you; he will stay behind his journal.'

'Newspaper,' Wortham said, automatically.

'Behind his newspaper. We must walk up and down,' she continued, 'and then sit next to him. So we have arranged.'

Wortham tried to work the whole thing out in his mind, as they walked up and down the gardens in silence. He felt more and more certain that he was being trapped; and yet Anyuta seemed sincere, even loving. He decided that it could only end in disaster, but that if that were the case, then he must play his part with as much dignity as he could muster.

They reached the bench, and Anyuta pulled him down beside her, so that he was sitting next to the man behind the copy of *Pravda*. Anyuta said, 'Tell him.' Then she moved away, to the far end of the bench.

From behind the shielding newspaper, the man's low voice began to recount the details of the morning's assassination, though he seemed to know nothing about the identity or motives of the murderer. Wortham listened carefully, making a strong effort to commit each fresh detail to memory. It was, he felt with some excitement, very good information indeed – if it were true. Finally the voice came to an end. A couple strolled down the path, past the bench where they were sitting, and Wortham waited until they were well out of earshot before he asked, 'But why are you telling me all this?'

There was no answer for some moments, and Wortham thought his question had been too low to be heard. He was starting to ask it again, when the man's voice cut across his own.

'I cannot tell you that,' he said, softly. 'But it is important to the future of this country, that the people of the West should know about it.'

Wortham thought about this for a little, remembering that he was supposed to be a journalist. 'Forgive me,' he said, 'but I must know who you are. My office in London won't publish this information unless I can satisfy them that I know who it comes from, and that I am sure it is reliable.'

He felt Anyuta turn suddenly towards them, and the man moved his newspaper slightly in order to glance at her. The thin sheet fell forward with the movement, and revealed the profile of a man of about Wortham's own age.

'Damn you,' Wortham hissed to Anyuta and began to get to his feet. 'This isn't your father – I've been set up.'

He looked around for the best way to escape. Anyuta reached across and put her hand on his arm, to pull him down again. The man laid the newspaper on his lap, and took something out of his inside pocket, which he passed over to Wortham. Wortham's hand closed over an oblong piece of plastic, with a thick matt magnetic stripe along the back of it. He turned it over and looked at it in the yellow light of the street lamp. It was an identity card. 'Belov Konstantin Stepanovich,' it read; and underneath, 'Chief Assistant (Economics) to the First Secretary of the Communist Party of the Union of Soviet Socialist Republics.' This was one of the closest aides of the Soviet leader. Wortham looked across at Anyuta. The lamplight fell full on her face, distorting the colours of it, and bleaching them to the blandness of a lovely mask. But there was pity in her voice as she put her hand on his.

'He is my husband,' she said.

Forty-five minutes later, the British Ambassador had authorized the telegram Wortham had written for the Foreign Office in London, and had sent a short note of his own indicating that the Embassy in Moscow had no objection to the news being made public. Wortham had made no mention of Anyuta's part in the affair, nor of his relationship with her – though as he hurried back to the flat, and to the dinner guests who were waiting for him, he could think of nothing else.

Moscow: Tuesday 16 July

A few minutes before ten in the morning, the black Zils began to converge on Red Square for the third Politburo meeting in two days. With redoubled police escorts, and detectives riding in each car, they swept across the grey cobbles of the square, their expensive tyres swishing in the rain. They swung round in front of the old place of execution in front of St. Basil's Cathedral and made the wide turn into the Spasskiy Gate of the Kremlin. The bells in the Spasskiy Tower performed their ungainly tumble down the scale, the clock struck the hour and the soldiers changed guard stiffly at Lenin's Tomb. The tourists from the provinces who had come to watch them scattered before the speeding Zils.

A few minutes later, the Politburo members were in their seats in the gold and white salon. Each one of them felt a sense of fear and of suppressed excitement. Each had political sensitivities which had been sharpened by years of successful infighting, and the signs that a crisis had been reached were plain enough, from the sensation created around the world by the leakage of the previous day's murder.

The Party Secretary nevertheless retained his habitually cool manner as he began the meeting with the usual preliminaries: a short account of what had been decided at the previous meeting – though he glossed over the circumstances of his defeat on the question of announcing the Chairman's death – and a brief reference to a series of regional appointments which would need approval. The meeting droned on for another twenty minutes, reviewing the situation in the steel industry and touching on the renewed unrest in Poland. The only time he succeeded in turning his colleagues' minds from the approaching clash was when he mentioned the difficult subject of the strikes in East Germany. That took a further fifteen minutes' discussion, before it was agreed to put the matter to a smaller Politburo committee for study. But no one expected that the composition of the committee would remain unchanged by the time the session finished.

The Party Secretary could string out the proceedings no longer. He began the closing section of the meeting, calling on each member of the Politburo in turn for any comments, or any matter he wished to raise – beginning as always with the man on his left, and moving clockwise round the table. Normally, a number of them would have brought up some item which affected their departments. This time, no one had anything to raise. As the Party Secretary went round the table, most didn't even look at him.

The Minister of Defence sat, by tradition, one seat away from the Party Secretary, separated from him by the Premier. No one, not even the note-takers, looked at the Minister of Defence when the Party Secretary called his name. There was a short silence, and the Minister almost seemed for a second or two not to know how to begin. Much too powerful to be dismissed, he had become the nucleus of opposition to everything the Party Secretary had done; but so far the Party Secretary had always been able to outmanoeuvre him. The Defence Minister had been waiting for a moment such as this for a long time.

'Yes, Comrade Party Secretary, I have a point to raise. A very serious point. It has been brought to my attention that a senior figure within the Party apparatus was the source of the anti-Soviet propaganda which has been pouring out at us from the West since last night. The evidence relating to his guilt appears to be conclusive.' Nobody said anything. The Defence Minister reached down to his expensive leather brief-case and pulled out a manila envelope. Inside were several blown-up photographs.

'This man – his name and details are printed at the bottom of the picture – is a First Secretary at the British Embassy in Moscow. Here is his accreditation photograph. He is the source of the defamation about our late comrade, the Chairman of the KGB. His report was sent to London at 10.15 yesterday night. An hour before that, he attended a clandestine meeting with the senior official I have mentioned, in the gardens close to the Sadovo Ring Road.'

He paused, and the other men around the table shifted in their seats. The Party Secretary, however, was looking straight ahead of him at the opposite wall. He gave no indication of what he might be thinking.

'Fortunately,' the Defence Minister's voice began again, in the precise and cutting accent of Leningrad, 'the security people in my ministry were sufficiently alert to follow the diplomat. They took these photographs.'

The Defence Minister handed round several copies. They had been taken from behind, and the graininess indicated that the photographer must have been some way away, perhaps inside a car. They showed Wortham in profile, leaning across the park bench and talking to the Kremlin official, whose profile could also be seen, outlined against one side of the newspaper he was holding in front of him. Another picture showed Wortham looking down at the identity card the official must just have handed to him.

'We have accurate recordings of their conversation, which I have heard, and will play for you at a more convenient time. Meanwhile, here is a photograph of the Soviet official in question. Some of you may recognize him.'

The Politburo members craned across to look; this time there was only one copy.

'How can you be so sure that these men are one and the same?' The Party Secretary had forced himself to pay attention to what was going on, and his voice sounded dry and anxious, though he seemed otherwise unmoved. 'The pictures of the man in the gardens don't seem particularly like the picture you have here.' He gestured at the full face of Belov, his economics adviser, whose photograph lay in front of him.

The Defence Minister smiled, not an unpleasant smile. 'I really don't think there is any doubt about it,' he said, in a voice which could have been friendly. He was in many ways a crude and unattractive man, but now that his point was almost won, he didn't gloat. His square, heavily-lined face, topped by a short brush of iron-coloured hair, bore a look which seemed something like regret. 'The official in question is waiting with some of the men from my department in the room outside. He can tell you himself what he did.'

He walked slowly over to the double doors, padded with green leather, and pulled them open. No one at the table moved or said a word, and only a few of them looked towards the doors. The Party Secretary scarcely glanced at Belov when he came in. Instead he looked, as before, at the wall on the far side of the room, where an oil painting of Lenin was hanging. It was an informal sort of picture, which showed Lenin standing in a relaxed way, with an ironic smile on his lips and a copy of *Pravda* sticking out of his jacket pocket. The Party Secretary had always liked the painting, and when he came to power he had asked for it to replace the much more formal and heroic picture of Lenin addressing a vast crowd in Petrograd shortly before the October Revolution.

Belov had started to answer questions about what he had told Wortham, claiming that his instructions had come from the Party Secretary himself. Scarcely listening to the ready flow of lies, the Party Secretary kept his eyes on Lenin's smile, and his mind wandered to the possibilities ahead of him. No shooting, certainly; that kind of thing had gone out when Stalin died. Perhaps a quiet *dacha* somewhere, in an area closed to foreigners. It would be slow and boring, and it might be hard to get books. It would mean being with his frumpish, corrupt-minded wife all the time. But, he thought with a flash of amusement, if that were the full extent of his punishment, he could face it. The majority of his fellow-citizens were punished that way, each day of their lives. It wasn't likely he'd be gaoled, he thought; the effect of such a thing on public morale made it impossible. It was all simply a device, after all; just such a device as he himself would have used against the Defence Minister, if he had had the opportunity. He listened for a moment to Belov's grovelling – how he had tried to refuse what the Party Secretary had ordered him to do, how he had been assured it was in the interests of the Soviet state. In distaste, the Party Secretary turned his attention back to Lenin.

Belov must have been planted on his staff, he thought, working all along for the Defence Minister; just as he, the Party Secretary, had himself planted or bought officials on the staff of other Politburo members. He should blame himself, he supposed, for not having detected Belov; but all that was over now. The Party Secretary trusted he had never behaved as badly as Belov and the Defence Minister. And then he remembered the moment in 1968 when Alexander Dubcek had been flown to Moscow after the Russian tanks had gone in. He had been partly responsible for the harshness of the Czechoslovak leader's treatment and, when Dubcek was hauled in front of them, it was he who had started shouting at him. Now, he regretted that moment very much indeed. He imagined himself standing there, shivering and white faced, just as Dubcek had stood there in that same room, with many of the same people round the table. Now, he recognized more than a little of Dubcek in himself. Perhaps Dubcek, too, had felt relieved when it was all over – the punishment, after all, could not have been as hard to bear as the tension of never knowing when it might come.

A hand fell on his shoulder, and the voice of Pokrovsky, a rising star who owed his present post as Minister of Finance to him, ordered him to gather his things together and get out. The Party Secretary looked across again at Lenin, standing smiling there with his hands in his pockets; then, remembering the smile but not quite able to echo it, he obediently put his papers into his document case and followed his escort out of the room.

Washington: Wednesday 17 July

It had been the Yugoslavs, invariably the most sensitive observers in Moscow, who had heard the first rumours of the coup inside the Kremlin. The rumours were passed instantly to Belgrade, and from there to the Yugoslav Embassy in Washington. The story had reached the desk of the Assistant Secretary of State within an hour. The Assistant Secretary of State waited a little before telling the Secretary of State himself. When he did, the Secretary of State decided to summon an immediate meeting of the heads of all the sections within the State Department which were involved in relations with the Soviet Union, and invitations went out to the CIA and the National Security to send their representatives. Then he put a final call through to a former pupil of his at Columbia University: the Director of the Research Institute for Communist Affairs, Dr. Richard Preger, who was generally regarded as the best authority on Kremlin politics in the United States. Preger was only forty-one, but his encyclopaedic knowledge made him something of a legend in the State Department, and he was regularly called in to advise the Department on Soviet matters. He would not be able to get to Washington in time for the meeting, but State Department officials worked to set up a closed-circuit television link which would mean he could still take part.

An hour later, eighty people trooped into one of the Department's larger conference rooms, many of them equipped for the meeting with files which had been hastily filled with notes, photostats and computer print-outs provided by their departments. A huge blown-up photograph of the new Soviet leader hung over the stage. The Secretary of State came in after the room had filled. As everyone dutifully settled back at their desks, the Secretary of State opened the meeting with the fussy touch that his critics found irritating, and then handed over to the Director of Eastern European Affairs, whose job it was to outline the known facts about the new Soviet leader. In a dry voice, he ran through the résumé which had been typed and distributed to everyone in the conference room.

'The new Secretary General of the Central Committee of the Communist Party of the Soviet Union (CPSU) was born on 15 April 1922 in Leningrad, the son of a metal-worker who had been a member of the Communist Party since 1904. That gave the family some privileges, though only until the mid-Thirties. He was educated to ninth grade in Leningrad, but then his father disappeared in the second big wave of arrests and executions, and the boy and his mother went to Moscow to live with her parents there. He studied at the Moscow Institute of Metallurgy until 1941, and joined the Communist Party in the same year.'

'Interesting, after what had happened to his father,' the Secretary of State broke in.

The Director of Eastern European Affairs looked down over his half-moon spectacles and said briefly, '1941 – the year the pact with Hitler broke down.' Then he resumed. 'He did his early war service in Moscow and the Ukraine, where he served with distinction and was decorated for gallantry and leadership. At one point in the battle for Moscow he rallied his men against a counter-attack, in spite of being badly wounded in the leg.' The Director looked up again, briefly. 'I'm told he still walks with a limp,' he said, as though he found such personal details slightly dubious.

'He reached the rank of Lieutenant-Colonel of Engineers, although he was only twenty-three when the war in Europe ended. By that time he had attracted the attention of Voroshilov, who had been Minister of Defence and then became Deputy Chairman of the Council of Ministers in 1940. He had served with a favourite nephew of Voroshilov's in the battle for Berlin, in the closing days of the war in Europe. For several years after he left the army, the young man worked on Voroshilov's staff. Then in 1950, probably with Voroshilov's encouragement, he entered politics and was made a member of the Party's Central Committee. For the next few years, his rise was not particularly spectacular. He was the First Secretary of the Orenburg Oblast Committee – an area he had little previous connection with – but in 1955 he got his first important post: Chairman of the RSFSR Council of Ministers.'

The Secretary of State shifted slightly in his seat and the Director of Eastern European Affairs, catching the movement, explained, 'Russian Soviet Federative Socialist Republic – like being Governor of California.' A titter ran round the room, which the Secretary of State tried to ignore.

'But even in that sort of job, a politician in the Soviet Union needs a major boost to get him to the uppermost levels. His boost came in 1956, when the Hungarian uprising broke out. Maybe he had some kind of Hungarian links from the War – there was a Hungarian partisan unit under his command at one stage – or maybe it was just influence from his patron. Whatever the reason, he turned up at the Soviet Embassy in Budapest in some official capacity when the uprising was at its height. And there he took part in one of the greatest coups the Russians have pulled off since the Second World War. The Hungarians had declared their independence, and they'd set up a government under Imre Nagy. The Russians seemed to go along with it. They'd begun negotiating with the Hungarians about pulling their troops out of Hungary; and our friend had been given the job of doing the negotiations. Possibly the fact that he'd fought alongside Hungarians, and was so young – he was still only thirty-four, remember – made it easier for him to trick them. Anyway, he invited the Hungarian Defence Minister round to dinner at the

Embassy and, while the Ambassador was negotiating with them over the banqueting table, in came the KGB and arrested them all. Several of them were later shot. That was his real start in life. But it only lasted until 1960.'

By this time the Director of Eastern European Affairs had dropped his formal manner altogether, and was plainly enjoying himself. 'Our friend's patron, Voroshilov, fell foul of Khrushchev, as did everyone who had had anything to do with Voroshilov, including our friend. It took him a long time to recover. Maybe, when Brezhnev and Kosygin took over in 1964, they didn't like the idea of someone so young and able around them. They certainly didn't help him any, and it wasn't until things started to loosen up in the early Seventies that he got anything like a good job again. He became Deputy Chairman of the USSR Council of Ministers, and then First Deputy Chairman – which made him a kind of deputy to Kosygin as Premier. A couple of years afterwards he got a seat in the new Politburo. At first, when he was made Defence Minister, most people thought it was all part of the liberalization of the new régime. He took Marshal Ustinov's place, and it looked as though we were going to get more of a civilian input into defence – something to make it more political. But no, he interpreted the atmosphere as meaning that he'd got to push the hard line if he was going to get on at all. All the evidence we have shows that he fought real hard when the Party Secretary – the last one, that is – cut back on the budget for the military. Now he's at the top, we'll have to see what line he takes.'

The Secretary of State broke in at that point to thank him, and the Director of Eastern European Affairs sat down, with apparent reluctance. But clearly the Secretary of State wanted other opinions about the way the new Soviet leadership would behave.

'Let's hear what our friends outside State have to say about that one.'

He turned to the large screen at one corner of the lecture-room, and the audio-visual technician obediently switched on the picture from New York of Dr. Richard Preger sitting impatiently in his office at Columbia University's Institute for Communist Affairs. A small, dark man with a nervous intensity in his manner, he scarcely waited to be asked.

'To my mind there can be no doubt about it. The new Party Secretary's speech in Minsk on October 25 showed that his one concern is to make sure that the Soviets have complete supremacy in chemical warfare, as well as tactical and strategic weapons and conventional ones too. He was speaking in Orenburg, where he'd once been head of the Oblast. What he said was this.' Preger fumbled on his desk for a typed sheet of paper. 'I'm translating,' he said, with a quick look at the camera.

'"It is the intention of the leadership to ensure that never again shall the Soviet state be open to blackmail or to attack from outsiders" – from people outside, that is. "There are dangers surrounding the progressive nations of the world which can only be matched with determination and with all the resources at our disposal." It goes on like that some way,' Preger said, almost apologetically, his face looming huge on the screen in the lecture hall, as big as the photograph of the man they were there to discuss.

'After that, weird things started happening. The speech itself wasn't reported in *Pravda* or *Izvestia*, nor on national TV. But he still had some pull locally, and the local *Orenburgskaya Pravda* and the local TV news broadcast both reported it. Copies were made of what he'd said, and they were put round the senior figures in the armed forces. But for a time it looked as though he was out altogether. That was the first time since he'd been Defence Minister, for instance, that he didn't go to Berlin for the East German national day. He was in his usual place in Red Square during the celebrations of the October Revolution, but his speech to the soldiers was a lot shorter. During the winter his name dropped down regularly in the lists, and he only once appeared on television – something almost every other member of the Politburo did five or six times. But he had friends – at least four on the Politburo – so he obviously couldn't be dumped. My feeling is that now he's come to power, he'll want to push the line that he got into so much trouble over. But he won't have the money to do it. We've seen what food shortages have done in Poland; he won't want to create the same kind of thing in the Soviet Union; not unless he can show people that they're really under threat from us. I would say that you can expect him to engineer something, to make us threaten him. Then he can say, "Look, we've got the West on our backs, you'll have to tighten your belts until we can get out from under." That's my guess. The one thing he won't do – you can bet on it – is to carry on cutting back on the guns and handing out the butter. He's tough, and he likes to play tough.'

There was plenty more discussion. The sharp, dark face of Richard Preger eventually faded on the screen, and a good many State Department officials took a more optimistic line, criticizing what he had said. But as the Secretary of State walked out at the end of the session, he said quietly to the Assistant Secretary, 'If I were you, I'd ignore most of what you've heard here. That guy Preger knows twenty times more than they do; and he started off smarter.'

Moscow: Wednesday 17 July

The Ambassador shifted uneasily in his chair as Wortham came in, and looked across at the small, fussy man sitting in the armchair in the corner of the room: Nuttley, whose duties were ill defined but carried over from security to administration. It was Nuttley who sent you notes querying the cost of a meal at the Aragvi Restaurant, and Nuttley who reminded you that you had not yet filled in form D179 to guarantee that you had submitted all your personal electronic equipment for inspection by the security people. It was as though the Foreign Office, having decided that such annoying functions had to be performed, had sought round to find the one man who could not be disliked any more for doing them. Nuttley was as close to a fixture at the British Embassy in Moscow as you could get; seven years of diplomats had been fussed and harried by him about their bills and their security. Wortham had already guessed that being called to the Ambassador's office must mean bad news; seeing Nuttley sitting there confirmed it.

'Oh, sit down, David; nice to see you.' The Ambassador, a mild-mannered man, was clearly embarrassed at the task he had to perform. He looked speculatively at the chandelier, while Nuttley fidgeted briefly in the corner. 'David,' the Ambassador began again, experimentally, 'we've – that's to say I've – been round to the Foreign Ministry this morning. I'm afraid they aren't very happy about the way we got hold of the news about the – uh – incident at the Lubyanka.' He made it sound like a parking offence. 'They went in for a good deal of loose talk about it all. Anyhow, the upshot of it is that they've got some photographs of you getting your information from this economics adviser, uh ...'

'Konstantin Belov,' said Wortham, tightly.

'Yes.'

His voice trailed away. Wortham could hear Nuttley starting to hand out a lecture about lack of security and giving the Russians an easy target, but he paid no attention. He looked steadily at the signed photographs of the Queen on a table beside the Ambassador, and tried to work out what must have happened. He felt very cold. Not even the memory of the way Anyuta had put her hand on his, and the way she had looked at him, as they sat on the bench with her husband, could take away a kind of rage at the way he had been used. Ever since that evening, he had been obsessed with the question of what her real part had been in it all.

Nuttley's voice was still lecturing him, as Wortham broke in, 'Did you see the pictures?'

Nuttley stopped talking, a look of surprise on his face, as though someone had poked a finger in his stomach. The Ambassador, embarrassed, said he had seen two of them. They showed Wortham and a man sitting beside each other on a park bench, he said. In one picture the man held a newspaper up in front of him. In the other, he was handing something to Wortham.

'It flies in the face of all standing instructions,' said Nuttley. 'You had no authority to make such contacts, and no way of...'

'There wasn't anyone else in the picture?' asked Wortham.

'No.' The Ambassador wanted to limit the whole affair as much as possible. Nuttley, however, picked up the hint.

'You mean there was someone else you've been in contact with? I hope you realize the problems you've caused us by this unauthorized behaviour of yours.'

Wortham decided he had been incautious. 'There wasn't anyone else,' he said, speaking to the photograph of the Queen. She seemed to approve, anyway. Wortham asked what was going to happen now.

'I'm afraid they're going to declare you *persona non grata*, David; there's nothing we can do to stop that happening. I shall be sorry to lose you, but there it is. I managed to persuade them that since you've got a wife and two children, one of whom is in a Soviet nursery school' – here Nuttley shifted in his seat to show his displeasure at a further breach of Embassy advice – 'you'll need more than the twenty-four hours to get out that they were originally going to give you. They agreed to Sunday: I don't think I've ever heard of such a long throwing-out time. Perhaps they aren't so angry with you as they seemed, now that the leadership business has been changed by it.'

Nuttley started to tell Wortham about the things on issue to him which he would have to give back to the Embassy, but this time it was the Ambassador who interrupted. 'Listen, David, I don't understand everything about this case, but what I do know is that somehow you've been drawn into the fringes of Soviet politics. I'd be extremely grateful if between now and Sunday, you'd give me a full account, for my eyes only, of how that happened. You can trust me to keep it to myself. But it could be very important to know.'

Wortham went out into the sunshine for a walk. The militiamen stationed at the gate smiled at him as he went past, but he scarcely noticed. He was going to be thrown out of a country he liked, but equally, it was clear that the Russians had wanted to keep Anyuta out of the whole affair, either because of her father's position – if he really did work for the Central Committee: Wortham now began to doubt everything she had told him – or for some other reason which he couldn't yet understand, and perhaps never would. That he had been used by her, he never for a moment doubted. It had, at least, deadened the love he felt for her. Even if she was sorry for him at the end, she had made a fool of him; there was something intolerable in the very thought.

He turned, and walked back towards the Embassy. A group of red-faced old women were sweeping the wide pavement. He said, 'Excuse me,' as he walked over a newly swept stretch, and one of the old women leant on her threadbare broom and made a joke about him to the others as he passed. He couldn't catch the sense of it, but he guessed that it wasn't altogether uncomplimentary, despite the mocking laughter of the others. Uncomprehending, he shot them a smile which doubled them up with laughter; and then he walked on, feeling as though he had made some particularly witty remark. He began composing his letter to the Ambassador in his mind, trying to work out which bits to leave out.

Chapter 3

When internal and external forces hostile to socialism attempt to turn the development of a socialist country in the direction of the restoration of the capitalist system...it becomes...a general problem, the concern of all socialist countries. *L. I. Brezhnev, speech to the Fifth Congress of the Polish Communist Party, November 1968: 'The Brezhnev Doctrine', justifying the invasion of Czechoslovakia.*

Moscow: Friday 19 July

The Polish Party leader had studied in Moscow, after going to the Central Committee's University in Warsaw. He had met his wife there and, unlike some of his Party colleagues, he was still happily married. He had much to be grateful to the Russians for. They had stood by him, pushed him forward and rewarded him, both during the troubles of 1976 and 1980/81. They had always had their eye on him, ever since the firmness he'd shown during the riots of 1970. He owed his present job to them. And after he had taken over as Party leader in Poland, they had been understanding and helpful.

And yet, as he approached his meeting with the new Party Secretary in Moscow, the Polish leader felt a hostility which he had never felt before. It wasn't true, he thought, to call it patriotism; that was a bourgeois emotion he was blessedly free of. But he detected within himself a kind of national resentment, as though the way he himself had just been treated was an insult to his entire country.

Walking into the headquarters of the Central Committee of the Soviet Communist Party, half way between the Lubyanka and the Kremlin, flanked by security men and all the panoply of honour the Soviet state could accord, he nonetheless felt that he had never been so patronized or treated in so offhand a manner. He had been careful not to talk about his feelings to the Polish Prime Minister, who had come with him from Warsaw. These were difficult times, and you could never be sure what might be used against you later. But the whole manner of the summons had been clumsily done. Of course, Soviet leaders expected their allies to drop everything and fly to the Black Sea or to Moscow at a moment's notice, but it was always arranged with a certain amount of tact – the fiction was maintained that, if it were an awkward time, then another arrangement would be made, though, of course, it never was. This time the call had been peremptory: he had been told to come, that was all. As the big bronze lift clanked upwards, the Polish leader smoothed his thinning hair and did his best to calm himself down.

Inside the large office at the top of the building, the new Soviet Party Secretary sat behind a huge mahogany desk. It had nothing on it except a small Soviet flag and a model of an SS-20 missile. As the Poles went in, he stood up and came round the desk to meet them. He shook hands and clasped their shoulders in the approved manner, and bent forward to give each of them a simulated kiss on the cheek; but his manner was distinctly cool and reserved. Soon the Chairman of the Council of Ministers, the Soviet Premier, came in, and the temperature warmed a little. As the vodka started to flow, and the choice caviare was handed round, the Polish leader found his own reserve gradually melting. This, after all, was the relationship he was used to: not equality, certainly, but a kind of intimacy. He knew the Soviet Premier a good deal better than he knew the new Party Secretary; to some extent, they were both men under authority, and had to recognize their limitations. He began to feel better.

The Party Secretary himself, though, never thawed and when, at one point, the Polish leader laughed at something the Soviet Premier said, he butted in coldly. 'I'm glad, comrade, that you can relax so easily when Poland is in such a dangerous condition.'

Instantly there was silence. The Polish leader put his glass down on the polished table, and sat back in his chair, his face empty of expression. The sense of resentment welled up within him again.

'Correct me if I'm wrong, comrade,' said the Party Secretary, 'but there are now forty-three factories and shipyards on strike in your country for higher wages and shorter hours. Seven cities in Poland are seriously affected by transport strikes. Yesterday, I think, there was a march of many thousands through a part of Warsaw. There have been demands for the withdrawal of Soviet tanks and soldiers. The Party is being criticized openly, even on Polish television. The Soviet Ambassador in Warsaw tells me that even worse things have happened today: that there have been ceremonies at the graves of fascists who died fighting the Red Army during the early years of the Revolution; and that some groups of reactionaries have been parading openly with weapons, and talking of "liberating" Poland from the Soviet Union. If a quarter of this is true, then I am amazed that you can take it all so calmly.'

The Soviet Party Secretary had spoken long enough to give the Polish leader time to master his anger. He merely said, 'The Prime Minister here and I have spent long hours in the past few weeks, negotiating and talking about these things. I was in almost daily contact with your predecessor as Party Secretary, who was in full agreement with the way we were handling the crisis. Am I to take it that you don't approve?'

'Listen, comrade,' said the Party Secretary, and the aggressiveness of the man showed as he spoke, 'don't get smart with me. I'm the one who's got to pick up the pieces after all of you have allowed everything to collapse. A socialist society, with people parading around with guns and striking for more money? Whatever sort of country do you think you're running? Do you think you're Great Britain, maybe? It's my task to put back a little order into the socialist group of countries. Things have been getting totally out of hand, what with scurrilous writers publishing fanciful accounts of how badly we've been treating them all these years, and the economy starting to look as though we've decided to copy the Italians. And then you come along, with your government falling about your ears, from a place which bears no relationship to the ordered and contented society it ought to be, and tell me it's all under control, and all part of the plan you and my half-capitalist predecessor dreamed up between you.'

The Polish leader said nothing, afraid that if he did start to speak his resentment would show itself irretrievably. So far the Party Secretary's tone had been cold, rather than angry. But the Polish leader's silence seemed to inflame him, and he leant his head forward across the table, only a few inches away from the Pole, and brought his fist down suddenly with a crash that shook the empty glasses and made them clink against one another.

'I could have you dismissed today. Lock you up, put you on trial, gaol you for life. Don't think I wouldn't, if I wanted to. That's the reality you've got to live with. Now there's only one choice ahead of you: are you going to do what I want, or am I going to have to sweep you aside and put someone else in your place? And don't fool yourself; there are plenty of people who'd jump at the job. I daresay even your good friend the Prime Minister here would take it if I offered it to him, wouldn't you?' He laughed, as the two men writhed under the torment. Then his face became threatening again. 'Are you going to work with me, or not?'

The Polish leader knew he had no alternative, and said so.

'Good. Well, you'd better go back and get ready for the arrival of the extra Soviet troops. Oh, I'm sorry,' he said with heavy irony, 'I forgot to tell you. From now on, there'll be Soviet troops based in Warsaw as well as Legnica and Rzeszow and –' the Party Secretary glanced down at a piece of paper in front of him '– and Elblag, which I see is close to Gdansk. That must be a great relief to you, I'm sure. No chance of Poland ceasing to be Socialist now, eh?'

There was little the Polish leader could trust himself to say. He stood up. 'I think you are making a mistake, Comrade Party Secretary,' he said. 'More troops may keep things quiet in the short run, but they won't help in the long run. They didn't the last time.'

'Neither of us may be around in the long run, my friend. I'm concerned with stopping the trouble in Poland right now, before it gets too big to stop, and you and your Prime Minister here and everyone else in the Party are all thrown out. You see, I'm thinking of your interests just as much as the Soviet Union's.' He laughed again. 'But you'd better sit down again, comrade; we must work out the details of the request you're just about to make to me.'

The Polish leader realized that this was his last chance of opposition. He looked across at the Soviet Premier, who had been sitting in uncomfortable silence beside his Party Secretary. The Premier made a self-deprecating little grimace of resignation. 'I, too, have to obey orders,' he seemed to say. 'Why give yourself all the trouble of resisting?'

The Polish leader sat down again, heavily.

West Berlin: Friday 19 July

Colonel Modin took the three top steps of the exit from the U-bahn station in one bound; more to show himself that at fifty-four he was still fit enough to do it, than because he was in a hurry. In his right hand he gripped a plastic and cardboard attaché case which he always meant to replace, and never did. It was packed with twenty thousand Ostmark notes, the currency of East Germany. This time, Colonel Modin thought, there should be enough profit for me to get a leather briefcase, without having to worry about the cost.

He strolled along, a vigorous, sharp-minded man with dark hair that was now greying fast. He was afraid of becoming old, and of being sent back to the tedium of office life in Moscow; and he knew that it would certainly happen to him one day, just as it had happened to all the others. A senior officer of Soviet military intelligence, the GRU, Nikolai Fedorovich Modin commanded the GRU's operation in Berlin from his office close to the Unter den Linden, on the eastern side of the dividing line. His career – he had had a long spell in Britain, and spent some time in Third World countries – had been unspectacular, disappointing even, and nowadays there were only two ruling principles in his life: to keep away from Moscow, and to make money.

He walked along the street in the sunlight, looking out for shops that sold leather goods and feeling waves of energy coming to him from the brightness and the crowded street and the noise. He would stop on the way back, he thought. He knew what he was doing was wrong. His younger self, the infantry lieutenant of thirty years before, would cheerfully have recommended that he be executed for thieving from the State. Even now his loyalty to that State was almost unimpaired. He had served it self-sacrificingly, often thanklessly, and sometimes at the risk of his life. But over the years there had grown up a parallel loyalty, a more secret affair that he was almost ashamed of: a loyalty to himself and to his son. Mostly the two loyalties could exist side by side. But now they had conflicted and, at a crucial level of behaviour and motive, the personal principle had defeated the patriotic one. He wasn't proud of that. Indeed, he thought about it as little as he could manage. And when he did, he comforted himself with a German saying that had no equivalent in Russian: *Geld verloren, nichts verloren; Ehre verloren, viel verloren; Mut verloren, alles verloren.* If you lose your money, you've lost nothing; if you lose your honour, you've lost a great deal; but if you've lost your courage, then you've lost everything. I have at least still got courage, Modin thought, even if my honour is lost; I shall just have to go on fighting.

The packs of one hundred Ostmark notes shifted in his attaché case as he started walking a little faster. They belonged to the GRU, and represented a week's cash for running the Berlin station. Ludicrously little, Modin thought; but then everything in the GRU is like that. The KGB never has such problems. Like dozens of East German officials, he came to the West every week to change his Ostmarks for hard currency. The officials had to pay for western goods essential to the East German economy. He had to pay informants. Informants, whether in East or West Berlin, weren't interested in unconvertible Ostmarks, which you couldn't legally take out of the country. They wanted West German marks, even if they got them at a discount.

It was the discount that rendered Colonel Modin liable to imprisonment or execution for embezzlement. The current rate of exchange in a West Berlin bank, or on the East German black market, was around 4.25 Ostmarks to the West German mark. The rate changed regularly, but Modin, following the example of his predecessor in the station, accounted for his Ostmarks at a fixed rate of 5.5 to the West German mark. So this transaction would give him a profit of a thousand Deutschmarks.

He was doing nothing unusual. Most GRU officers who

were based along the borderland between the Soviet bloc and the West managed something of the sort. And since the fiction was maintained in Moscow that one Ostmark equalled one West German mark, as East Germany's official propaganda maintained, someone must be cooking the books somewhere. Everyone did it, and the officials turned a blind eye to it – but that was the kind of reasoning the young lieutenant would have despised. The ageing colonel, however, had a need for money that his younger self couldn't have visualized. It wasn't to pay for expensive living; Modin was unconcerned with such things, and only wanted a new leather briefcase because it attracted less attention than his utilitarian East German one. But his nineteen-year-old son, who was studying in Moscow, suffered from a rare form of liver disease regarded by Soviet doctors as incurable. A specialist in Vienna had been claiming remarkable results from a new form of treatment; Modin believed it was his son's only chance of living a normal life. If it had been his wife or his daughter, or even himself, he wouldn't have taken the risk. But Vasily was different. And Modin needed the equivalent of US $45,000 to make the operation and the associated treatment possible. So far he had amassed $22,000 of it. He gripped the handle of the cheap attaché case a little tighter, and pushed open the glass doors of the bank.

Warsaw: Saturday 20 July

There had been barricades in the streets during the night, flimsy things for the most part, often little more than heaps of building materials lugged from nearby sites, together with the occasional burning car tyre or length of iron railing. One or two of the more ambitious rioters had pushed and dragged cars into the middle of the streets and set them alight. Bus crews had left their ungainly blue vehicles skewed across the road before setting fire to them. There were some attempts to get people to man the barricades all night long. But as the hours passed, people melted away; and when, not long before dawn, there came the sound of tanks rumbling through the streets, the remaining defenders disappeared as well.

To stop a tank in a city street requires two or three rows of tank-traps reaching across the full width of the road. The barricades in the streets of Warsaw scarcely stopped the scout-cars. The T-72 tanks simply crushed their way through and over the obstacles, grinding into the burned-out cars and snapping the iron and concrete beneath their treads. Not even the buses held them up; the tanks simply thrust them aside, and the ungainly blackened skeletons swayed and toppled to the ground in a cloud of ashes and sparks. Many of the tanks, equipped for warfare rather than civil disorder, were fitted with metal studded tracks, and they chopped a wide double line out of the tarmac down the centre of the streets. The clashing, grinding noise of them filled the centre of the city, and the heavy exhaust fumes hung among the buildings long after the tanks had passed.

At last, the noise stopped. Fifty or more tanks took up positions in the centre of the city: on each side of the River Wisla, around the Seym – the parliament building – in front of Warsaw University, and at the intersections along the main thoroughfares. In all these places tough-looking Russian soldiers were standing up in the open hatches of their T-72s wearing the leather helmets that made them look like pre-war aviators, and the green and brown combat uniform which marked them out as members of the best trained and best equipped army in the world. But one thing was different this time from the last Red Army invasion of Warsaw: this time the demonstrators had guns. Plenty of people claimed to have heard the guns being fired, though there was no serious evidence that this had happened. But some people had certainly seen guns. They had been brought out and ritually paraded, like saints' relics, at the head of one or two of the demonstrations. No one knew where they had come from. That morning there were a few acts of defiance, as small groups taunted the Soviet tank crews or pelted them with stones from a safe distance. If possible, the soldiers tried to ignore the incidents; if not, they called in the *milicja*, who in most cases obeyed orders if it was obvious that Polish lives would be saved. The Russians were under strict orders not to fire on crowds or on individuals unless they were coming under direct fire themselves. During the day a number of foreign television crews were arrested, and occasionally beaten up, for trying to film the Soviet tanks. The *milicja* acted fast to break up any crowds that were starting to gather. For the most part, though, the day passed fairly quietly. People were watching and waiting for one thing only: when would the guns be used?

Chapter 4

After the uprising on June 17th
The Secretary of the Authors' Union
Had leaflets distributed in the Stalinallee
Which said that the people
Had forfeited the government's confidence
And could only win it back
By redoubled labour. Wouldn't it
Be simpler in that case if the government
Dissolved the people and
Elected another?

Bertolt Brecht, *The Solution.*

East Berlin: Saturday 20 July

When the world heard that Soviet troops had been moved in from their bases in Poland, the effect everywhere was immense; but in East Germany it was strongest of all. East Germany, too, had been undergoing a series of strikes, not on the scale of the Polish ones, since there was less pressure on the system in East Germany – but startling, nevertheless, in a country which had been quiescent for the previous twenty years. There were protest demonstrations in several big cities in East Germany: Potsdam, Dresden and Karl-Marx-Stadt. The biggest took place in the Alexanderplatz, not far from the foot of the great telecommunications tower in the centre of East Berlin. But the *Volkspolizei* arrived in force within minutes, to take the names of the demonstrators and disperse the crowds that had gathered to watch. At that stage the authorities had clearly decided not to make any arrests.

The picture became a great deal more serious that evening, with a series of incidents close to the Wall on the East Berlin side. Small groups had gathered at several places, to hold silent protests. None of these lasted for more than a few minutes. Most weren't even broken up by the police, but were brought to an end by the protestors themselves.

But not far from the Brandenburg Gate there is one stretch of the Wall where, because of the way the road runs on the eastern side, it is impossible to maintain the usual wide strip of no-man's-land. As a result, the distance from East to West is only about forty yards and visitors to West Berlin can climb up on to a wooden platform and look across at the other side.

At seven o'clock that evening, about forty demonstrators converged on the eastern side of the Wall, appearing unexpectedly from the small side streets of mean houses in that part of the city. There were more of them than the border guards at that point could easily deal with, though they were peaceful enough, holding hand-written placards which accused the Russians of aggression in Poland, and demanding greater political freedom in East Germany itself. In the normal way, this demonstration, like those earlier in the day, would have passed off more or less peacefully. But what turned the incident into something serious was the fact that a much larger group of people began to assemble on the other side of the Wall at the same time.

The Wall on the western side is marked with crosses, where people have died over the years in the effort to escape from the East. Today there were fresh wreaths and bunches of flowers lying at the foot of the Wall below the crosses. When the demonstration on the eastern side gathered, a massive cheer went up from the west and a group of ten or so on the observation platform started singing a popular West German protest song, which had been written by an East German exile. The crowd on the eastern side knew it too, and they took it up. And, in the enthusiasm, they moved closer towards the Wall.

At that moment the first shot was fired. The border guards had received no warning of the demonstration, and they were caught off balance, assuming that some mass escape attempt was going to take place. The most senior guard on the eastern side was only a sergeant, and he it was who fired the shot into the air. That made people panic, and they started running in all directions, some moving towards the Wall itself. The guards fired another six or seven shots in all, and as the demonstrators disappeared, three bodies were left lying in the street. Only the people who were standing on the observation platform had seen what had happened, but the shots and screams from the other side told the whole story. At first there was a shocked silence on the western side, and then a howl of rage. In spite of the sizeable number of West German police who had appeared, precisely in order to prevent any kind of cross border trouble, the crowd began hurling bricks and anything else they could pick up on the waste ground nearby. Few of the missiles reached the border guards on the eastern side; the sanded gap with its straight rows of buried landmines, its barbed wire and its tank traps was far too wide for that. But one of the demonstrators, unnoticed by the West German police, produced a petrol bomb and threw it, flaming, over the twelve-foot wall. That too smashed harmlessly down into the no-man's-land between the double line of walls. But the border guards, already rattled, caught sight of the flame from the petrol bomb as it arced down from the West, and reacted with fresh panic.

One guard raised his rifle and fired a shot at the group on the wooden observation tower, hitting a nineteen-year-old girl in the throat. That was enough for the West German police, who baton-charged the crowd clear of the Wall. But as the sirens started to wail on both sides of the divide, it was plain that the damage had been done.

Moscow: Saturday 20 July

The first thing that Abramov became aware of was the stench, his own stench. He had no conception of the length of time he had been in the small room, but he assumed that it must have been for days. The second thing he became aware of was the appalling swelling of his body. It was difficult to move his head, but as he looked down at himself, at the filthy underpants which were all that covered him, and at his bloated and bruised stomach and ulcerated legs, he became frightened for the first time since his arrest. And, with the fear, there came a third awareness: pain. He groaned weakly as it filled every filament of his body and his brain. It was impossible even to distinguish the different strands of the pain: it merged together into a great wave, which swept over him and left him retching and shivering. There was a thin trail of watery vomit, flecked with blood, on his chest and on the mattress he was lying on. He did not move, but looked up at the ceiling, with its single light-bulb glaring down at him.

In the immediate aftermath of the killing, he had had the worst of the beatings-up. He had been taken to an office and punched and kicked repeatedly until he lost consciousness; the KGB guards were waiting for orders and were simply venting their violent fury on the man who had murdered their chief. He thought that most of the injuries to his legs and chest must have occurred then. After that, the beatings became more systematic. They would ask him questions about the help he had received, and who his friends were; and, almost without being interested in his answers, two KGB men in green overalls had taken turns to beat him in the face and testicles with rods of some kind. At that stage, too, his finger had been broken. All Abramov had to do was to keep his nerve and scream with pain, and the thugs would attack him again without waiting for him to give a proper answer. But he knew this phase must eventually end.

In his windowless, soundless room, with its chipped enamel bucket, its concrete floor and its mattress, the passage of time was impossible to determine. Abramov had often lapsed into something like sleep between the beatings. But then a man in civilian clothes had come in, and after examining him carefully, had produced a hypodermic syringe from his bag, filled it from a small bottle, and injected Abramov in the arm.

There is no such thing as a truth drug; but the man was using a fast-acting barbiturate known as thiopentone, in order to anaesthetize him and make him lose his inhibitions, without making him completely unconscious. The injections made Abramov feel pleasantly drowsy and slightly drunk, and the questioning was relaxed.

Not that he remembered anything of what he had said afterwards. He would wake up with a slight headache, remembering only the pleasure of relaxation. He had no more control over himself than a paralysed child. There was a shameful luxury in the feeling, like relieving himself where he lay.

And yet he must somehow have resisted, even under the influence of the drug, because there were other times when the syringe contained not the relaxing thiopentone, but a massive injection of the standard Soviet tranquillizer, aminazin. These injections did different things to him. Some filled him with wild pain, lasting for hours, so bad that he could neither think nor speak, and only babble with incoherent pleading. At other times the injections would be followed by long periods of sleep, after which he would have the memory of elaborate dreams, with voices ringing in his head from time to time.

Sometimes, instead of being given injections he would be rolled in wet canvas from head to foot, so tightly that he could scarcely breathe. Over the next few hours the wet canvas would begin to dry, and to contract. The folds in it hardened, and cut into him harder and harder. At each advance of pain Abramov tried to scream, but there was no air in his lungs and he tore his throat with the effort. He tried to feign unconsciousness so that the two thugs would cut him free; but they laughed, and poked at his eyes with their finger-nails, and the smaller, localized pain of that made him cry out. Finally he would sink into genuine unconsciousness from the pressure and the lack of air; and then they would cut him free. It happened three times before the man with the syringe came back and started work on him again. But the thugs had told him what they wanted: it was to know where the gun had come from. He had, he realized, given them the names and addresses of his companions in the Volya group, but had not said anything about the gun. Abramov couldn't decide whether that was a matter of chance, or whether something in his mind had really blocked off any answers to the question, in spite of the reactions induced by the barbiturates.

In fact, he knew very little about the gun and where it had come from. That was Volodya's job, and he himself had deliberately kept out of all the discussions. He knew Volodya well, and could make guesses about the origin of the gun; but the drug didn't take account of guesses. For a time Abramov felt as though he had scored a victory. He giggled about it, as he lay in his dirty underpants on the mattress, and even though it reawakened all the pains that had been inflicted on him, he went on giggling.

Abramov had no inner resources to keep him going: no hope, no faith, not even a great deal of affection for the others in the group. But, he thought, with another weak giggle, I have will – *volya*. And my will tells me not to say anything about the gun. After more immeasurable time had passed, it was clear that the authorities felt he was too weak to undergo any more treatment with the drug. They left him alone, and fed him pulse porridge and a weak, thin soup. They even emptied the enamel bucket. Abramov lay on his mattress, dozing in the luxury of being under no pressure, and of having no immediate pain. It felt as though he were floating between one world and another, dead to both. No fear, no sensation, no anxiety, no emotion of any kind. During the time it lasted he saw nobody; his tin bowl and mug were shoved through a small flap at the foot of the door. Sometimes the floating feeling would leave him, and he would hallucinate with violent suddenness, shrieking and sobbing. Those moments, though, were mercifully few and only increased the later luxury of lying and thinking of nothing.

The end of the peaceful period came without any warning. Four men, none of whom he had seen before, filed into the cell and stood round looking down at him. 'You know what we want, Abramov. We won't be playing any more games with you. Everyone else has been arrested. All we need before we kill you is the information about how you got the gun.' Abramov cackled, but was cut short by a kick.

'If you've arrested all the others, why do you need any more information from me?' He was answered with another kick.

'Listen, Abramov, if you give me what I want, I can promise you that we shall kill you quickly and easily. You won't suffer a thing – a bullet in the brain is instantaneous. If you hold out on me, you will still die, but it will take a lot of time, and give a lot of people a great deal of trouble. It may be that you don't know where the gun came from, but you must have an idea of how it got to you. Are you going to tell me?'

Abramov lay there. No one said a word. The faces with the electric bulb behind them looked down at him as though he were already dead – meat on a slab. By now he was incapable of too much coherent thought; he was too tired for it. He couldn't any longer make out a profit and loss account of the whole thing. Everything was too much effort. He chose the way of least resistance and the least amount of thought.

'All right,' he said.

Warsaw: Saturday 20 July

The ten men gathered in the municipal cemetery in Wola, a dreary industrial suburb in western Warsaw, had been chosen partly for their discretion, and partly for their military record. Three of them, including their leader, had fought in the War. All the rest had done their two-year military service. The municipal cemetery had previously been the military cemetery of Poland; and it gave an air of theatricality and absurdity to the proceedings which appealed to their leader, Adam Wysocki. But it had a more practical side as well. Wysocki was chief overseer at the cemetery, and stored his weapons there. Most of the men gathered in the half-hour before the gates shut, though two had been there all day, like Wysocki himself; they also worked at the cemetery.

Wysocki was in his late fifties, a slightly built, good-looking man with carefully combed, spiky, iron-grey hair. Even as a boy he had been an ardent Communist, and had joined the Polish Workers' Party when it was founded, in 1942. He escaped from Warsaw in June 1944, after his father had been taken hostage and publicly shot. After a long and difficult journey, Wysocki had arrived in Moscow and joined the Polish People's Army, which fought alongside the Russians. He took part in the liberation of Warsaw in January 1945, shortly after his seventeenth birthday. It was a city of ruins, and 800,000 of its inhabitants had died during the War.

Wysocki, like many other young Poles, found that his zeal for the Party began to disappear amid the daily compromises which the system demanded. A fundamentally honest man, he soon refused to keep pretending that conditions in Poland were in sight of the perfection which the authorities claimed. In the early years he had made no complaints when men and women who had fought bravely and hard against the Germans for a different kind of Poland were arbitrarily arrested; he accepted that the building of a socialist state required such things. But when the socialist state remained unbuilt, he insisted on saying so.

In 1952 he was himself arrested, and worked in labour camps until he was amnestied in 1956. His sentence was relatively light, but it turned him into a bitter enemy of the authorities. After that he was regularly in trouble, and in 1970 he took a leading part in protest demonstrations supporting the workers in the Baltic towns who were on strike over higher prices. This time he was gaoled for seven years. By training he was a tool-maker, but his record of dissent made it impossible to continue working as one. He lost his union membership, and the only work he could find was in the cemetery. He remained something of a Marxist in his attitudes, and had little sympathy for the Catholics who provided the strongest opposition to the régime; rather he adopted a sceptical, amused approach to the task of resistance. In 1980 he refused to bury members of the Party who died. But he was ruthless, and his small group was probably the best disciplined of any among the activists and boasted the tightest security. That was not something the other groups were noted for; by the morning of the sixteenth the names of several of the men who had been out with guns the evening before were known across the city. But Wysocki's men had stayed at home and waited for orders. No one knew of the existence of their group, nor of their weapons.

And yet that night Wysocki was to risk his whole organization – and his life – in what was essentially a romantic gesture: a show of resistence to the Soviet tanks. He knew that this was not the start of the final revolt against the Russians that he had worked for, but perhaps he had come to the conclusion that this would never happen. Perhaps he simply felt it would be worse for his men to sit at home when there were Russian tanks in the centre of

Warsaw, than to resist in vain.

Wysocki had always carried out the intelligence work for the group himself, and he oversaw the supply and care of weapons and ammunition. For this night's work he had procured three motor cycles and two cars, all stolen, and from his private arsenal, which was kept among the graves, he brought out an array of weapons: 9 mm pistols, a heavy .45 revolver of pre-War German make, a shotgun, several Soviet grenades, and two elderly American M-1 carbines. He himself took the revolver and the shotgun, and distributed the pistols to the others. Then he allocated them their jobs – two to drive the cars, three to drive the motor bikes. The men who were to ride pillion were given a couple of aged stick grenades each, the reliability of which was unknown. He himself was going to be the passenger in one of the cars, taking with him one of the grenades. The other car passenger got the two carbines and a grenade.

Everyone knew his own target, and his own escape route. Two of the motor cycles and one of the cars would be working independently of each other, and were to attack one tank each. Wysocki's own car would be accompanied by the other motor bike, since their target was the group of tanks stationed around the Seym building. All the attacks would be made at the same time, and an eleventh member of the group had already been given the job of planting three small bombs in the main shopping area, timed to go off then as well. Wysocki made them check for the last time that they were carrying no identification, and nothing that would incriminate them or anyone else. Then they went out in pairs through the side gates of the cemetery which Wysocki had ensured were left unlocked. The cars and motor bikes were parked outside, carefully separated from each other.

The driver Wysocki had chosen for his own car was Josef Konieczny, an unmarried man in his mid-twenties, who had the reputation of being a fanatic. He was the youngest man in the group. Wysocki, not normally given to sentimentality, had taken him in because he had known his father during the liberation of Warsaw. Josef was Wysocki's link with younger groups of activists, and had supplied the 9 mm pistols. Wysocki sat behind him in the car. By having the freedom of the back seat, he could fire out of either window, and could wield the shotgun more easily. They took a roundabout route, past the Kasprzak radio works, then up to the Muranow area. There were thirty minutes before they were due to rendezvous with the motor bike near the Seym building. Josef took the small side streets that ran parallel with the big north-south avenues, since Wysocki suspected that the police would be stopping cars on the main roads. He was right. As they crossed the Al. Niepodlegosci, heading west, they could see road blocks further up to their left and right.

They reached their rendezvous, the corner of Mysliwiecka and Wronskiego streets, without trouble, and waited in a side street until they heard the motor bike. With no signal of recognition, they drove together the few hundred yards to the main road where the Seym building and the tanks were: Piekna Street. The Seym, a replica of its pre-War self, was floodlit. Around it, the park was in darkness. Five tanks were drawn up, out of the light of the Seym building, between it and the road.

Josef turned the car slowly into Piekna Street, and headed towards the Seym. In the warm evening air, a group of Russian soldiers lounged between the tanks talking idly, while a couple of others stood in the opened turrets of the tanks. They looked bored and relaxed. Wysocki slowly wound the right-hand window down and rested the shotgun on his knees. The stick grenade lay on the seat beside him. In front, the motor bike was almost level with the tanks, moving quite slowly. It passed the first couple of tanks, and then, as it came level with the group of soldiers, the pillion passenger raised his pistol and fired three times at them. Then the gun seemed to jam and he dropped it angrily, and threw the grenade. By this time the motor bike was pulling away from the tanks, and the grenade fell on the grass beyond the last tank in the line. After a full second or more, it exploded with shattering force. The Russians, meanwhile, had thrown themselves to the ground and, showing a creditable speed of reaction, were already starting to fire back. The motor cycle roared off at full speed, but Josef eased his car alongside the main group of soldiers and Wysocki blasted them with the shotgun as they lay on the ground. Then, awkwardly, he leant out and threw his grenade. As he did so, a series of shots hit the side of the car, wounding him in the arm and the stomach. The next moment, the grenade exploded, but Wysocki had not thrown it far enough. The blast caught the car as it started to pick up speed and made it swerve across the road and bounce against the kerb on the other side. For a moment the car was brought to a total stop, and more shots hit it. Wysocki fired three times out of the back window, and Josef gunned the car backwards very fast, making the tyres scream on the warm tarmac; then he slammed it into first gear and raced off.

Josef had stayed remarkably cool, and he was unhurt. Wysocki punched him weakly in the back in congratulation. As he did so, the sound of an explosion came from the main shopping centre, followed by another some seconds later. The eleventh man had done his job well. Burglar-alarms, set off by the blast, began to wail, and then came another noise: police sirens. While Josef drove, Wysocki cursed and tried to bind up his arm. There was nothing he could do about the wound in his stomach. They headed back to Wola.

Chapter 5

The Western Powers, far from having made any efforts to normalize the situation in West Berlin, on the contrary continue to use it intensively as a centre of subversive activities against the GDR and all other countries of the socialist commonwealth. Nowhere else in the world are there so many espionage and subversive centres of foreign states to be found as in West Berlin. *Declaration of Warsaw Pact Powers on Berlin, August 1961.*

West Berlin: Saturday 20 July

The Association for Peace and Freedom was a small, right-wing organization with a headquarters in Munich, and a branch office in a small apartment in a square not far from the Kurfürstendamm in West Berlin. The apartment was crammed with filing cabinets and towers five feet high of yellowing newspapers from eastern Europe. The foundation's funds came partly from West German industry, and partly from the United States; it had frequently been linked with the CIA. Its main objective was to help people who had escaped from eastern Europe to find jobs and settle down in the West, and most of its money was spent in this way. But not all. A more secret purpose of the foundation was to promote the growth of resistance to Soviet rule in eastern Europe. Almost certainly, its operations had been penetrated over the years by both West and East German security organizations, and perhaps by others. But its West Berlin representative, Dr. Werner Gartner, had kept one operation entirely in his own hands over the years, cut out from the rest of the organization, and apparently secure. It was an operation to smuggle weapons into eastern Europe and the Soviet Union.

Gartner began with a remarkable piece of good luck – in fact, the piece of luck had sparked off in his mind the idea for the rest of the operation. In 1971, two government ministers in the Irish Republic were arrested and charged with trying to supply weapons to Catholics in Belfast. They were found not guilty. The weapons in question were a consignment of five hundred Hungarian 9 mm pistols, bought from a dealer in Hamburg with shadowy funds provided by Irish businessmen. The dealer had obtained them from the official Czechoslovak arms concern, Omnipol, which is remarkably liberal and undiscriminating in its sales policy. When the Irish operation collapsed, the weapons were re-sold to a dealer in Latin America; and five years afterwards, towards the end of 1976, Dr. Gartner bought them through yet another middleman, and stored them somewhere in West Germany. Despite their comings and goings across the world, they had been kept in perfect condition.

It took him more than a decade to smuggle even a proportion of the pistols into eastern Europe. If he had been prepared to use more couriers, and to put more effort and money into the operation, it could have been done much sooner. But Gartner was well aware that his section of the foundation might be penetrated, and his plans – unknown even to his colleages – demanded total security. Many of the weapons were taken one at a time by tourists going to Romania and Bulgaria. Carried in suitcases, in flat boxes, rather than in hand baggage, they were hardly detectable, since incoming luggage wasn't X-rayed at the airports in Sofia or Bucharest; and once within the eastern bloc, security was relatively lax.

This part of Dr. Gartner's small private enterprise arrangement was, therefore, highly successful. The couriers didn't know what they were carrying to Romania and Bulgaria, and the people who took the guns on from there would not neccessarily have known either. Most of the guns ended up in Warsaw, though others reached Budapest, and Moscow itself. Wysocki's group used the 9 mm pistols, and P. D. Abramov used one to shoot the Chairman of the KGB.

As Modin drove into the centre of West Berlin, he looked out at the garish signs, the sex shops, the outrageous cinema shows, the streets filled with crowding, impatient consumers. It gave him a strong feeling of distaste; on balance, he still preferred the austerity of East Berlin, in spite of its shortages and its dreariness.

The GRU worked closely with the KGB, was indeed dominated by it; but the new Party Secretary in Moscow obviously felt he could rely more on the GRU, having himself been Minister of Defence, and had personally ordered it to investigate a possible western dimension to the incidents in Warsaw, Moscow and East Berlin. Colonel Modin was to examine the four anti-Soviet groups with offices in West Berlin for any signs of a link with the troubles. Normally such an operation would be spread carefully over a number of weeks, but this one had to be completed in a night. The twenty-three full-time agents of West German nationality whom the GRU employed in West Berlin had done a certain amount of surveillance of the four groups over the years, and they had watched them more closely since the trouble broke out in East Germany. Yet Modin's task was a difficult one. If he was not able to raid the offices of all four organizations thoroughly in one night, those that were not touched would take fright immediately, and hide or destroy anything that might be incriminating. Modin would have to select his targets with considerable skill. He had seen the briefing information circulated by Moscow headquarters, and was well aware that the rewards for success in an operation put in motion by the First Party Secretary of the USSR in person would be considerable – as would be the rewards for failure. He knew the history of the consignment of Hungarian 9 mm pistols. The sale by Omnipol to the dealer working for the Irish fund-raising group, the shipping of the whole consignment to a dealer in the Central American state of Honduras, and the resale to a dealer in Europe with an address in Brussels – all were fully documented. But the Brussels address was that of a building which had been pulled down in 1972, and the trail had then petered out completely.

And yet Modin felt that Dr. Gartner was the most likely source for the guns. The curiously tight security which surrounded the whole affair strongly implied precisely the kind of one or two-man system that Gartner might run. This meant a small organization, one that was run semi-autonomously. There was, of course, no reason why the organization Modin was searching for should be based in West Berlin at all; it could just as well have been in Frankfurt, or Vienna, or conceivably in Belgrade. But Modin's patch was West Berlin; and since he had received his orders he was determined to check out his theory. He planned to send his men to search two of the larger organizations which dealt with eastern European dissidents that evening. He himself would go to the Association for Peace and Freedom – Dr. Gartner's office. Modin drove to a flat on the north side of the city, which had been rented for six months and kept as a safe house, and briefed the six West Germans who were to take part in the night's operation. They left at 12.30. A bar on the far corner of the street from Gartner's office was disgorging its last few customers. Otherwise the street was quiet. Modin had a Russian house-breaking expert with him, and was taking one of the Germans as well.

The preparations had been meticulous. The previous morning, the German had gone into Gartner's office, on the pretext of offering him some small snippet of information about a dissident East German writer. Gartner may have suspected something, but the visit gave the German agent a chance to inspect the lay-out of the place, and to check out the locks and the alarm systems. There were people in the apartments above and below the office but, when Modin and his two men arrived, the Association's windows were dark. The fire-escape at the back gave them access to the floor, and the Russian house-breaker, knowing the alarm system, had little trouble getting a window open. Still, the alarms were good ones. Another system protected the filing cabinets, and a third the area around Gartner's desk. Each had to be painstakingly disconnected. In the corner, set into the wall, was a safe: a strong, ten-year-old Schralb.

It was a long wait for Modin. He went carefully through the filing cabinets, but found nothing more useful in them than press-cuttings and transcripts of interviews with people who had escaped from, or travelled in, eastern Europe. He made a few notes, but that was all. Finally, just before 4 a.m., the safe was opened. Inside was a large amount of money in West German marks and dollars, and an even larger amount in Ostmarks. There were also several box-files, and twenty-five or more cash-books dating back to the early Sixties. Modin had not been expecting anything like lists of addresses or names of contacts, so he wasn't disappointed. If Gartner even kept such things, they would be stored in a bank vault somewhere.

But the files and cash-book would be useful and there were dozens of letters from sympathizers within at least three government ministries in Bonn, often containing bits of sensitive information which had come the writer's way. Most were anonymous but one was written on headed notepaper, and signed.

Modin decided to keep that one, and photograph the others. If it were ever necessary to prove collusion between the Bonn government and the Association, that letter would be adequate proof. But the files contained nothing else of value – and certainly nothing to show any link with the Hungarian pistols.

Modin turned to the cash-books. There were no names in them; most of the entries were restricted to an initial or a number, with an amount of money set against it. Some words were in code – groups of capital letters. Modin flicked idly through the books, looking for something he might recognize. Suddenly a group of three letters caught his eye: LHR. His time in London told him what that was – not a code after all, but the abbreviation that airlines use for Heathrow airport. In his neat way, Dr. Gartner had listed a number of destinations for airline trips. Modin checked in some of the other books. In each, Gartner's small, unvarying red ink capitals had indicated several such trips. There was even a MOW for Moscow among them. With growing excitement now, Modin turned up the cash-book for 1972: the year the unknown buyer had sent the consignment of pistols from Honduras to Brussels. There, in February, was the evidence that Gartner had paid for an airline ticket to Brussels. The entry BXL was clearly marked. That was something, but not conclusive. On the line above, there was a more puzzling group of letters: TGU. Modin turned it over and over in his mind. Then it came to him. The capital of Honduras was Tegucigalpa.

He could have shouted aloud. Instead, he said nothing to the other two and immediately began the boring job of photographing each separate page of the cash-books. Modin himself had been told nothing about the later history of the guns, but he knew that a list of the trips Gartner or his agents had taken must be of considerable value. Other entries indicated Bucharest and Belgrade as the pistols' possible destinations.

In the grey light, an hour and a half later, Modin pushed open the metal gate that led to the customs office at Checkpoint Charlie. He was carrying his camera and the film he had shot in his new leather brief-case. The letter from the ministry in Bonn was in an inside pocket. The customs man was annoyed at having his early morning interrupted, but his brusqueness changed to servility when Modin pulled out his official pass in its hard black cover. The pass said nothing about the organization Modin worked for, but the customs man knew a Soviet intelligence officer when he saw one. Modin brushed aside the offer of an official car. A fifteen-minute walk to his office in the building off the Unter den Linden was what he needed to clear his head.

Warsaw: Saturday 20 July

Wysocki knew a doctor who would treat him, but he insisted on sticking to plan. The fewer people who were involved now, the better. Josef protested, but Wysocki ordered him to drop him by the side entrance to the cemetery, and then to drive off and hide the car on a disused building site they knew, further out of the city. Wysocki headed back to the only place where he felt secure: the hut in the cemetery. He had prepared a small cache of clothing, food and medical supplies there.

The other teams had been less successful than Wysocki. One of the motor bikes had crashed, killing both men on it, the other car had been stopped at a police road block afterwards and the men in it were captured alive after a brief shoot-out. One of those men had later given information about the meeting in the cemetery, not realizing that Wysocki had taken refuge there.

The raid was carried out four hours later by the Polish security police backed up with ordinary *milicja* and dogs. Wysocki, who had sunk into a doze, was roused by the excitement of the dogs. Picking up his .45 revolver, he found the strength to creep out of the hut in the darkness and slip away among the graves before the search party got too close. If he had not been wounded, he could have got completely away, for the security men, with characteristic carelessness, had failed to block off the side gate which Wysocki had left open. But he had no real intention of escaping. He headed for the well-to-do end of the cemetery, where the graves were more imposing and would give him better cover.

The dogs found the hut, and were following his track across the graves, the *milicja* and the security men following clumsily in their wake. Wysocki sheltered beside an expensive, life-sized marble angel, and waited until they were a few yards away. Then he fired. The security men were easy targets; like their Soviet counterparts, they wore fedora hats even when they were hunting a man in a cemetery at night. At that range, he killed one and wounded another before they could work out where he was. But he had no time for a third shot. The story goes that the bullet which killed him blew away the angel's upward-pointing hand.

Josef was never caught, and neither was one of the other members of the group. All the rest were killed or executed. Between them, they had killed three Soviet soldiers and a security policeman, wounded three others, and done a little, easily-repaired damage to a T-72 tank.

Chapter 6

C'étaient des fous, mais ils avaient cette petite flamme qui ne s'éteint pas.
They were madmen, but they had in them that little flame that never dies.

Pierre Renoir on the men of the 1871 Commune.

Chelm, Poland: Sunday 21 July

The strikers had made no effort to barricade the doors. They sat in between their buses, playing cards, or talking, or just staring into space. For a decision which could well mean their life or death, they had taken it remarkably quietly, and with none of the excitement that had characterized their strike before the Russians had moved in. There was a crucifix on the wall, and a great poster of the Pope: a picture taken a long time ago, perhaps even before he had left Poland to go to the Vatican. His arms were out to the men, and some of them hoped that they still were, even though they were about to commit what appeared to any sane man to be suicide. It hadn't even been the idea of a bus driver. The wife of one of the inspectors had started the whole thing, and she was there in the depot too, sitting in her Sunday best beside her husband, who looked distinctly uncomfortable. Once she took his hand, but he seemed ashamed to let everyone else think he might need his wife's comfort.

Still, everyone knew about Henryk's wife: she was something of a joke at the depot, and it was as much through fear of her tongue as through patriotic determination that some of them were there. The idea of being reviled by such a woman, even a woman who might soon be in prison, or dead, was enough to make some of the men stay. Others were there out of genuine conscience. The Chelm bus depot had an honourable tradition, having been involved in strikes during every single round of trouble there had been since the Russians had arrived in Poland. This was no time to let the tradition slip. Someone started singing a song, a wailing, tuneless song, which several of the others around him took up immediately. It spread until the gamblers, too, put down their cards and joined in. The song was a long one, and many of them knew only a few words; but they went on humming while the few who knew all the twists and turns of the old rhyming story, about the greatness of a prince and his slow downfall, went on singing, sometimes contradicting each other in the words, but never stopping. No one looked at anyone else. Some of the men had tears in their eyes as they sat and sang; and this time, when the inspector's wife put her hand in his, he let it stay there, no longer ashamed of the gesture or of the tears which streamed down his face.

When the security police burst in through the doors, and pointed their sub-machine guns at the lines of men sitting between their empty buses, there were some who tried to edge away, and others who stopped singing. But a few stood up and went on singing or humming the sad tune, regardless of the policemen. Other security men had opened the great wooden doors at the end of the garage so that the buses could be driven out. The captain in charge came through behind the men with their machine-guns, and curtly ordered the singing to stop. Gradually it faded away – even the most determined men there wanted to hear what the captain was going to say.

'You will now get into your buses and drive them out. The strike is over.'

For a moment, no one did anything. Then the inspector's wife pushed her way through and stood in front of the captain, her small, aggressive frame filled with fury.

'This is nothing to do with you, or with your men with their silly guns,' she said. 'Get out. This is the people's garage, and no one is going to take it away from the people. The Polish people,' she added, after a moment's thought. 'I'm not taking your claptrap about the people's this and that.'

The captain pushed her to one side, without replying. There was a murmur of anger, and then one of the busmen, normally a quiet and peaceable fellow, lunged at the captain, and caught him on the shoulder with a wild punch. The captain stepped back, and one of the security men pushed a gun in the man's stomach. The force of it knocked the wind out of him, and he sat heavily down on the ground. The rest of the busmen, taking their cue from him, sat down as well. The captain had had orders that he was to get the buses out, no matter what force he had to use; but he was not altogether an unfeeling man.

'Listen to me,' he told them, 'sooner or later, in one way or another, you are going to drive those buses out on to the road. I have come here to make you do it. There's no point in waiting around, you're simply wasting everybody's time.'

Nobody said anything. Nobody, not even the more reluctant of the busmen, wanted to be the first to stand up and volunteer to drive. While they sat there on the ground they were in control. The captain, realizing this, ordered his men to force a couple of the men to their feet. They hung limply on the security men's arms. Finally the captain lost patience. He moved in, kicking and cursing, trying to find someone who would stand up. One man did; but the howling and shouting from everyone around him made him sit down again. That brought the captain to the point.

'Shoot that man,' he shouted. The security man closest to him hesitated. 'Do what I tell you,' the captain yelled again. The busman started to stand up, horrified at what was happening to him. As he got to his feet, slowly, he watched the finger of the security policeman tighten on the trigger. Then the bus garage seemed to explode with the noise of the gun, and his body was flung back a little way, and lay against the front wheel of a bus.

The inspector's wife screamed with rage, and then went very quiet. Slowly, in a sharp but tuneful voice, she began singing the only words she could remember of the song again. The words were wrong, but the tune was right. Soon everyone there was singing it, except for the security men. They shot first one man, then another, then the inspector, and still the singing went on. After that the security men refused to shoot any more, and the captain had to order them out. The sad, meandering song trailed out of the garage after them, and continued even when the noise of their boots had died away.

Sheremetyevo Airport, Moscow: Sunday 21 July

The worst of it was over. The goodbyes had been said, the last drinks taken, the arrangements made, the rows with Janet patched up. She needed another couple of days to get everything ready, but there was no immediate need for her to leave. Wortham was required to report to the authorities at the airport in time for the afternoon flight to London. As his friend Horwood drove across the bridge on the Moscow River, Wortham caught his last glimpse of the people fishing and swimming and sun-bathing on its banks. He stared at the monument which marked the closest point the Germans had reached to Moscow in the Second World War. He tried to take in every detail of the sagging wooden houses along the roadside, built before Chekhov wrote his short stories. He peered at the birch trees, fixing them in his memory. He had the melancholy certainty that he would never see any of these things again.

Horwood broke the silence. 'You always liked it here, David, didn't you?'

'Well, yes, I know a lot of people think Moscow is the arse-end of the universe, but I've always liked it. Partly it's friends, I suppose, but what I really enjoyed was being in Russia with Russian people.' For a moment, Wortham almost felt like going farther; but then he withdrew, as he habitually did, into the conversational shallows, where it was safer. 'For one thing, you know how they can cut loose from all the jargon and you suddenly realize they don't give anything more for it than you or I do. And then there's the way they enjoy themselves, and the way that they can drive you mad.'

His voice trailed away, as he thought about Anyuta. He was tempted to speak about her to Horwood, who was the only really close friend Wortham had in Moscow, and the only man in the entire foreign service who might, he thought, sympathize with someone who had taken such a stupid risk. But he was wary nowadays of the compulsion to confess: far from unburdening yourself, you simply loaded an equal weight on to someone else's shoulders.

They drove on in silence, passing the heavy goods trucks which were grinding their way towards Leningrad and the Finnish border. Horwood said, as they turned off the motorway on to the airport road, 'Is there anything I can do?' Both of them knew perfectly well what he meant, that he'd guessed that there was something else in the episode.

'You could make a noose out of red-tape and hang Nuttley with it,' Wortham said. Then he added, 'No, I don't think so. But it's good of you to ask.'

Neither of them looked at the other.

The airport was as crowded and disorganized as it always was. They fought to get through a crowd of Uzbeks who were camped noisily on the floor of the domestic departures building, and they worked their way through to where a stolid, sour-faced policewoman was standing, guarding the narrow gap which led to the international side of the terminal. Wortham shook hands awkwardly with Horwood, and then clapped him briefly on the shoulder. He couldn't think of anything to say, until he caught sight of the policewoman's face.

'At least she's sorry to see me go,' he said. But at the sight of Horwood's grin, even the sour face of the policewoman broke into a smile, punctuated by the flash of gold teeth.

Normally the formalities would have been endless, but Wortham's dubious status as a diplomat who was about to be expelled smoothed the path for him. I should have tried this before, he thought. The senior immigration officer of the KGB to whom he reported ensured that each of the usual barriers to speedy progress was cleared in record time: changing money, going through customs, getting his ticket accepted, passing through immigration. A boy in uniform stared at him as though he were a photofit description, and asked a question in incomprehensible English. The KGB officer told Wortham to ignore it. The officer was even obliging enough to stay and watch his hand-luggage while he wandered over to the souvenir shop in the departure lounge.

Wortham leafed idly through the poorly-made records, and the books which split down the spine as soon as they were opened. He glanced at the chess-sets and the samovar-warmers, and then moved across to the best things on display, the amber necklaces and ear-rings. He ran a dark line of amber beads through his hand, and wondered whether he should buy them for his mother.

'So in spite of everything you buy me a present.'

He spun around, reddening at the sound of Anyuta's voice. 'What in the devil's name are you doing here?'

'Be careful, my friend: already you are a dangerous foreign agent. Now they will think you are robbing the Soviet Union of jewellery.' Quickly he turned, and handed the necklace back to the curious girl behind the counter. When he looked at Anyuta again, her mood had changed completely.

'David, my dear David, I came to say goodbye to you, and to tell you that I am very sorry for what has happened. Will you forgive me, David?'

Already, the anger and resentment which had built up in him had dissolved. He took refuge, though, in the familiar bantering tone. 'I suppose I owe it to you that I won't be making these things in a labour camp somewhere.' He waved his hand at the chess-sets and the carved animals. Anyuta looked at him steadily, then dropped her eyes and played with her belt of purple fabric.

'Please, David.'

'Nothing has changed,' he said, gently, and felt he almost meant it.

She went over to the café in the departure lounge to get them a table, while Wortham had a word with the KGB officer. Obliging as ever, the man agreed to remain with the luggage. Wortham hurried over to the café, where Anyuta had already cleared a couple of Soviet travellers from a table and was busy tidying up the plates and ash-trays they had left behind.

'I should like a Scotch whisky with ice,' Anyuta said, keeping to her British traditions.

As he waited to be served at the counter, Wortham found all the old delight returning at the thought of a few minutes with her. He was conscious of her eyes on him as he stood there, and he tapped his fingers impatiently because he thought she would find his impatience amusing. It was several minutes before he got back to the table, carrying the appallingly expensive whisky and a cup of tea for himself, which he bought for sentimental reasons because the hot water came from a samovar. He was moved, as he always was, by her face, and by the lines that would intensify as she grew older. 'And delves the parallels in beauty's brow,' he quoted to himself, uncertain whether he had got the words quite right. She patted the seat beside her, as once she had patted the bench at the Lenin Hills. But this time the gesture was authoritative, and showed that she wanted to talk seriously.

'David, I am very sorry for what happened. I want to ask you to understand that it was not my fault. I am sorry also that I never told you that Kostya was my husband. He had to do it because – well, in our system and perhaps in yours, too, there are pressures which one cannot ignore.' It sounded like a prepared speech.

'How on earth did you manage to get in here, to the departure lounge? Are you flying somewhere too?'

She laughed, moderately for once. 'I have a card which can break all those rules,' she said. 'I came, just to say goodbye. And sorry.'

'Did you plan it all out, right from the start, so you could reveal all that stuff to me?' He had wanted the question to sound slightly amused and worldly, but in his own ears it was merely plaintive.

'No, my dear,' she said, and traced a word, or a letter, on his hand with her scarlet fingernail, distractedly. 'My husband thought you were from that newspaper in England.'

'You mean Reuters news agency?'

'Yes, Reuters. When he found out you were a diplomat, he got very angry.'

'Did you say you knew?'

'No, I said you had told me you worked for this English newspaper.' Anyuta laughed loudly, and the woman at the samovar looked across at her and scalded her hand by accident.

'Don't you tell anyone the truth, Anyuta?'

'Oh, the truth,' she said, dismissively, 'that is too boring, and anyway it hurts people.'

'Hurts them more than they have been hurt by all of this?'

'Who can say?' She looked at him, and smiled sadly. 'Listen, my dear friend. My husband is a servant of the State. Not just working for them, but slaving for them. He would do anything the State wanted him to, if it helped him. He has no morals about it. I, however, tell lies because it suits me, and because I choose to. Sometimes the lies hurt me. Sometimes they hurt people who I love.'

'Whom I love,' said Wortham.

'Whom I love. That is you. I'm sorry.'

Wortham looked away. He wanted to believe that she meant it, and was anxious not to be shown that she didn't. 'I shan't ever see you again.'

'No,' she said. 'That is why I came to see you, before you went. It will not be easy, now that you are gone, David.'

Her voice had lost all its playfulness, and she wouldn't say any more. They sat there, her hand on his, the whisky and the tea untasted, looking at each other. The confused voice from the loudspeaker finally broke in on them, announcing the departure of the flight to London. Wortham started to move.

'I have something for you,' she said at last.

She fumbled in the large red carpet-bag which she carried over her shoulder, and pulled out an envelope. Wortham looked inside: there were three photographs of Anyuta in it: one snap-shot, taken at a party, one of her making a face and wearing a fur hat, and the third a formal studio portrait. He looked back at the slightly older original, sitting opposite him.

'I don't have any pictures to give you,' he said.

'I shall have to get the ones they took of you in the park last Monday,' she said, and she laughed again, briefly. 'Now you must go.'

She looked at him for a long moment, and then he walked away, back to the KGB man, who was reading a free copy of *Pravda*. Absent-mindedly, Wortham shook hands with him, and went towards the final security check. As he went through, he glanced back at the café. It was a long way off now, but he could see the fair hair, the green jacket, the red bag. She was still sitting at the table.

Moscow: Sunday 21 July

The first thing the surviving members of the Politburo noticed as they moved in to take their seats at the familiar table was the new picture of Lenin, which hung at one end of the room and almost filled the wall space. The informal picture of him with *Pravda* in his jacket pocket had gone. Instead, the painting the new First Party Secretary had selected was one that dated from the Thirties, before the cult of personality took over, and it showed Lenin standing on a balcony, exhorting a crowd, while a vast red banner fluttered around him. If any of the other Politburo members needed a sign that the days of liberalism and compromise were gone, they had only to look at the painting.

When everyone else was seated, the Party Secretary walked in stiffly, and lowered himself into the seat at the head of the table. It was an unnerving moment for most of his colleagues. Few of them had been his allies during recent years, and many had sided with his predecessor at significant moments. His two closest colleagues had already received their reward: one sat on his left hand, as Chairman of the Presidium of the USSR Supreme Soviet. The other sat further down the table, as the new Minister of Defence. Beside the Party Secretary sat the increasingly isolated figure of the Chairman of the USSR Council of Ministers, the Premier.

There were now two posts vacant on the Politburo, and the Party Secretary began, not with the usual reference to the previous meeting, but with a brief announcement of the men he wanted to fill them. Both were conservatives, and their appointments would ensure that the Party Secretary would have a majority on the Politburo. No one dissented. For one thing, the time was scarcely suitable to start a new feud; but there was, anyway, an acceptance of the idea that a Party Secretary had the right to put his own men into key positions. That was the way the system had always worked. With careful management, the Party Secretary would in future be assured of a block of five votes out of the fourteen, and everyone knew that the powers of patronage would very quickly give him the unquestioning support of at least three more. His position was secure.

The Party Secretary waited until the ritual discussion of the new appointments had run into the sand, then he made his second main announcement of the meeting.

'Comrades of the Political Bureau, I should tell you now as a matter of urgency that information has been brought to me which clearly links the outrages which have been perpetrated against the Soviet Union, and our friends and allies, the fraternal peoples of Poland and the German Democratic Republic. This information makes it clear that western agents were responsible for all three of these vicious outbreaks.'

For a moment around the room there was total silence. No one had expected that the new Party Secretary would go beyond the formalities at this first meeting of the new régime. Most of them, since his coup against the previous Party Secretary just a few days before, were aware of what use he could make of intelligence work if he wanted. Then each of them recalled what was expected of them and made little noises of incredulity and shock.

The Party Secretary continued. 'The alertness of the officers of the *Glavnoye Razvedyvatelnoye Upravleniye*, stationed in Berlin, has uncovered clear evidence that the weapons supplied to the criminals who attacked Soviet soldiers rendering fraternal assistance in Warsaw and elsewhere in Poland, were supplied by western intelligence from a group working in West Berlin.' There were more sounds of consternation.

'The GRU officers have also provided information showing conclusively that the weapon used to murder our late comrade, the Chairman of the KGB, was supplied by the same group. Comrades, it was in effect the CIA which carried out this outrage.'

This time the consternation was completely unfeigned. The seriousness of the accusation was such that everyone round the table knew the Party Secretary could not be inventing it completely. He pressed the button on the desk in front of him, and an aide came in carrying two small piles of paper.

'Before you, comrades,' said the Party Secretary, as the aide went deferentially around the table, handing out two documents to each Politburo member, 'you will find the report of our senior GRU commander in Berlin, giving the full details of the fascist organization which, with the help of the CIA, has been supplying weapons to terrorists not only in Poland, but even here in the Soviet Union. You will also find a full confession from the assassin of the Chairman of the KGB. We have confirmed that the weapon he used was one of those supplied by the group in West Berlin.'

Neither report was long. Each had, in fact, been considerably slimmed down by the officials the Party Secretary had brought with him from the Ministry of Defence. It took the men round the table about five minutes to finish reading. Despite the editing, it was clear to most of them that even if the CIA had funded the organization which supplied the weapons, it had not itself been involved directly in the supply. The distinction was a real one, but the Party Secretary was not inclined to allow it to be made.

'Comrades,' he said, when the faces turned back to him from the documents, 'we cannot permit international crimes of this magnitude to go unpunished for an instant. We see our fraternal allies in Poland and the German Democratic Republic suffering the onslaught of hooliganism and violence, supported by western intelligence organizations. It is essential that we take action, both to support our allies and friends, and to punish this criminal conspiracy against socialism.'

The new Party Secretary had rarely spoken much during Politburo meetings under the previous régime. His formal phrasing and heavy seriousness recalled the days of Bulganin or Molotov. The rest of the Politburo tried to peer through the wordiness and work out his intentions. 'This is an intolerable provocation,' the Party Secretary said at last, his heavy eyebrows contracting over the heavy nose. 'What should our response be, comrades?'

At last they understood, or thought they did; it was to be a test of their toughness, and their willingness to follow his line and reject what he believed to have been the weakness of his predecessor in foreign affairs. For an hour or more the debate went backwards and forwards across the table, as a whole range of possible responses was examined. The Party Secretary only revealed his own plan at the end.

'It is essential that we demonstrate our firmness, in my opinion. Anything else will simply increase the provocations which the West will plan against us. The comrades in Warsaw and Berlin will be looking to us for action. If we fail them, their own position will be weakened and the reactionaries' thereby strengthened. The plot against us had its origins in West Berlin. We must show the western powers that they cannot use this enclave of theirs to undermine our allies. We must begin by restricting their access to West Berlin.'

There was a pause. Then the men round the table began to voice their agreement; some more enthusiastically than others.

Heathrow Airport, London: Sunday, 21 July

It had never occurred to Wortham that the outside world might find him and his experience interesting. In the small-scale world of diplomatic Moscow, the news had soon leaked out about his involvement in the fall of the Party Secretary. The colony of western journalists in Moscow had asked to interview Wortham, and the Ambassador had refused; and although Wortham had disliked the idea of keeping away from the friends he had made, particularly among the British and American journalists, he had accepted the Ambassador's ruling.

But as the days passed, the desire to see and interview the British diplomat who had brought down a Soviet leader did not diminish; and when Wortham arrived in London after the flight from Moscow, he found himself in the terminal building, engulfed by television lights and faced with a thicket of microphones close to his face.The Foreign Office officials who had been sent to pick him up dealt with the confusion as best they could, promising a press conference later and pleading with the journalists to give Wortham a chance to rest and recover. They took no notice. Questions were shouted at him, as he was pushed through the crowd by the Foreign Office men; cameramen fell back on each other, cursing the umbilical cords that roped around their legs, their faces snarling with the heat and the effort of walking backwards and keeping the camera steady and focused.

'What's it feel like to change a government, Mr Wortham?'

'Do you think it could have been a KGB plant, Mr Wortham?'

'What does this mean for East–West relations, Mr Wortham?'

'Over here, Mr Wortham!'

'Could you just look this way, Mr Wortham?'

'Mr Wortham—'

'Mr Wortham!'

He could scarcely think, in the din and the heat from the lights. When he saw himself later that evening on television, he felt deeply embarrassed at the bemused way he had simply waved his hands in front of him repeating, 'I can't say anything for the time being.'

That was in the bedroom of the hotel. There was no going back to his house in Kew, which was let for another year to a couple from Norway. The Foreign Office would put them up at the Hyde Park Hotel until something could be done with them. What that something was, Wortham had no idea. He imagined they would give him an allowance of some kind, to pay the huge rent on a house somewhere reasonable. He was deeply uncertain how the Foreign Office regarded him anyway. He knew they disliked it when diplomats were thrown out of countries, and it was always said that even if it wasn't your own fault that you had been thrown out, an atmosphere of displeasure could hang around you for several years. You could languish at a desk in London, waiting for someone to move elsewhere in the world; hoping that the Office would forget that you had once transgressed somebody else's rules, and release you from limbo.

After he had switched the television off, and groaned a couple of times at the picture he had presented of himself at the airport, Wortham lay back on the bed and thought it all out: how he had been trapped into it all by Anyuta; how, right down to the final meeting at the airport, she had been able to do precisely as she chose, without falling foul of the officialdom which normally clogs everyone's feet in the Soviet Union. There could be only one conceivable explanation for all of that: the explanation which he had always preferred to hide from himself when it was a question of stealing out to meet her, day after day. Clearly, the Soviet authorities must have known all about their relationship.

And the Foreign Office: how much did they know? Not a lot, he was inclined to think. He had managed to cover his tracks fairly well, and it was inconceivable that the appalling Nuttley could have known about it and managed to keep it discreetly to himself. There will undoubtedly be a regulation in Nuttley's book, Wortham thought, that bears on meetings with foreign nationals that may in the opinion of an outside observer lead to sexual intercourse between the parties of the first part. If Nuttley didn't frame it, he must certainly know it off by heart.

He pulled out the pictures of Anyuta and laid them on the bed, examining them carefully, one after the other. He smiled at her expression in the one with the fur hat, and thought of her singing *Waltzing Matilda*. Then he remembered that she had told him at the airport that she would get copies of the pictures of him on the bench with her husband. She had laughed, but was she serious? The only people who possessed those photographs were the Soviet security men who had taken them. And from what the Ambassador had told him in Moscow, the photographs must obviously have been doctored or cropped in some way in order to leave Anyuta out of the whole affair. Wortham began to go through the possible reasons for that: if she had been telling the truth about her father's position, for instance, that might be a reason to leave her out of the affair. It would certainly operate to her father's disadvantage, otherwise. Wortham's mind began to cloud over with the mass of possibilities and the sheer impossibility of proving any of them. As for the way the Foreign Office regarded him, that was a matter which would soon be made clear.

Chapter 7

As a result of a technical interruption of the railway line, the Transport Administration of the Soviet Military Administration in Germany has been obliged, during the night of June 23–4, to suspend all passenger and freight service on the Berlin-Helmstedt section of the railway in both directions. *Announcement of the start of the Berlin blockade, 1948.*

West Berlin: Monday 22 July

The green telephone in the small, expensive flat in the suburb of Zehlendorf started to shrill at 6.35. The Mayor had been asleep for no more than three hours. At the other end was an excitable voice; it belonged to the Commissioner of Police, the Mayor decided after a couple of seconds. What were his instructions? The autobahns had been blocked, the canals too. The Mayor struggled to inject some firmness into the conversation.

'I shall be at my office in an hour from now. Try to have a complete picture for me then.'

'An hour? That might be difficult. You see ...'

'Try.'

The Mayor put the phone down, and lay there deciding whether to phone the Chancellor in Bonn then, or leave it till there was more information. It seemed more sensible, and more humane, to do it later; the Chancellor had had as much trouble as the Mayor over the shootings at the Wall the night before last, and he had probably stayed up even later. The Mayor of West Berlin was one of the most powerful politicians in West Germany. The curious status of the city, which the Russians had never accepted as forming part of the Federal Republic of Germany, meant that the Mayor was its sole ruler, since it was governed not from Bonn but from the Rathaus in Schoeneberg. The Mayor was in charge of the police, of finance, transport, housing and labour; and the present holder of the job was the best known woman in German public life.

She set great store by being punctual, and was duly at her desk in the Rathaus by 7.30. There was no sign of the Police Commissioner. She sat at her desk, as her secretary sleepily rearranged the details of the office day, and stared out at the rain falling on the ugly Fifties brick buildings surrounding the Rathaus, which in many ways was the ugliest of them all. She was a handsome woman, with a famous mane of red hair and a strong, heavy face. It was her fifty-second birthday.

The police commissioner came in at 7.45 accompanied by the Commissioner for Transport. The picture was a gloomy one: unless things changed as the day wore on, the closing of the autobahns and the canals would mean no more coal or oil coming into the city, and very little food. The Mayor asked whether the gas link with the Soviet Union was cut as well; a phone-call established that gas at least was still flowing. The Mayor thought about it. It was starting to look as though some specifically political point was being made – a point to do with the Four-Power Agreement between the wartime Allies in West Berlin.

That was worrying enough itself. The Four-Power Agreement had established the right of West Berlin to secure communications with the rest of the Federal

Republic, and had given it, and West Germany, stability.

There were still pontoon bridges stacked on the river bank where East Germany adjoined West Berlin, just in case Soviet policy were to switch radically and it became necessary to carry out an attack on West Berlin and its garrison of 12,000 Allied soldiers; but no one had seriously thought the bridges would ever be used. The Four-Power Agreement had been West Berlin's basic guarantee; and now, thought the Mayor, it could no longer be taken for granted – not if the Russians could set it aside in the course of a morning.

She knew the Russians had changed; that they were no longer subject to the impulses of a Stalin. She knew, too, that if there were to be a blockade, it would be far easier on the Berliners than the one of 1948. She remembered it all vividly: the anxiety and the cold and the hunger, and the constant noise of planes landing and taking off for the airlift. Then there was still rubble in the streets, and men begging, and people with terrifying war wounds. Now there was only wealth. The city had supplies of food for a month, and oil for six weeks; and it generated all its own electricity. Unless the Russians were to cut them off for a long time, they couldn't starve or freeze them into submission. It was a comforting thought.

Around her the Mayor heard the preparations she had ordered for an incident-room to be set up. Already the phones were ringing in the next office, and the brief interlude of peace would very soon be over. Ahead of her lay a long day of conferences – with the Chancellor, with the three Allied generals, with her officials, and with the government in East Berlin, if it proved possible to contact them on the roundabout telephone link between the two halves of the city. People would be frightened, just as she was. They would need the kind of reassurance which she would have to summon up all her will-power to give them. She was in charge of a city that had been marooned, cast adrift from its contacts with the real world. She looked out at the rain, which was starting to fall more heavily, and wondered why it was always assumed that things were going to get better and more peaceful in the world. Then the phone started to ring beside her.

Moscow: Monday 22 July

There had been no injections now for a long time. Abramov's system had become so dependent on them that the pain caused by their absence outweighed the relief. He rarely ate anything from the tin plate that was pushed at intervals through the door of his cell. He stared up at the light bulb on the ceiling.

He had, he supposed, told everything he knew. But it hadn't been done voluntarily, or even fully consciously. He often thought about the others in the group, wondering where they were and whether they had escaped after the assassination; but they belonged to such a remote period of his life now that he could scarcely remember them as individuals. They were separated from his small white-painted glaring cell – from his whole world – by an unbridgeable gap created by physical pain and total isolation.

His life, he supposed, had been a poor affair: unsuccessful in terms of the way some of his contemporaries at Moscow University had already become successful; and unsuccessful, too, in the hidden, dangerous way he had himself chosen. He wasn't prepared to let himself wonder whether the murder of a senior member of the Soviet Politburo amounted to success. But it did seem to him that he had never entirely thought the thing through.

Certainly, he had planned the murder with great thoroughness; but he had never visualized what would happen afterwards. It was so foreign to anything he had ever experienced that it had been completely impossible to imagine the moments that followed the shooting. To encourage him, two of the others had said they would wait in a car in a nearby street, so that if he could get to them they would drive him to a safe house on the outskirts of Moscow. He hadn't rejected the offer, but he had known it would come to nothing, that it was only being said because the others felt guilty at leaving him to bear the entire burden. No doubt the car was there, waiting for him; but he had had no real reason to run to it.

It was becoming difficult for him even to remember the life outside the walls of the cell: the summer life, which was going on all round the Lubyanka, where he assumed he still was. That seemed to him to be completely dead now; as dead as he himself was, lying on his mattress, unable to feel his arms or legs, unable to turn his head away from the burning filament of the light bulb which filled his entire existence.

The door opened before he had noticed the sound of feet in the bare corridor. The two uniformed thugs came and stood over him, looking at him and then at one another. Behind them stood a third man, someone Abramov hadn't seen before: a small, apologetic-looking man in his fifties who ducked his head and seemed to smile.

'Come on, sonny,' said the third man, 'it's time for you to be moved to another room.'

The two thugs pulled him up, and he said nothing, in spite of the pain in his arms. They got him into a slouching position, hanging from the two of them, his arms round their necks, his feet dragging on the stone floor of the cell. Without a word they pulled him along the corridor and down a flight of concrete steps, then along another corridor with boiler-rooms and cupboards opening off its length from time to time.

The corridor seemed endless to Abramov, and the pain from his arms and legs welled up and filled him with nausea. And yet, he found to his amazement, he was able to observe things with a remarkable intensity: the pattern of cracks along the floor, the marks that the individual hairs of the paint brush had left on the walls, the writing on a tin which had been left in a corner.

At the end of the corridor was another white-painted room, empty except for three rough chairs and a table, and a cupboard in one corner. The two thugs dumped Abramov on to one of the chairs, and walked out. He stayed there, slumped down, with his elbows on the table and his head in his hands.

'Now then, sonny,' said the other man, in a voice that sounded reasonably sympathetic, 'you just wait there for a bit.'

Abramov felt momentarily like crying, with the pain and the relief and the hint of sympathy; but he said nothing. The man was fumbling about in the cupboard. The room was hot, so close to the boilers, and Abramov started to sweat. It made him feel almost healthy, that his body should respond in its old way to external circumstances. The smell of oil and polish came to him. He felt as though he was not after all a dead man.

Perhaps he felt the muzzle of the revolver as it touched the back of his head experimentally; perhaps he felt the slight movement, as the man's finger tightened on the trigger. But the shattering noise as the round went off came instantaneously with the blackness of his death; and he would not have felt that.

Part Two

Gulf Summer

Chapter 1

No one tells the soldiers what the generals are planning, yet they always know perfectly well whether they are deployed on the main line of advance, or on the flank. *Alexander Solzhenitsyn, 'The First Circle'.*

Moscow: Tuesday 23 July

Colonel Modin propped open the rickety door of the wardrobe, so that he could see to do up his tie in the mirror. He tightened the fat knot, and folded down his collar. He had wanted to wear his GRU uniform, but the protocol officials had insisted on a lounge suit. One had been brought round to the hotel for him the night before. It didn't fit, but at least it was new. Modin was vain about his stocky figure and his fiftyish good looks. He combed and brushed his greying hair with unnecessary attention, and then put on the dark blue jacket of the suit, pulling it down a couple of times sharply to make it sit better across the shoulders. He wasn't successful. Modin sighed, and polished his shoes on the fallen bedspread, before gathering up the things he might need and distributing them in the pockets of his suit. Finally, he put on a clumsily handsome gold watch from Switzerland, his award for discovering the links between the West Berlin front organization run by Dr.

Gartner, the pistols used in Warsaw, and the assassination of the Chairman of the KGB. He stretched his wrist out to show off the watch to himself, then covered it with the inadequate cuff of his shirt. A final glance in the mirror, and he shouldered his way through the double doors of his hotel room and out into the corridor.

Although he lived well in East Berlin, he had never been inside an expensive Moscow hotel before. He felt strange and rather uncomfortable; and it didn't surprise him at all that at breakfast he was ignored until all the foreign guests had been served. The waiters had sized him up directly he came into the dining-room: a parvenu Russian, no matter how important, wouldn't be paying for his breakfast with foreign currency, or leaving a tip. It didn't bother him greatly. As a soldier, he was used to having to take his place in the line. The pleasure of staying at a big Moscow hotel lay in the honour that was being done to him, not in the couple of nights of limited comfort, away from East Berlin.

By 9.20, he had still not been served with the sour yoghurt *smetana* he had ordered, and he was getting anxious about the car which was to pick him up in ten minutes' time. Even though it was only to take him to the Kremlin, whose walls were visible from the windows of the dining-room where he sat, there could be no question of missing it. He stood up abruptly, having swallowed down his tea, and left no tip: the waiter's assumption that he wasn't worth paying attention to became self-fulfilling. Modin walked downstairs, and waited in front of the hotel for several minutes. The car, fortunately, was later than he was. It was 9.45 before it appeared: an ancient black and chrome Chaika, with thick, comfortable leather seats and a talkative driver.

'What are you getting, then?' the driver asked, as soon as Modin had settled in and they pulled out into the traffic.

Modin tried to keep his voice matter-of-fact. 'Nothing – just an introduction to the Party Secretary.'

'Oh yes?' The driver was unimpressed. 'At 10.15 I've got to be back for a couple of Order of Lenins.'

They drove past the Manège, going right round in order to get into Red Square. 'Live near Moscow, do you?'

Modin said shortly, 'I always think it's best not to ask too many questions, my friend.'

The driver kept quiet after that.

The officials who received him and the twenty or so others who were to be honoured weren't particularly impressed either. They put him through his paces, and paired him off with an Ethiopian whom no one spoke to; Modin felt it was something of an insult. The ceremony itself was upon them almost before he had realized it. They were brought into a gold and white room, marched along a dark blue carpet, and then the Party Secretary shook hands, and gave them each a couple of perfunctory kisses on the cheek. The Ethiopian he scarcely bothered with, but he looked at Modin, and said, 'I am very pleased with you, Nikolai Fedorovich.'

Modin got the impression of a pair of penetrating brown eyes, looking at him from under the heavy eyebrows. There was a television camera in the room, but it wasn't for them, and the technicians stood and chatted at one side. Modin and the Ethiopian each shook the Party Secretary's hand again, and walked back along the blue carpet, in step.

For the first time, Modin felt let down. Twenty years of difficult and occasionally dangerous operations, culminating in some of the best intelligence work he had ever done or heard of, had ended with a peck on the cheek and a handshake. Outside, however, a senior official was waiting for him.

'My dear Colonel Modin,' he said, 'many congratulations on your mission. I have been asked to tell you that you have been recommended for the Order of the Red Star. I'm sure it will be only the first in a series of honours. The Party Secretary, I may say, was extremely interested in your success; and he read a copy of your report himself.'

They headed off in the direction of a quiet office. The Ethiopian looked lost; no one had been detailed to look after him.

The official settled down, and fussed with a green file which he had been carrying under his arm. 'The Party Secretary, as you know, had a great deal to do with the GRU, when he was Minister of Defence. He always felt it didn't have quite the independence it might have enjoyed. However, that is over now.'

The official needed to say no more to a GRU man. For twenty or more years, Soviet military intelligence had in effect been controlled by the KGB, following the traumatic revelation that the GRU had been penetrated by agents of the CIA and the British SIS. In the days since the new Party Secretary had come to power, it had been expected that the KGB, which had been closely associated with his predecessor, would in some way be cut down to size. Modin knew that nothing would happen quickly; but, with a new leader in the Kremlin the possibility now existed that GRU men like himself might be able to come out from under the shadow of the KGB. And the discovery he had made in Dr. Gartner's office in West Berlin must, he knew, have been of value at a crucial moment. The official opened the green file, and started talking about a new mission that the Party Secretary himself wanted Modin to perform in Saudi Arabia. Modin had never been back to the Middle East since his days in Beirut, ten years before, but he listened with a pleasant sense of self-congratulation. There would, he knew, be any number of ways of earning hard currency there. He wished now that the morning's ceremony had been televised. That way, his son Vasily could have seen him shaking hands with the First Party Secretary of the Soviet Union. Perhaps, he thought, I can bring Vasily with me when I get my Red Star.

London: Tuesday 23 July

Wortham ran up the shallow marble stairs two at a time. He was late, in spite of his best endeavours. Somehow, he had misjudged the time it took nowadays to get across London to the Foreign Office. He cast around for an excuse, but by the time he reached the top of the staircase he had decided that there was no point. He ran down the corridor, and when he reached the door, he had to stand there for a second, chest heaving, to get at least some of his breath back. As he walked in, a woman in her late fifties looked dubiously at him, and then at the clock. He was six minutes late for one of the most important occasions of his career, he thought – if career was quite the right word, any longer.

'You'd better go straight in, I suppose,' she said, putting down a small plastic watering-can and opening the door at the end of the room.

'Don't say they've started without me,' said Wortham.

The secretary ignored him, and announced to the group of three men sitting at a mahogany table at the far end of the room, 'Mr Wortham is here, *now*.' She looked disapprovingly at him, and closed the door behind her. The Head of the Eastern European and Soviet Department had not reached the senior levels of the Foreign Office by being late for meetings, but he seemed prepared to be tolerant of those who were.

'Sit down, David,' he said. 'Traffic difficult, I expect?'

'The tube, I'm afraid,' said Wortham. 'I'm terribly sorry.' He smiled as winningly as he could manage. The smiles he received in reply varied in warmth, but the Head of the Department at least seemed moderately human.

'Newspapers seemed to think you've been pretty hard done by, David. Agree with them?' The question caught Wortham slightly off balance. For the second time that morning, he opted for honesty.

'Not entirely, I suppose. After all, if you get

photographed in the way I was, you can't expect much else. I was set up, no doubt about it. But I still think I was right to go that evening.' There was a touch of defiance in what he said, not aimed at the Head of the Department, nor at the man from Personnel who was sitting on the left, and who gave something which could have been interpreted as a nod of agreement, but at the man on the right, whom Wortham didn't recognize. Wortham thought he looked like the man who came into the interview room and knocked the lighted cigarette out of the prisoner's mouth.

'Forgive me, David, you may not know Gregory Stallard.' No indication of where he worked: that meant that he must be on the security side. It wasn't looking good; no better than Stallard himself looked, Wortham thought. Glancing at the Head of the Department, by way of asking his permission, Stallard opened the serious questioning. He picked up a red pencil and carefully sighted down it to the pad of paper in front of him.

'I'm not altogether clear in my own mind why you did go.'

'Because I was asked to.' Wortham thought it would probably be better to camouflage any mention of Anyuta's involvement by using the passive voice as much as possible.

'The man who rang you,' said Stallard, expressionlessly. 'Did you know him?'

You bastard, thought Wortham. You've found out from someone in the flat that night that it wasn't a man at all. Wortham knew it as much from the way Stallard was trying to balance the pencil on his forefinger, as from the deliberately off-hand way he had asked the question.

'As a matter of fact it was a woman who rang.'

No one did anything, particularly. But Wortham knew he had passed the test, as certainly as if the three men at the table had suddenly held up score-cards with numbers on them.

'This woman, then,' said Stallard, as though it didn't

matter, 'did you know her?'

Wortham was careful not to lose his grip on himself. 'No, I didn't. And my wife didn't recognize her voice either,' he volunteered, as though that would clinch it.

'And she didn't turn up with this Belov?'

Now is the moment, Wortham thought. He hadn't told the ambassador in Moscow that the call had been from a girl, and he certainly hadn't included any mention of Anyuta in his written account. If they know in some way, Wortham thought, I'm a goner.

'No, there was just him, sitting on a park bench reading his copy of *Pravda.*'

'At night?'

'He was sitting under a street-lamp.'

'The Ambassador didn't say you'd told him that the person who contacted you was a woman.'

Wortham thought he'd brazen it out. 'I think I did.'

'Look,' said Stallard, and he passed over a photostat of the Ambassador's report. Wortham read it. He was, he himself always admitted, a ready liar.

'It was stupid of me. I suppose that since I knew it and took it for granted, I just assumed I had told him.'

Stallard put the pencil down and turned to the Head of the Eastern European Department, as if to say, 'No further questions.'

The Head of the Department pursued the subject for a little longer but there were no more traps. Soon they got off on to other areas of discussion: what Wortham would do now, where he and his family were going to live. By the end the atmosphere was positively friendly, and the personnel man, who hadn't wanted Stallard there in the first place, was clearly relieved that everything had gone well. He passed on his best wishes to Janet, and as Wortham stood up to leave, exchanged a look of satisfaction with the Head of the Department. Stallard looked at his pencil, though when Wortham walked down the long room to the door he watched his departing figure carefully. Neither of the others at the table spoke.

'Well, that's that, then,' Stallard said. The other two were arranging their papers. 'All the same ...'

But the Head of the Eastern European Department had had more than enough.

'About that Budapest case,' he said, firmly.

Helmstedt, West German border: Tuesday 23 July

At 10.30 in the morning, the customs men on duty on the West German side of the border at Helmstedt noticed that the VoPos were starting to heave the red-and-white painted oil drums away from the middle of the road on the far side of the East German customs and police post. It took more than half an hour to clear the road. After that, the extra VoPos who had been drafted in to man the road block were picked up in trucks and driven off. Fifteen minutes later, one of the West German customs men decided to stroll across to the line of the frontier and ask someone on the other side what was happening. Instead of ignoring him, as the East Germans had been doing for the past couple of days, the West German's counterpart shook him by the hand over the border line, and told him the road was free. He gave no explanation. The road blocks had been in position for just one day.

It was past midday before the first cars made their way hesitantly down the autobahn in the direction of West Berlin. None of them was stopped. Before that, the barges which had been held up on the canals were allowed through into West Berlin. The Mayor gave orders that the incident room in the Rathaus with its maps and its array of phones, could be dismantled. Now it was over, some of her advisers were inclined to dismiss the whole thing as a piece of theatre which the Russians had mounted because of the shootings at the Wall, and the subsequent accusations against the Association for Peace and Freedom. Others, including the British and American generals, suspected that the real Soviet aim was to try to soften up the Western Powers, and force them to withdraw from West Berlin altogether, as Khrushchev had tried to do in 1960.

But the Mayor thought the reason was slightly different: she believed it was a warning to West Germany that the Soviet Union was now in a position to do what it wanted, both with West Berlin and with the Federal Republic as a whole; and that the government in Bonn had better recognize the fact, and come to terms with it. When she telephoned the Chancellor at 7.30 that morning, she found he had already drawn the same conclusions from what had happened, and, like her, he had found little comfort in the reflex outrage from the Americans. As things got back to normal during the day the Mayor was too busy to think about the long-term implications; even the interviews she gave to West German television, and to several of the foreign stations, gave her little chance to expound her views.

But one thing stayed with her all day long, and it was the last thing she thought about before she finally got to sleep that night. The customs and immigration people at the Helmstedt border had reported that the red and white oil drums hadn't been taken away with the rest of the special equipment that had been brought in for the road blocks – the radio vans, the trailers and so on. The drums were still lined up along the side of the road. Ready, the Mayor thought, to be used again, whenever the Russians wanted.

Chapter 2

Clutching a little case,
He walks out briskly to infect a city
Whose terrible future just may have arrived.
W. H. Auden, *Gare du Midi.*

Riyadh, Saudi Arabia: Thursday 1 August

There had been no time for the usual careful back-up, the painstaking creation of a legend, the meticulous preparation of a network of contacts. From their experience in war-time, the British and Americans call such an operation 'parachuting in'. The KGB, on the basis of a slightly different kind of war-time activity, calls it a 'hit and run'. No one as experienced and methodical as Nikolai Fedorovich Modin could possibly enjoy a hit-and-run mission. It was, he knew, a gamble, and there was insufficient time to make success likely. But he also knew that if you were given a mission at the personal invitation of the Party Secretary in the Kremlin, you had very little alternative but to accept.

The airport, with its self-consciously Arabized facade, shone too brightly in the afternoon sun for Modin to be able to look at it directly, as he walked from the plane. With his free hand, he smoothed his hair down. Then he felt for the West German passport in his jacket pocket. It was the only passport they had issued him. He walked into the building, past a couple of watchful Saudi soldiers, and waited quietly for his travelling bag to emerge on the carousel. Most of his fellow-passengers were what he himself professed to be: businessmen from West Germany.

He felt moderately at ease with his cover. Having lived so long in East Berlin, his German was fluent and marked by only a little of the thickening that Russians give to German consonants. To anyone who wasn't born in Germany, he would pass muster very well. His clothes had been provided for him by the GRU commissariat, and were all western, if not actually West German. He had brought some addresses sewn into the binding of a Konsalik novel which the Commissariat had also found him. The set-up was by no means perfect, but at least it was moderately professional. That meant a good deal to a man like Modin.

There was no difficulty at the immigration desk; the green-stamped visa, which filled one entire page of his German passport, had been arranged at short notice, but that was quite usual for businessmen with unexpected meetings to go to. Modin caught a taxi and headed for the InterContinental Hotel, where a room was booked for him at a cost equivalent to a hundred roubles a night. Modin wasn't given to comparing things unfavourably with the Soviet Union, but he could see very clearly the differences between the InterContinental and the National Hotel in Moscow he had stayed in a few nights ago.

He wandered around the shops in the cool arcades of the hotel, worrying vaguely about the mission. No one knew very much about it; a senior army officer, a Saudi, had approached the military attaché at the Syrian Embassy in Jedda, to pass a message on to Moscow: a query about the likely attitude of the Russians in the event of a military coup against the royal government of Saudi Arabia. It was Modin's task to assess the likelihood of the coup so Moscow could give a considered reply.

Modin waited until nearly five o'clock, and then took a taxi to the market area. Stopping the driver in the main road, he told him to stay there while he took a walk. Modin then headed off down a small, dusty side street. Everything was going smoothly.

At the prearranged time of 5.12 precisely, after he had passed a decaying mosque which was set in a row of cafés and small shops selling electrical goods, Modin came to a coppersmith's booth, with the wares set out on the street. A man was bending over, looking at the inevitable coffee-pots; he straightened up as Modin came level with him. The usual recognition signals had been arranged by the KGB resident, but for some reason – nervousness, perhaps – the man launched straight into conversation.

'I'm very glad to see you; I was afraid you could not arrive, so fast.' The man was clearly an Arab, but he spoke in English. Modin, angered by the lack of security, stuck to the convention, and used the words about buying a coffee-grinder which had been agreed upon. The man pulled himself together, and gave the necessary response in the careful, meaningless antiphony. Modin wished, more than ever, that he was back in Europe. They walked together into the shop.

The owner, wearing a dirty white *ghotra* on his head, bustled around and gave them each a cup of coffee. Then he walked out, tactfully, and started to rearrange the wares on display. Modin sat, sipping the hot coffee and looking carefully at the man he had come to meet. He was clearly a lot younger than the man who had made contact with the Syrian military attaché. That made it likely that he was a junior officer, perhaps a dispensable one. He was dressed in a neat lightweight suit, and was sweating heavily. Modin spoke English, not fluently, but well enough to keep up a conversation with another man whose native language was not English either. Despite his stay in Beirut, Modin's Arabic was poor.

'I must know who you are,' Modin said, brusquely. 'I was expecting to meet somebody older' – he meant more senior – 'and I must know everything before I can get an answer from my friends.'

The younger man looked anxious. 'But it is late. The Syrian men we talked to here took very long to speak to your friends. It is not possible for my leader to speak to you – he is too busy. But I am perhaps not as little important as you believe.' He smiled, and for the first time seemed more at ease. Modin felt somehow relieved. The man's reassurance meant nothing to him, but he sensed the relaxation in his mood, and felt almost inclined to believe that he was, after all, talking to someone of significance in the plot. You mustn't judge people necessarily by age in such countries as this, he reflected.

'It is not possible for me to give my friends' opinion on what you are doing,' Modin said, feeling the need to inject a little discipline into the negotiation, 'unless I am given the full details in advance.'

The other man seemed shocked. 'But this is a secret thing.'

'Those are my orders.' Modin calculated his abruptness of tone skilfully.

The Arab said, after a pause, 'I shall have to go back and talk about this.' He played with a gold ring on his forefinger, allowing it to slip off on to the table. 'But you see the thing that is to happen will happen very soon now. This is an important time.'

'Those are my orders,' Modin repeated. The conversation went backwards and forwards, unsatisfactorily, for a few more minutes. Finally Modin decided that the time was right to press for a little more commitment on the other's part. 'You must tell me your name,' he said finally.

The Arab at first refused. But Modin had sized him up, and knew that he would not want to break off contact over something like that, dangerous though it might be for him. After more argument, he pulled out an army identity card. It was printed in Arabic only, and Modin was unable to read it. The man spelt it out: 'Major Faroukh Ismail.'

London: Thursday 1 August

By the time David Wortham got back to his desk, the afternoon post had arrived. There seemed to be rather more than usual. A bill from American Express, a reminder about personal insurance and pension rights, a request for more details of a trip Wortham had taken some months before to Estonia, a belated summary of Soviet radio reports from the previous day. And a private letter, something of a rarity for him. He left that to the end, as something to look forward to after the administrative chores. When, finally, he turned to the letter, he examined the handwriting on it carefully. There was, he thought, something vaguely familiar both about it, and about the coarse paper of the envelope. The postmark was London. It was only as he was opening it that he realized what was familiar: it had the bold swirls and rounded shapes characteristic of someone who had been brought up to write the cyrillic alphabet; and the envelope was of Soviet manufacture.

There was another envelope inside, a pale green one, carefully sealed with adhesive tape, with a signature scrawled both across the tape and the back of the envelope, as a precaution against opening. Wortham felt a sudden cold shaft of fear go through him. He knew who it was from, as surely as if he could read the impossible signature. There was only one person in the world, he thought, who was bold enough – and foolish enough – to send him a letter from Moscow.

For once, Anyuta chose to address him in Russian, and she was as careless of spelling as she had been of rules of common sense. She explained that she had asked a friend who was coming to London to take the letter with him and send it on from there. Wortham couldn't decide whether he was glad she had taken the risk, or angry, and it was only gradually that he realized he was glad. The letter was a despairing one. Without his company, without the relief he had represented from the daily conformity of life in Moscow, her existence had become intolerable. Her husband had, she wrote, been rewarded for his part in the incident in the park. It was clear from what she wrote that he had been a plant, an agent working for the other faction within the Politburo, and that he had done his work well. Anyuta complained bitterly that her husband was nothing more than a servant of the State and of his own career. The imposition of silence was intolerable to her. To be the wife of a slave, and a slave oneself was, Anyuta wrote, a kind of death. Her letter tailed off with a wild denunciation of the system and equally wild professions of love for Wortham.

He read it twice, examining the carelessly pencilled words on the ugly lime green paper with great attention. Now that he was away from her, he could see the absurd side of her character clearly. He thought it almost certain now that she was involved in some way with Soviet security; it was impossible to explain the arrival of the letter in any other way. He had always thought that was the most likely reason for her appearance at the airport to say goodbye to him, and of the KGB officer's tactful agreement to keep away from them.

And yet the letter's emotions seemed genuine enough. After all those meetings in Moscow, he felt he knew her well enough to be sure that, however much she might lie, she never acted a part. Her lies were always about matters of detail, never about emotions. In that way, she could be fearsomely honest, and take no account of her personal interests. For the time being, he locked the letter away in a drawer and decided that when he went home that evening he would find a better place for it than that. If his own people were watching him, the arrival of a letter addressed in a Russian hand would be of great importance to them, and they would search for it very carefully. Later he examined the outer and inner envelopes for any sign that they had been tampered with, but they both seemed to have been untouched. He got hold of a box of matches, and took the envelopes to the lavatory with him. There he burned them, and flushed the few ashes away. For a moment he almost did the same with the letter itself, and even lit one corner of it. But as he saw the flame spreading its way towards the big, childish writing, with its desperate words, he changed his mind, and snuffed it out with his fingers.

Three times that afternoon, before he left, Wortham took the letter out of its locked drawer and re-read it carefully.

Ta'if, Saudi Arabia: Thursday 1 August

The one man who might have prevented the coup was the Minister of the Interior. He was a shrewd man, renowned for his peace-making abilities within the royal family. He had known about the rumours of dissatisfaction within the National Guard for several weeks, but had all along resisted the suggestion that he should take action. His tactic was to wait until the leaders had shown themselves; only then, he argued, could the government move decisively.

The National Guard was a paramilitary force of 20,000 Bedouin, set up partly to act as a counterweight to the regular armed forces in Saudi Arabia. Like so much in the country's life – the government, the administration, the education, the all-important oil policy – the basic division was between those who wanted to modernize faster, and those who thought that modernization had already gone too far, too fast. The regular armed forces, and particularly the air force, were on the side of the modernizers; the National Guard was the bulwark of the conservatives. Most members of the government fell into one or other of the categories, but not the Minister of the Interior. And his influence with his brother, the King, was paramount.

The Minister sat in his small golfing cart and drove over to the glass pavilion, between the trees, a good way from his palace. Heart disease had robbed him of his other passions, the stories of which had once circulated distantly in Riyadh and Jedda after his lengthy trips to London and New York. In spite of the careful diet he was obliged to maintain, he was still a big man and as he sat upright in his electric car, the motion of the air billowed his white robes, and his thin beak of a nose over the greying beard was pushed sternly forward.

Here in the mountains, the heat of the summer season was easily bearable. The flat stones beneath the wheels of the electric car were cool despite the morning sunshine, and the shade from the tall trees was pleasant. Like every minister in the government, the Prince spent six months of the year in Ta'if, accompanied by only a handful of his most senior civil servants. From May to October each year, the business of governing Saudi Arabia was left to the clerks sweltering in Riyadh. The Prince and his fellow ministers spent a couple of hours each day at their offices in Ta'if, but there were few matters of importance to settle, and almost no foreign visitors to see. No one who wanted business done in Saudi Arabia chose to travel there in the summer.

The Prince had that morning received a phone call from the head of security, about a German who had been seen in the company of an officer who was a known Islamic militant. The head of security thought it was possible that the man was working for East German or perhaps Soviet intelligence. The Prince was interested, but reassured the head of security. There were always dissidents, and sometimes Soviet agents would come to talk to them. It was better, however, to allow them to think they were undetected, rather than pick them up the instant they showed themselves. Keep an eye on this German by all means, the Prince had said; but be careful not to cause any incidents by arresting him or showing that we are interested in him.

The head of security had other, more important matters to attend to; if the Prince wasn't particularly interested in the German, he wasn't either. He put a man on the case, and turned his mind to something else.

The Prince navigated his car to the glass doors of the pavilion, and left it in the care of the doorkeeper there. Inside, it was cool and a little humid. The atmosphere was regulated to the constant mean temperature of the Prince's favourite resort in southern France. He walked carefully through the ranks of his vintage cars: this was the last delight which age and illness permitted him. The two German mechanics who worked for him ensured that all twenty-eight of the cars he owned were in perfect order, though the thought of trusting his 1923 Isotta-Fraschini or his 1920 Hispano-Suiza to the roads of Ta'if was intolerable. Still, he had the pride of the collection, ten cars in all, shipped carefully down to Riyadh each year when the weather cooled and the government of the country moved back there.

The Prince wasn't a mechanic. Sometimes he liked his two Germans to take out an engine and strip it down for him, or show him some recondite delight from the braking system; sometimes he would sit in the back seat, and have them start the engine of one of them; but it was the pleasure of having his agents discover some rare automobile for him, in Europe or Central America, and getting it sent back and reconditioned, which attracted him. He would sometimes speak sardonically of the lusts of a sick man for things he could no longer drive. But it was the possession of the cars, not the driving of them, that he wanted.

The Prince spent two hours every morning before going to his office in visiting his cars. In so rarefied a setting, the immediate problems of controlling potential subversives seemed a little unreal. He gave the possibility of a coup his attention between the hours of eleven and one each day; and even then the reasons for doing nothing seemed stronger than the reasons for taking energetic action. His brothers and cousins in the royal government agreed with his analysis. No one thought that the discontent of a few Bedouin officers in the National Guard could be so serious as to upset the somnolent rhythm of a Ta'if summer. The Prince had moved some senior officers around, and put a man he trusted in the office of the National Guard's commanding officer. That, he thought, should show he was watching things carefully. If anyone wanted to continue plotting now, they would soon be flushed out. The Prince had every confidence in the balance of the system.

Experimentally, Modin opened the plastic box the stewardess had handed him, and poked at its contents with a fork. After years of travelling around eastern Europe by Aeroflot, he was finding it hard to get used to the habit they had on western airlines of fussing over you. At least, he thought, as he bit into the veal, the stewardesses didn't retreat into their curtained enclave, as they did on Soviet airlines, and chatter and laugh throughout the flight as if the passengers didn't exist.

As he ate, he thought about the report he would have to make when he arrived in Rome. He hadn't been altogether impressed by what he had so far seen of the various conspirators in Riyadh. For one thing, their security was abysmal. He suspected that the same lack of discipline would apply to everything else they were doing.

On the other hand, from what he had seen, and from what the KGB residents had told him, the chances of success were moderately good. They, at least, were firmly in favour of supporting it, and their opinions counted for a good deal. The great advantage, Modin thought, as he dutifully packed up the remains of his lunch and handed the box to the stewardess, was that the plotters didn't want anything specific from the Soviet Union: no weapons, no manpower, just support once they had succeeded. Indeed, from their point of view, open aid from the Soviet Union could be a distinct disadvantage. The core of their resistance to the Saudi government was religious, and in the past Islamic hostility to Marxism had been just as strong as to western ideas – and after the Soviet move into Afghanistan it had been stronger. But the revolutionaries knew that they would need friends after the coup, especially if the Americans decided to stage a counter-coup. Modin doubted whether the Politburo in Moscow would sanction any kind of military support for a coup in Saudi Arabia, if it seemed likely that the Americans would move in. But it was no part of his duty to tell the conspirators that. He stretched himself out as best he could.

For a man of his build, he noticed, western aircraft were no better nor more comfortable than Soviet ones; that gave him a sense of satisfaction. He had been a little too exposed to the advantages of the West in the past week or so, he decided; that was what made Soviet citizens feel inferior to westerners. He shifted uncomfortably in his seat, and in doing so woke the man sitting next to him. From the copy of *Der Spiegel* on the man's lap, Modin assumed he was German. His apology was therefore a muttered one; the last thing he wanted to do was to get into conversation with a genuine German. But the man dropped off to sleep again, and Modin's mind returned to his report. It would, he thought, be as well to suggest that he should keep in discreet contact with the coup leaders, without making them any firm assurances. If the coup succeeded, Modin would be the indispensable link between Moscow and the new revolutionary régime. If it failed, he would be sufficiently in the background to be able to slip away. There was always South Yemen, the Soviet satellite which bordered on Saudi Arabia; Modin had no idea how he would get there, but he assumed that the KGB residents in Riyadh would have a system prepared. The more he thought about it, the better the prospect looked. And all because I remembered the name of the capital of Honduras, he thought.

His neighbour stirred again, and came to life. Modin thought it was a good moment to try to sleep himself. There was only one last thing to consider: the coup leaders would want a sign that the Soviet Union was interested in their case, a gesture of some kind. A show of naval strength in the Gulf, perhaps? He fell asleep before he could work out how big he thought the force should be.

CHAPTER 3

To fit in with the change of events, words too had to change their usual meanings. What used to be described as a thoughtless act of aggression was now regarded as the courage one would expect to find in a party member; to think of the future and wait was merely another way of saying one was a coward; any idea of moderation was just an attempt to disguise one's unmanly character; ability to understand a question from all sides meant that one was totally unfitted for action. *Thucydides, 'The Peloponnesian War', Book III.*

Camp David, Maryland: Saturday 1 September

Dr. Richard Preger had been happy to get away from Columbia University and the Institute for Communist Affairs there. The constant, silent combat in which he was engaged with his deputy, a man of Hungarian extraction, had been getting worse. The Hungarian disapproved of the links Preger had tried to forge with the Administration and the State Department, on the grounds that they damaged morale at the Institute and got in the way of its real work. There were times when Preger felt that there was something in that; but he wasn't, all the same, prepared to sever the links.

Not even the Hungarian, with his lugubrious silences and his expressive shrugs, could complain when Preger decided to spend the Labor Day weekend at a seminar held at Camp David. The only person who might have complained was Mary Preger, who had been hoping that she and her husband would spend the holiday with friends on a farm in rural New Jersey. For a time, relations at home had been as bad as they were at the Institute. But Mary Preger shared some at least of her husband's ambitions for himself; and she never came close to suggesting that he shouldn't go to Camp David.

He woke at 6.30 on the Saturday morning, in a narrow and uncomfortable bed in Hawthorn Lodge, one of the guest cabins. The sketch-map pinned to the inside of his door showed that Hawthorn was almost as far as you could get from the President's own cabin, Aspen Lodge. Preger didn't need to be told that the closer you were to the President, the more important your services to him were felt to be. But it didn't matter. Preger lay in bed and listened to the faint shouts from the more enthusiastic officials there, who shared, or pretended to share, the President's own liking for early morning exercise.

The first session of the weekend began at eight o'clock. It was to be the kind of seminar for which the President had become famous. It gave the impression that each major decision, each central aspect of policy, was carefully weighed and evaluated in the light of a range of expert advice; though in practice, Preger suspected, the impression was more important than the actual process itself.

Preger guessed that he had been selected because he was known to be something of a dove on East-West relations. The range of experts from the State Department and from organizations like his own Institute was a broad one, and stretched as far as people whom Preger himself regarded as being very far to the right. But he could see that, although the President opened the seminar by telling everyone they should speak straight from the shoulder, he seemed quite uninterested in strongly outspoken judgments. For all the President's much talked-of toughness, Preger decided that what was really wanted was a gently modulated debate, in which everyone shaded off from a central position, leaving the President himself to pinpoint just where he believed the central ground lay.

As the morning wore on, Preger spoke briefly a couple of times: once to correct a point of fact about Soviet trade, and once to give his own opinions on the value of a trade boycott against the Soviet Union. He realized afterwards that there had been no need to speak as long or as earnestly as he had.

It was hot, and insects droned occasionally through the fug of ideas and made their way out again through the open windows. Preger could smell the grass outside, and he caught himself concentrating on the truncated view he had through the window opposite, rather than on the views that were being put forward. In spite of the talk about toughness – which most speakers appeared to sense was what the President wanted – Preger felt that everyone was beginning from a position of actual weakness. In spite of the billions of dollars that had been spent, the assumption was still that the Soviet Union was militarily stronger than the United States. Preger's guess was that Soviet discussions started from precisely the same viewpoint; that they, and not the Americans, were the weaker power. We're like two elderly gladiators, he thought, circling round each other in the arena. Each of us thinks the other is strong enough to end the fight with a single blow, while in reality we're each as weak as the other. And what we should really be afraid of is missing our footing in the sand. For a moment he almost thought of saying something about it. But he jotted down some notes instead, and looked out of the window again.

The day dragged on, and the President finally summed up what he said was the consensus of the day's discussion: that the Soviet Union was urgently looking for a way to get off the hook of its high military spending, and that a firm policy of warning and confrontation was required to show the Russians that they would have to take a less aggressive stance. A useful opportunity of making this clear, the President agreed, was provided by the recent arrival in the Gulf of the Soviet Union's newest and most powerful warship: the Rostov-class aircraft carrier, *Irkutsk*, and the cruiser and two destroyers which accompanied her. Their presence in the Gulf was totally unacceptable, the President said. Sitting and listening to him, Preger reflected that few things were sadder to witness than weakness and indecision masquerading as strength. But a general murmur of agreement went around as the cocktail hour approached and the late afternoon sunshine beckoned. Preger thought there was little to look forward to except the film show that evening.

Riyadh: Saturday 1 September

As the first streaks of red and gold came into the sky over the Ministry opposite his room, Faroukh Ismail heard the rumbling of the three lorries which were bringing his detachment of fifty men along Abdul Aziz Street to the rendezvous at the crossroads nearby. The lorries pulled up just short of the junction with the Airport Road, and Ismail, immaculately dressed, and carrying his swagger-stick under his arm, made his way out into the hotel compound and across the road to meet them. He first inspected them, in best parade ground manner, then marched them up to the gates of the Interior Ministry. By this time a short fire-fight had started, farther up the Airport Road, as the detachments taking over the Saudi naval headquarters and the Military College met with a brief show of resistance from the guards on duty there. But that was over a mile away, and the sound of gunfire was too faint in the noise of the wakening traffic to alarm anyone in the Interior Ministry. As for the attacks on the two compounds on either side, Defence and Communications, they were planned to follow only when Ismail had succeeded.

The paras on the gate at the Interior Ministry assumed that any detachment of National Guardsmen must be there with official approval, and they opened the gates to them directly Ismail gave the order. The detachment marched in, still in parade-ground order, and then fanned out. Some arrested the astonished paras on duty at the gatehouse, while others moved towards the main buildings, which were some way from the road in a desolate compound filled with parked cars and discouraged, scrubby trees. Even at this stage, most of Ismail's men didn't know what it was they were taking part in, and they weren't to find out for another hour or so. But their discipline held them together, and Ismail had taken the precaution of informing one hand-picked group of ten men the night before. These ten marched up, with Ismail at their head, to the ornate doors of the Ministry, while others spread themselves out in the warm dust of the compound and took up firing positions to give them cover if necessary. It wasn't. Ismail was able to walk into the marble entrance hall, and demand the surrender of the Paratroop Major in command. The Major, who had been asleep, was too bewildered to resist. Ten minutes later, the entire guard of twenty paras were marched off, stripped of their belts and boots, to one of the smaller buildings in the compound. Ismail and his men had gained command of the most important and best guarded ministry in Riyadh without firing a shot; and they were now in a position to provide cover, if any should be needed, for the attacks on the Ministries of Communications and Defence on either side of them.

But force was unnecessary. The architect of the coup, Colonel Mazouhi, had done his work well at the one, and the other was poorly guarded. The shooting up the road at the Military College and the naval headquarters had been brief, and no one had been seriously hurt, let alone killed, on either side. The first phase of the coup in Riyadh was over by six o'clock in the morning, an hour after it had begun. All the other objectives, the airport, the television station, and the air force base, had been captured in their turn. By eight o'clock, five key generals based in Riyadh had been arrested, and peace-feelers were being put out to military bases in other parts of the country. Everything now depended on the reaction of the King.

CHAPTER 4

The worst news imaginable. *President Jimmy Carter on the Iranian revolution.*

Camp David, Maryland: Sunday 2 September

Once, President John F. Kennedy and his wife had called it 'the cornball motel', and had preferred to escape to the New England coast. But none of the presidents who followed had the same dislike for the folksiness which surrounded Camp David. Nixon thought it improved the popular view of him as a big city lawyer. Carter had valued it less for its image-enhancing value, that for its security. But the incumbent President had taken to Camp David enthusiastically, precisely because it was a refuge in the mountains. He ordered the great presidential seal to be restored to its Nixonian place of honour over the chimney-piece in the panelled sitting-room, which had a view southwards into the valley of the Catoctin mountains, several hundred feet below.

The atmosphere of relaxation suited the President's nature. An early riser, and an enthusiastic walker, he was up as usual at five the next morning; the only person in the Camp who was, apart from his mess-steward and the secret servicemen who guarded him.

He walked briskly along the line of the triple wire fence and its electrified barrier, as close to it as the security men would allow him to go. That meant he could avoid the lodges and get the best view. The lonely figure in the grey tracksuit passed from the surveillance of one security man to the next, his progress monitored on the shirt-cuff microphones and the plastic ear-pieces of each of them. As he walked he caught glimpses through the trees of the fields and valleys below. It gave him a patriarchal feeling to gaze down at a small corner of the vast country he governed; and in the early morning, before he was obliged to assume the self-confidence and reliability which people wanted of their President, he would often feel a shiver of inadequacy at the thought of the hundreds of millions of people depending on him and on the quality of his decisions for their safety. The President was not a philosophical man, and these thoughts never struck him later in the day; such moments were linked with the cool air of the mountainside, the scent of the pine-needles under his feet and the occasional sight of the world beyond the security fence.

He had been walking for a few minutes only, when the distinctly less athletic figure of his Chief of Staff, wrapped in a white terry-towelling bathrobe, came running across from Laurel Lodge, towards the northern end of the camp. Pushing past a nervous secret serviceman, he ran into the President's path, forcing him to stop.

'Sir, there's a call from the NSC – there's been some kind of trouble in Saudi Arabia.'

Five minutes later the President stood in front of the seal over the chimney piece, looking down at the unlit logs and allowing himself to think for the first time about the implications. Then the telephone sounded, and the Army Signal Corps operator on duty plugged him through to the Washington headquarters of the National Security

Committee. The US Embassy in Jedda was in full-time contact with the State Department in Washington, feeding each new item of information on the telex machine as it was received. But all communication between Jedda and the royal palaces in Ta'if had been cut, and the relatively small US liaison office in Riyadh itself was equally unable to get through to Ta'if. The details were far from clear but the American Ambassador was inclined to believe the worst. By six o'clock the President's National Security Adviser had made up his mind on the basis of the Embassy reports, and was advising the President to send in the Rapid Deployment Force, which was kept in reserve for just such an emergency as this. There would be no problems with Congress. It would, he argued, be hours before even the first troops could reach Riyadh, but the situation would not have stabilized by then, and the force could be seen as coming in at the request of the King. The President felt it was impossible to take such a decision so quickly, and he was relieved when the Secretary of State was shown in by the mess-steward.

'Does State have any idea who these revolutionaries are yet?' The Secretary of State did up a button on his sports shirt before answering. 'No one has any idea, Mr President. Maybe some Islamic purists, is all.'

'Because NSC says we must send in the Force right away.'

'That's an option which exists, Mr President, but we simply can't exercise it until we're certain just what's going on down there.'

'Even if it may be too late?'

'You know as well as I do the dangers of some half-assed trick that goes wrong. Remember Carter and the "rescue" of the Iranian hostages?' His voice was heavy with irony.

The telephone rang. The State Department reported on a crackling line that it looked now as though the Saudi army had given its backing to the coup.

'Where does that leave us?' asked the President, a little

plaintively, as he put the phone down. 'Makes it more difficult just to move in, that's for sure.'

The moment for action passed, imperceptibly. The President was a man who selected advisers because they were likely to give him the advice he wanted. It almost never occurred to him to go against their advice.

The telephone sounded again. The National Security Adviser was impatient about the lack of a decision, and was calling, at the risk of further irritating the President, to try to get him to commit himself. But the President would do no more, with the Secretary of State standing beside him, frowning and nodding, than to agree that the forward units of the Rapid Deployment Force, based on Masirah Island, off Oman, should be placed on stand-by. The argument went backwards and forwards for a few minutes, and at one stage the President put the Secretary of State on the line to give the counter-arguments. Finally the President took a decision which was no decision at all.

'The first essential, Dave,' he told the National Security Adviser, 'is to find out what's happened to the King. We can't do anything without him; there's no question of the RDF being sent in without his agreement. I shall be leaving here for the White House in twenty minutes. Keep the telephone line open until then.' The National Security Adviser, faced with a direct order, had to obey.

All over Camp David, people were waking up to be told the news. There was an anxious crowd at the breakfast hall, passing around such information as could be gleaned from the Secretary of State's party. The idea of carrying on with a seminar about the United States' relations with the Soviet Union, at a time when the entire balance of power was changing in the Middle East, seemed ludicrously irrelevant. Cut off as they were at Camp David, people began to talk about returning to their offices; but until the President and the Secretary of State were on their way, the harassed transport officers could do nothing for anyone else. Richard

Preger turned out with the others, but felt that it was better to wait quietly until after the big rush. There would be no immediate call on his services.

The President walked out of Aspen Lodge fifteen minutes later, hand in hand with his wife. His family would be staying on at Camp David over the Labor Day weekend, to complete the holiday. He kissed her goodbye, and climbed into the back seat of the waiting Buick. The convoy of cars moved off, the Marine sentries saluted, and the remaining secret servicemen settled down with relief to the quieter task of guarding the presidential retreat without the President.

As he got into the helicopter on the landing-pad at the side of the Camp David complex, the President vaguely returned the salute of the Navy Commander who had only just finished buttoning his uniform. The helicopter flew across the face of the mountain, and the President looked down at the patches of woodland and the Catoctin mountains, and the small hamlet of Thurmont which he had glimpsed during his walk that morning. All he could think about was the decision that still awaited him over Saudi Arabia.

New York: Sunday 2 September

The news was slow in reaching the outside world. The first indication they had at the CBS television newsroom that something major had happened was a message from the pool group which always staked out presidential visits, whether to Camp David or anywhere else. The President had suddenly broken off his working holiday there and had flown back to Washington with the Secretary of State. But at eight o'clock on a Saturday morning – given that it was Labor Day weekend – there were only seven people in the CBS newsroom.

It would normally have taken a few minutes to find out why the President had left, but instead a patient assignment editor, with no contacts worth mentioning, worked away for a good forty-five minutes. And before he had finished the news came through on the AP wire.

'Holy shit,' said one of the other assignment editors, as the two-line message came up on the teleprinter. 'Hey, you wanna hear this?' He read it out. 'Flash. Coup attempt in Riyadh reported by diplomatic sources.'

'Could be good,' said the producer, who had just got in. 'If it works. What a time to stage a coup.'

'Maybe they don't have Labor Day in Saudi, Bert.'

'You don't say. I thought CBS were the only ones who didn't have Labor Day.' The line brought a rueful laugh.

As the morning wore on, further details came out. No one had been able to find out who the coup leaders were, or what they were planning to do. Saudi Arabia is not the kind of place where most of the big international news organizations have full-time correspondents, with the exception of the agencies. On the other hand, Saudi Arabia had brought in a number of western journalists to work on its English and French language services in television, radio and newspapers, so the standard of the stringers was higher than it would have been in other places. But such western journalists as there were tended not to have the kind of experience that was needed on a story as big as this.

Within minutes of getting the first message, the CBS foreign editor had telexed their full-time Middle East correspondent, who was in Cairo, to tell him to get to Riyadh as fast as possible. The flights, though, weren't particularly favourable. The foreign editor sighed, and thought about his air travel budget, which was already overspent for the year. They were going to have to charter a plane to get into Riyadh. He rang the other networks to see if they were interested in coming in on the charter. Neither of them was. NBC had a correspondent and a crew in Turkey; ABC were glumly trying to locate their Middle East team, who were thought to be in Cyprus. If CBS could get their people to Riyadh, the chances were they'd have a beat on the other nets; and that, thought the foreign editor more cheerfully, would take care of the money problem. He got to work on the telephone, setting up an aircraft and starting the long business of asking permission for it to land in Riyadh.

Across the newsroom, the producer and associate producer were trying to work out the scale of the story.

'If this really is a major coup, and the King gets thrown out on his goddam ass,' Bert, the producer was saying, 'then screw Labor Day, we're going to have to get everybody in here, but quick. We're gonna need the special reports unit in, everyone except the sport guys. And even they'd better hang around, in case the new guys in Saudi play baseball.' Another tired smile went round the group. No one liked to ignore Bert Howardson's jokes entirely, because he took them so seriously himself.

'We're gonna need an executive producer, and all the library tape we've ever shown on Saudi, and get some guys going through that to find the pictures, since we sure as hell aren't going to get any pictures out of Saudi television today, or maybe ever.'

The associate producer slipped away to ring the list of correspondents in Washington who were going to be needed: the White House staff, the State Department staff, the defence correspondent, the economics correspondent, the diplomatic correspondent – the list went on and on, and each of the specialists as they came on the telephone line showed a different degree of irritability at being disturbed on what should have been a quiet, private weekend – until, that is, the story was outlined.

Richard Preger had just arrived home when the diplomatic correspondent called him; and after a brief consultation with his conscience and his wife about breaking up the family weekend still further, he agreed to participate in the programme.

For the rest of the afternoon the correspondents hammered away at their scripts, grumbling at the shortage of hard facts, stretching out other people's opinions as far as they could make them go. The defence correspondent was the only man who had an easy run; his material was the least hypothetical, since the United States had the capacity to intervene in the Middle East, and he had been on exercises time and again watching the Rapid Deployment Force test its readiness for just such an operation as this. His only doubt was whether the President would use the RDF in Saudi Arabia to put the King back on his throne; and that was more a question for the White House correspondent, whose best contact, a man in the President's private office, had told him that he simply didn't know.

It was past three o'clock before the final confirmation came through that the King had left. The foreign editor had been trying to think of every possible destination the King might choose, and there were CBS crews on stand-by at as many western European airports as possible, in case the King did not make the trip to Washington that everyone was expecting. The news that the King was likely to leave had caused the correspondents, working away with the special projects unit, to revise a good many of their assumptions. The feeling, influenced mostly by the hopes at the White House, had been that the King would stay and fight. His escape changed the whole picture. People for interview started to trickle in. The maps and other graphics were assembled, and the last minute edits on the videotape inserts were made.

Afterwards, when the ritual congratulations had been given, several of the correspondents agreed among themselves that it had been a fairly uninformative show. They had gone through the events of the day as best they could, describing the King's departure dramatically enough by means of a telephone interview with someone who had been at the airport, but unable to say with any kind of certainty who had taken the country over and forced the King to leave in this way. No one knew, or was prepared to say, anything about the leaders of the coup or their real motives.

Richard Preger had said it was his opinion that the Russians were not involved, and that the presence in the Gulf of the largest and newest ship in the entire Soviet navy was a coincidence. A former US Ambassador to Iran had disagreed, and spoke of the red shadow stretching across the whole western end of the Gulf. The diplomatic correspondent said that the White House and the State Department would agree with the Ambassador. Nobody felt able to say for certain whether the United States would decide to send in its Rapid Deployment Force.

Ta'if: Sunday 2 September

The coup was an extraordinary blend of confidence and confidence trick. A group of no more than fifty officers all told, none of them above the rank of colonel, managed to convince their own men, their superior officers, and their government, that they had control of the country, when in fact they had no more than physical possession of the buildings of a dozen government ministries and three airfields. But two things were in their favour: they had appealed successfully to the discontent and the religious anxieties of the men in their own force, the National Guard, and in the armed forces; and the King and most of his senior ministers lost their nerve.

Important in that loss of nerve was the total lack of bloodshed during the first crucial hours of the coup. That convinced the government, far away in the rarefied atmosphere of Ta'if, that the conspirators had far more support than they in fact possessed. And there was the manner in which the news was broken to the King. If it had come from some loyalist source first, he might have been reassured, and been persuaded to fight back. But luck continued to favour the leaders of the coup. The first news came on an emergency line from the Ministry of Communications to the office of the Interior Minister in Ta'if. All other lines from Riyadh had been cut. Colonel Mazouhi spoke to the Minister at around 10.30 in the morning, claiming that the armed forces were solidly behind the coup, and that everything was in the hands of the revolutionaries. That this was no more than a bluff should have been obvious to the Minister: Ta'if, after all, was completely unaffected, and Mazouhi quite clearly lacked the ability to mount any show of force there. But something else worked in his favour, too.

The Minister was normally a cool enough figure, but the frequent warnings he had received from his specialist about the effects of strong emotion or sudden exertion on his heart condition made him the more inclined to accept what he was told, rather than contest it. And Colonel Mazouhi, unlike Ismail and several of the other coup leaders, took the line that the King and some members of the royal family – including, it seems, the Interior Minister himself – should not be overthrown, but forced to accept a constitutional role and hand over the day-to-day running of the government. The Minister cannot have wanted to accept such an offer, but he clearly thought it was worth while trying to negotiate with Mazouhi, instead of urging an immediate counter-attack. As the only member of the Cabinet who had been in touch with the conspirators, his views had a particular weight.

But by the time the other ministers arrived, together with the service chiefs, the atmosphere was one of open panic. The navy and the air force remained loyal to the government, but the navy's support was useless and the government's belief in the loyalty of the air force had been undermined shortly before the Cabinet meeting, when three F-14 fighters from the main base near Riyadh, which was in the hands of the rebels, screamed low over Ta'if and fired several rockets at the royal palace. No one was hurt, but the incident clinched it. In fact the F-14s were at the full stretch of their capability, and had to risk a landing at the apparently loyal air base near Jedda. But by that time the enthusiasm generated by the coup had affected even the air force, and the pilots were given a hero's welcome.

By mid-afternoon there were reports of big anti-royalist demonstrations in Riyadh and Jedda, as people hurried out to support the coup. Soon the King was convinced he had no alternative but to escape. A move by the Interior Minister and one or two others to delay until the following morning, and to mobilize popular support in Riyadh and Jedda, failed to get much backing. The King was determined to leave.

It was left to the Interior Minister to tell the leaders of the coup. Late in the afternoon he managed to contact Colonel Mazouhi in Riyadh and give him the government's reply.

The Colonel listened in silence, and then said, 'You have acted correctly, and in the interests of the country. You will not be hindered in your flight.'

It is doubtful whether, in any case, the conspirators had enough control over the air force to stop the royal party leaving, but by that time it was too late for second thoughts. Nothing, the Interior Minister said later, with some bitterness, could stop the instinct for self-preservation. He himself bore a good deal of the responsibility for the King's decision, by trying to persuade him to negotiate rather than counter-attack; but it had been no part of his intention to encourage an outright collapse.

There was panic at the airport, as several hundred senior court officials struggled to get on board the three Boeing 707s of the royal flight. Many didn't make it. In the small terminal building at Ta'if the smell of fear and sweat mingled, as people shouted and tried to buy their way on to other planes, or gave up the effort and turned to other ways of leaving. Huge sums of money changed hands, and even then harassed airport officials had to pull some people off the steps to the aircraft, and there were fights about the amount of baggage the lucky passengers were allowed to take with them. One man, in a magnificent gold and white robe, handed out his luggage as presents to the ground crew. In a corner of the airport building, the wife of a senior official was desperately trying to find her small son, who had wandered off into the maze of small offices while she was trying to help her husband get seats for them all.

It was shortly after eight o'clock that night before the Boeing 707 carrying the King into exile was finally able to take off. The sky was a brilliant display of red and gold, with the darkness stretching across from the west, the direction the planes took, one after the other. In silence, the airport staff stood and watched them go. Then they turned away, to try to put their own affairs into some sort of order.

Further off, the palaces of Ta'if were left deserted; the guards and lesser functionaries did what looting they could, and escaped themselves. The German mechanics at the palace of the Minister of the Interior reluctantly locked the doors of the pavilion where his vintage cars were kept, and went out to look for something more modern to drive to Jedda in.

Riyadh: Wednesday 5 September

Abdul Aziz, the founder of modern Saudi Arabia, had begun the long task of conquering the land from his tribal and religious opponents in 1902, staging a sudden raid on Riyadh with a few companions, and capturing it against all the odds. In his way, Abdul Aziz had a good deal in common with the man who was to supplant his dynasty: Faroukh Ismail. But for the moment, Ismail still ranked second to Abdullah Mazouhi, the man who had convinced the King that he could no longer remain.

The first three days after the coup were taken up by an almost continuous meeting of the revolutionary council: a body composed of twenty of the leading conspirators, with one or two co-opted men from the army, senior officers who had sympathized with the coup, and several civil servants. Their meetings were held at the Ministry of the Interior. Occasionally Colonel Modin would slip in to talk with them there; though he kept very much in the background, waiting for the coup to settle down. The leaders were in constant communication with units of the National Guard throughout the country; and particularly in the oil-fields, which were under the sole control of the Guard. The council members met in what had been a large waiting-room on the first floor of the Ministry, drinking endless cups of coffee supplied to them from the kitchens by Guardsmen, and from time to time breaking their meetings for two or three hours' sleep, each of the members lying down on the thick carpet of the room.

Faroukh Ismail slept only rarely. He disagreed profoundly with the attitude of Abdullah Mazouhi, who was anxious to reassure the outside world that the Arabian Islamic Republic, as it was now to be called, had not changed its general alignment. Mazouhi, in spite of the loud protests of Ismail and one or two of the younger officers, telephoned the American Embassy in Jedda several times to assure them that there would be no interruption of oil supplies to western countries, and no major dislocation of his country's relations with the United States. At one stage Ismail tried to wrench the telephone out of Mazouhi's hands as the council sat and listened to the call, but Major Achmad Wazir, who was Mazouhi's closest ally on the council, pulled out his revolver and threatened to shoot Ismail if he didn't sit down. From that point on, the hostility and suspicion within the revolutionary council grew stronger, until Ismail and his sympathizers took to meeting in a smaller anteroom – only coming into the main council room for the long sessions – which took on the nature of a negotiation, rather than a discussion of policy. And from the second night, the brief breaks for rest saw Ismail and his allies walking out of the room and sleeping elsewhere. Their door was carefully guarded.

On the third night Ismail went out into the courtyard – the first time he had shown himself there for thirty hours or more. He was immediately mobbed by his supporters, who shouted to him to lead them back into the council-room to arrest his opponents. Ostentatiously, because he knew that guardsmen loyal to Mazouhi were watching, he told them that the divisions on the revolutionary council were only disagreements on policy between comrades, and that the main objective of everyone was the victory of the revolution, not the victory of personality. That brought a cheer, grudging enough from some, but one which Mazouhi's supporters took up enthusiastically. After half an hour, Ismail turned to go back into the building. He was followed by several of the men who had been with him on the night they had taken the Ministry over – fellow-tribesmen of his. He had only a few seconds to speak to them, because Mazouhi's supporters were responsible for security within the building itself. But before he went up the wide marble staircase, he was able to whisper a time to them: 4.30.

The council meeting carried on, as usual, into the small hours, as the different members argued and shouted with each other about the policy they should adopt on oil depletion and on the rate of modernization that should be allowed, given the lower income from oil. By three o'clock they were exhausted, and someone suggested that they should adjourn for a couple of hours' sleep. There was general relief at that, and Ismail as usual led his small group out of the room, together with their bodyguards. He didn't tell the members of his group what was to happen in ninety minutes' time, since he couldn't finally be certain of the loyalty of all of them. As the bodyguards watched the door, inside and out, and the rest of them settled down on the floor to sleep, Ismail himself lay awake, trying to work out what his followers would do when they stormed the building.

At 4.30 he heard a slight noise, not from the courtyard, but from above: a squealing sound which wasn't enough to make anyone else turn his head, much less wake up. Ismail knew what it was: the sound of a pulley, as his men were lowered from the roof of the Ministry, which they had reached from the roof of one of the other buildings in the compound. For a time there was silence. Then, from several places in the Ministry at once so it seemed, came the appalling racket of submachine gun fire, as guardsmen loyal to Ismail opened up almost simultaneously on the guards at the main door to the Ministry and inside, at the door to the council-room. Ismail lay on the floor, facing the others in the room, and waving his revolver at them; as much in menace as in a gesture to them to keep their heads down.

Very soon, the firing became desultory, and then stopped altogether. The whole incident had probably taken no more than a minute, from start to finish. Ismail's closest comrade opened the door, and grinned wolfishly at him. The man was dressed, like the other guardsman, in a blue boiler suit, but his had splashes of blood on the front, and he was holding a commando knife in his hand.

'Come and see,' he said.

Ismail walked slowly, tiredly, into the council-room. The bodies of Mazouhi's guards lay at the doorway, riddled with bullets. Ismail couldn't avoid treading on the outstretched hand of one of them as he made his way into the room. The only living people in the room were Ismail's own companions. There were gouts of blood on the wall, to shoulder height, and the plaster was heavily pocked with lines of bullets from the Stirlings the men had used. Mazouhi's body was a little separated from the rest. He had bled from a wound in the shoulder, but that wasn't what had killed him. The head lay a good yard away, severed by the commando knife of Ismail's closest friend.

Chapter 5

If we fail to meet this challenge, all other nations will be on notice that despite its overwhelming power the United States, when a real crisis comes, will be found wanting. *Richard Nixon, justifying the invasion of Cambodia, April 1970.*

The Gulf: Monday 10 September

At four in the morning the decks had still not entirely lost the stored heat of the previous day, but the cold air cut through the Marine Captain's green flight suit and flak jacket which covered him from waist to throat. There were no lights on the carrier's deck, and the cold and the darkness made the nervousness and the fear infinitely worse. He climbed into the helicopter, remembering a line from Shakespeare: 'As cold a night as 'tis, he could wish himself in Thames up to the neck.' The Captain hadn't seen the Thames, but he knew his *Henry V*, from the days before he went to boot camp in Pensacola.

He had never flown a mission on active service before, and neither had any of the forty-three other men who would be flying with him, as crew or as dumb troops. He settled himself uncomfortably in the right-hand seat, his throat dry with nervousness. As he was putting on his fibreglass helmet and doe-skin gloves, the second pilot, the H2P, slipped into the seat beside him and gave him a grin that seemed confident enough. He and the H2P had always got along well on the countless training missions they'd flown together. But this time there would be shooting, and the danger of losing more than a reputation; and the thought made each of them wonder how the other would behave when the bullets started flying.

The helicopter kicked and shifted as the infantrymen climbed aboard and settled themselves, clumsily and noisily. A voice barked an obscenity, and the noise died down a little. The Captain scarcely heard them. He was finding that he needed to think carefully about everything, that none of the usual procedures was coming naturally to him, and it was like early training days again. There was a line in *Henry V* about that, too, he thought; but he was too busy to disinter it from his memory.

The Captain's face glowed weirdly in the red light from the instrument panel in front of him, and the red reflected off the bubble of plexiglass that held them in, backed by the darkness of the night sky. Then, as the folded blades of the helicopter sequenced into flying position, the blade-locking lights changed from red to green. Outside on the deck the plane handlers held up the three tie-downs to show him that the helicopter was free of its shackles. In the last seconds before the noise of the rotors hit them there was no talk as the Captain and the H2P prepared themselves for take-off. They got their instructions from Pri-Fly, no longer individuals, but part of helicopter Bonny-Sue 1-1, and of the squadron she herself belonged to. They moved clumsily out across the sea, into the greater darkness of the sky. The few small lights and the green and red glows from the cockpits of the other helicopters in the squadron on the flight deck of the great carrier faded beneath them and the Captain had other things to concern him.

He knew nothing of the days of argument and anxiety in

Washington which had led to the decision to send in Bonny-Sue 1-1 and the rest of the Rapid Deployment Force: the threatened resignations, the fierce political in-fighting, the struggle for the ear of the President. Faced with a total lack of agreement among his advisers, the President had followed his own instincts and ordered the RDF to move in. And even before he had taken the decision, the preparations had been made, just in case.

All during the bitter early stages of the revolution in Saudi Arabia, the carriers based on the British island of Diego Garcia had been heading westwards to the Gulf, while other carriers, from the Operations Support Establishment at Berbera in Somalia, headed north-west up the Red Sea, to station themselves off Jeddah. Massive 130-CX jet transports had brought several thousand troops from the headquarters of Readiness Command at Fort McDill Air Force Base, Florida, and had deposited them at the other major Support Establishment, on Masirah Island off the coast of Oman. Pre-positioned ships in the Indian Ocean had stored sufficient heavy equipment and supplies, sealed and dehumidified, for three brigades of US Marines. Altogether, the plan was to funnel three divisions of troops, and two dozen squadrons of F-15 fighters, into the area.

The Captain looked across the darkness from Bonny-Sue 1-1 at the other eleven helicopters in the squadron, humming angrily over the sea like great burdened insects. Ahead of them, less than a mile away, was the coast of Saudi Arabia and the peninsula where stood the second largest oil refinery in the world: Ras Tannurah. In the warmth and comradeship of the briefing in the carrier's ward-room, eighty minutes before, the Captain had looked at the aerial photographs, and anticipated this moment when, in the darkness and discomfort of his seat at the controls, he would see in reality what the black and white photographs showed – closer, darker and far more menacing than any photograph.

They had seen the missile launchers which had been hastily installed in the desert around the refinery, and the tents where the National Guardsmen and their reinforcements were billeted. Now the waning moon gave sufficient light for the Captain to see the refinery clearly outlined against the pale sand. Excitement had taken over from the nervousness. The Captain called the crew chief, back in the aft of the helicopter with the infantrymen, 'Everybody buckled up, Jeff?'

The answer, familiar from a hundred training sorties, came back, 'Yessir, ready back here, sir.'

The Captain nudged the H2P and signed to him to pull the visor down on his helmet. Over the UHF network came the voice of the Lieutenant-Colonel in the command gunship: 'Bonny Sue 1-6 to Bonny Sue 1-1 through 4: head in now, and don't forget this time it's for real.'

They went down to two hundred feet, the refinery in front of them looking like a ruined city of spires and towers and domes. But not uninhabited.

Two things happened, almost simultaneously: a storage tank, one of dozens on the side of the refinery nearest the sea, blew up with a stunning concussion and a white and scarlet sheet of flame; and the Captain saw a dozen cherry-red balls of fire coming up towards him from the ground. Almost before he had registered them, they had passed. Anyway, he could have done nothing to avoid them. Instead, they hit Bonny Sue 1-2 beside him. She went down immediately, falling sideways, with smoke and fire belching out from her in the fierce light of the burning storage tank. Somehow the pilot switched on his UHF transmitter, and the Captain's head was filled with the pilot's screams. When it came, the crash and explosion of the helicopter, packed with men, was a sick relief.

Now there were other explosions, other trajectories of cherry-red golf-balls, but somehow none of the other helicopters in the squadron was seriously damaged. The

Captain, gripping violently on the controls, put down with the others and landed in a loose trail, each fifty yards from the next.

The crew chief threw the doors open, and the laden infantrymen, rifles in hand, jumped out in groups, roaring with fear and aggression. Elsewhere another group of helicopters from the squadron, all four of them, were putting down on the south side of the refinery. The Captain watched them come down, waiting for the crew chief to give him the word that everyone was out of their own 'copter. Directly the word came, he jerked them up into the sky again. Helicopters coming down are vulnerable enough, but there is nothing more vulnerable in war than a helicopter on the ground.

Bonny Sue 1-1 and the two other survivors of the group headed off together, and the four from the parallel group rose with them, like flying ants from nests in the grass. Beside them in the air billowed the great columns of black and red smoke from the two storage tanks which the National Guardsmen themselves had blown up. Over the refinery they left the command gunship orbiting, with the Lieutenant-Colonel in radio contact with the men on the ground, regulating the course of the battle and still keeping in reserve four other helicopters, which hovered not far away. They would be brought in directly the Lieutenant-Colonel saw where the balance of advantage lay. The Captain headed off with the others, back to the carrier. For twelve hours or more they would be ferrying men and material to the refinery, returning every forty minutes or so. Each trip would be less dangerous, as the resistance on the ground was worn down. When it was light, they would have the help of four F-15 fighters, which would scour the desert for any tanks or armoured personnel carriers which the revolutionary government might have sent. And directly the refinery was under the army's control, the helicopters would switch to bringing in oil experts from the carrier to man the pumping stations and keep some sort of flow going.

The Captain pulled the doe-skin gloves tighter on his hands, and tried not to listen to the sound of his friend's screams, which still echoed in his head louder than the noise of the rotors above him.

Riyadh: Monday 10 September

The air strikes began shortly before nine o'clock.

The awesome scream of the American 'Tomcat' fighters, as they shot overhead at a thousand feet a second, close enough for every detail of their fuselages to be clearly visible, with the pilots crouched tensely over the controls, split apart the silence in Modin's new room at the Al Yamamah hotel, opposite the Interior Ministry. The next second, the rockets from the 'Tomcats'' sounded their brief high-pitched whistling note, and then exploded with a violence that brought part of the ceiling down on to Modin, as he lay on the floor, his arms ineffectually sheltering his head. He still lay there, as the planes came back again and again, each time followed by screams and the terrorized wailing of people who had found themselves out in the open, and were unable to get to cover. Modin could distinguish, he thought, between the different screams. Up on the second floor of the hotel, he had precious little cover himself, there being little measurable difference in the resistance which concrete and mud brick put up to the penetration of an air-to-ground missile.

There was a pause in the attack. Modin decided to stay where he was, rather than be caught somewhere even more exposed. But he could hear people running out of the ministry opposite, in the sudden silence which had fallen after the 'Tomcats' had withdrawn. Afraid that they would soon be back, he pulled the mattress off his bed and wrapped it around himself. The floor was covered with slivers of glass from the windows, and his hair and clothes were full of them, too. As a last gesture to security, he pulled the pillows over his head.

But even before he had made sure that he was fully covered, the scream of the 'Tomcats'' engines came back; and for a moment they mingled with the screams of the people outside, before those smaller sounds were subsumed into the one vast scream of the attacking aircraft and the renewed whistling and exploding of the rockets. This time the attack appeared to Modin to be less precise. The rockets were landing further away, he thought; and then one seemed to strike the hotel where he was. He felt himself thrown against the bed. Before he lost consciousness, the stench from the high explosive filled his nostrils.

His black-out lasted no longer than a few seconds, though by that time the fighters were already several miles away. He groaned, and tried to work himself free from the crushing weight that lay across his chest. Two of his fingers seemed to be broken; he wasn't able to tell whether he was injured in any other way. The mattress must have helped, though it was split apart, and flock from it filled the air and made him cough painfully. The movement, however, appeared to dislodge some of the masonry. It shifted, terrifyingly, but somehow its new position made it possible for Modin to pull himself painfully out of the rubble. There was no longer any outer wall – that seemed to have disappeared completely. The wind blew up in his face, filling it with dust from the shattered buildings and from the street. There was, for a time, very little noise. It was starting to get hot. Modin heard a car driving very cautiously along the road. A child's voice, curiously natural, came to him. Then, without warning, he started retching, aware of a violent pain in his chest. It was five minutes or so before he made his way over to the door, uncertain whether the floor would bear his weight. It did, but there seemed no possibility of making his way down the rubble-blocked staircase. He couldn't hear any other movement in the hotel.

He went back to the gaping front of the hotel, and gingerly looked down to see whether that might be a better way out. The drop seemed impossibly far, but he thought that, despite the pain in his fingers, he might be able to edge his way along the wide ledge on the outside of the building, and so make it to the iron staircase which was still in place, at an alarming angle but otherwise apparently secure, at the corner of the building.

His foot crumbled away a whole section of cracked concrete, which fell the eighteen feet or so to the ground and left him hanging by his good hand on to a ruptured pipe that was sticking out of the wall. That was enough. He decided to wait where he was. By this time, ambulances and fire engines were starting to arrive. For the most part, they were busy on the other side of the road, at the Interior Ministry and the other buildings on either side of it; but one fire engine stopped as close as it could to the hotel, and men started to push an extending ladder up towards him. As they did a lump of falling masonry hit one of the upper flights on the iron staircase, and knocked it away from the side of the hotel. For a moment it stood almost upright then crumpled deafeningly down to the ground.

Modin felt that his fingers and aching chest, painful though they were, didn't justify his taking a place in one of the ambulances. There were many far worse cases. About a dozen ambulances had now assembled and the whining of their sirens filled the air. He wandered across the road to see what, if anything, remained of the ministry. From the road, it seemed like little more than a heap of rubble, with a plume of dust and smoke hanging over it still. A small group of people moved around, directing the rescue operation. Even from a distance, and even covered with dust, the figure of Ismail, demoniacally active as always, was clearly visible. Modin's sense of security prevented him from going up to Ismail and speaking to him. Instead, he started walking, heading for the office closer to the centre of Riyadh where the KGB resident worked. Already, the ever-present flies had discovered the blood from Modin's damaged finger-ends. As he walked, he waved his fingers slowly and painfully in the air to keep the flies away. To put his hand inside his shirt would, he felt, have been intolerable.

Paris: Tuesday 11 September

The double line of CRS riot police, in their dark blue boiler suit uniforms, could hear the noise of the demonstrators when they were still in the Place de la Concorde: shouting, chanting, playing loud horns and trumpets. There were ten or twelve thousand of them, enough to fill one side of the Place, as they came down from the Champs-Elysées; mostly young, but with some older men and women, supporters of the Communist Party, the PCF, with them, and a sizeable number of anarchists, waving red and black banners. They had been refused permission from the police to turn off the Champs-Elysées earlier, since that would have brought them past the Elysée Palace, farther up the Rue Saint Honoré. Instead, they had been directed to come through the Rue Royale. But as the march turned into the Rue Saint Honoré, the mood changed.

A small group pushed forward, through the frontmost ranks, and began the measured chants of 'Et-ats Un-is ass-ass-ins' and 'U-S hors d'Ar-ab-ie'. An atmosphere of seriousness, of menace even, came over the march. Some people who had brought young children with them sensed the new mood and moved out of the crowd. When the demonstrators spotted the lines of CRS guarding the front of the American Embassy farther along, a roar of angry challenge went up from them. They pushed on, past the British Embassy, scarcely noticing it, even though the plan had been to halt in front of it and chant slogans about British support for the American intervention in Saudi Arabia. There were a few CRS men and a group of gendarmes, twenty-five men in all, on duty in front of the massive gateway to the British Embassy, prepared for just such a contingency; and when one man, aged eighteen or nineteen, pushed his way through the side of the moving crowd and started to paint a slogan on the wall of the Chancery building, the CRS men, freed from the task of having to guard the gateway, spotted him immediately. Five of them ran across, their batons in their hands, and started to club him to the ground and kick him before he had been able to spray more than two hurried red-paint letters, 'CH...' With a roar, the crowd turned and surged around the CRS men, pinning them to the wall. One of the policemen lost his footing in the pressure of bodies and went down, grunting with pain as people jostled with each other to kick him. Two of the others, close to panic, pulled out cans of tear-smoke and ripped the rings off. The smoke fizzed out of the cans, billowing upwards and outwards and enveloping the people nearest the group. The CRS, temporarily freed, scrabbled to pull their breathing masks over their heads before the gas blew back and took effect on them. But the unprotected demonstrators caught the full force of it.

The gas burned into their throats and nasal passages, giving an intolerable sensation of heat and pain. It made its way into the muscles of their eyes, and made them swell and bulge and burn, so that crying was no relief but made the sensation all the worse. Some people tried to vomit; others staggered into the safety of the crowd, their faces inflamed, their noses and eyes and mouths pouring and weeping. The worst effects took ten minutes to pass away.

By now the front ranks of the demonstration were almost opposite the gateway of the American Embassy. The crowd turned awkwardly in the narrow street to face the ranks of CRS men, and started to compact as people crowded up into the Rue Saint Honoré behind them and pushed forward against the leaders. Soon a length of wood which had supported a banner came flailing over the heads of the crowd, and fell on to the helmeted heads at the back of the CRS ranks; then more and more pieces, some of them falling short and dropping on to the demonstrators themselves. Light battens of wood weren't dangerous; but the bottles which followed were, and the heavy square cobbles which some people, deep in the shelter of the crowd, were beginning to hack out with crowbars from under the tarmac of the roadway. The sight of blood on the faces of some CRS men stirred the crowd further. The front ranks started to pull back, arms linked, before surging forward against the dark blue line of the CRS. Recruited mostly from the rural poor, the CRS are the most brutal of the various bodies of French police with no love whatever for Paris intellectuals or the left, and a tradition of violence which their officers positively encourage. As the crowd linked together and surged forward towards them, the CRS men picked up the pieces of wood which had been thrown at them, broke the ends off to make them jagged, and held them out waist high, pointing at the demonstrators. It was an effective tactic. The line broke, and, depending on the pressure from behind, parts of it fell back or were forced on to the makeshift spears of the CRS.

And then, just as the crowd was wavering, and the shouts of pain and fear could be heard from the front, a much larger body of CRS men in full riot gear moved out of a side street a few yards further down the road, and marched straight at the flank of the demonstration. This attack rolled up the line: the demonstrators fell back and, step by step and yard by yard, they were pushed back on themselves and gradually lost all order.

The pattern was similar in a great many other capitals. In London, Bonn and Rome there were big demonstrations outside American Embassies, though for the most part they were peaceful enough. There was a whole series of protests in the United States itself, mostly by Arabs. The response in Muslim countries was explosive: the American Embassies in Baghdad, Islamabad, Ankara and Damascus were all attacked and damaged. In Baghdad, in particular, soldiers and policemen joined in, and the Embassy was completely burned out, though the staff had been evacuated beforehand.

In Libya, the crowd scaled the walls of the American Embassy compound in Tripoli and went through the buildings smashing and burning. But the anger in Tripoli turned to a kind of rejoicing when it was announced that evening that the leader of the short-lived coup in Saudi Arabia, Faroukh Ismail, was to come to Libya after his escape from the American counter-coup.

London: Tuesday 11 September

Most of the cars which had been parked all day at the meters in King Charles Street, between the Treasury and the Foreign Office, were gone, as David Wortham left for home. He walked towards Whitehall. One car which was still parked on the Treasury side had someone sitting in the driver's seat, reading an evening paper. The man watched carefully as he passed on the other side of the street, and when Wortham reached the archway near the corner of Whitehall the man got out, locked the door carefully, and hurried after him. Wortham crossed over Whitehall and headed down the side street opposite in the direction of the Norman Shaw building, which had once been New Scotland Yard. Then he turned right, up the slight incline of Cannon Row which points directly towards the Houses of Parliament. A few yards farther on, the man caught up with him.

'I'm sorry to trouble you,' he said in almost flawless English, with a hint of an American accent. Wortham turned, slightly irritated at being stopped in the street. 'You don't know me, but we have friends in common.'

Wortham sized him up. The clothes appeared to be English, but the face, with its fair hair and its bulbous nose, was certainly not. Perhaps a Scandinavian, Wortham thought. It would explain the good English.

'Perhaps we could go somewhere for a drink.'

That annoyed Wortham further. 'No, really, I'm afraid I have to get on.'

'That seems a pity when I've already been such a reliable postman for you.'

'Postman?' Wortham repeated dully; but he knew immediately what the man meant, and what country he came from.

'Why don't we drop in here, at the end of the street, Mr Wortham? There's a rather comfortable little bar in the basement, I think.'

Wortham said nothing and they walked in silence towards Bridge Street. A few yards before the corner, they came to the entrance of the St. Stephen's Street Dive Bar and Wortham, still without saying a word, headed down the stairs to it.

In the bar itself, the man became overpoweringly cheerful, and insisted on buying Wortham a pint of bitter to match the one he ordered for himself. 'Nothing like English bitter, I think. I miss it when I'm away, you know.' His cheerfulness became more disturbing to Wortham than anything more overtly sinister could have been.

Wortham sat at a table in the corner, listening to the man enthuse about different types of English beer, and trying hard to work out how he should respond to him. That he was some kind of Soviet official was certain. That he was working for the KGB seemed more than likely. That he was going to put some kind of pressure on Wortham was almost inevitable.

Wortham looked briefly round the bar. At that time of the evening it was filled with the kind of soaks who couldn't face the journey home without something to help them on their way. He didn't recognize any of the faces, which was a relief. Everything seemed so unremarkable, with the low drone of tired men boring one another, and the quiet shuffling of tired women drawing their drinks for them. The Russian had moved on to comparing the beers of other countries, but Wortham cut him short.

'What do you want?'

The man paused for a moment, looking almost hurt. 'Just to talk.'

'Well, let's get on and talk, for God's sake. What is it you want to say to me?'

'Take it easy, Mr Wortam,' said the Russian, mispronouncing his name in his mid-Atlantic accent.

'It's Wor*th*am, as in Worthing,' said Wortham

mechanically. 'What's all this about? Why were you following me?'

'I just wanted to pass on to you somebody's love, that's all. Nothing to get sore about.'

'Whose love?'

'I think you can probably guess that without me telling you.'

There was a silence. So Anyuta had, after all, betrayed him. All the business about needing to be independent and hating the slavery of her husband: it was just another of her lies. She's as much of a slave as any of them, and she's trying to make me one as well.

'Look,' he said to the Russian, 'if you've got some deal to offer me, you can just forget it. I'm not interested. I'll report you directly to the authorities.'

The Russian leant forward and put his hand on Wortham's arm. 'You've got it all wrong, my friend. I don't have any deal to make. I work for Aeroflot, I spend a lot of time travelling, and I promised your friend – I knew her at college, by the way – that when I was here I would post her letter to you. Then it occurred to me that you might have some message for her in return. The only way I could get in touch with you was to wait for you. Your friend told me what you looked like, and I just waited. Don't be so suspicious. We aren't all spies, you know. Some of us are human beings. Believe me, I sympathize very much with you and your friend.'

'Don't keep calling her my friend, if you don't mind. And do you really want me to believe that you watched outside the Foreign Office for me, on the basis of a vague description from ... from someone who knows me?'

'I have a confession to make,' said the Russian. 'I rang your office this afternoon, and you weren't there. And when I asked your secretary what time you left the office, she said 6.45. You were a little late.'

Wortham remembered that the secretary he shared with

several others in the department had told him that someone had called to ask what time he was leaving. It didn't make him believe the Russian's good faith, but it made the whole thing a little more plausible. Wortham felt he had been rather abrupt.

'I'm sorry if I seemed suspicious,' he said. 'It's just that these things happen with some regularity nowadays, and one can't be too careful. It was kind of you to pass me the letter, and please thank Mrs Belov for it, but tell her I think she's running too many risks.'

'And you want to send her anything?'

'Absolutely not,' said Wortham.

'Not even your love?'

For a moment Wortham thought how Anyuta would despise him for not daring to say anything to her; if, that is, she were not working against him. 'Yes, all right; please send her my love.' He felt as though he had committed himself dangerously in talking to the Russian like this, but then the whole thing was dangerous. Life itself is dangerous, he remembered Anyuta saying to him once, at their second meeting; you don't protect yourself from it by refusing to take part. She was wrong, of course; you could at least limit the damage as much as possible.

The Russian was talking about beer again. Then he said, 'I shall bring you another letter the next time I come. Only maybe I won't post it.'

Wortham again felt pulled in two directions. The safe thing would have been to tell the man not to bother; and yet Wortham couldn't bear to think of his telling that to Anyuta. He could imagine her angry reply. Even if she were betraying him, he wanted to cut a reasonable figure in her eyes.

'No,' he said, 'better not to post it.'

Chapter 6

Those that have embraced the faith and fled their homes and fought for the cause of Allah, and those that have sheltered them and helped them – they are the true believers. *Holy Koran, Chapter VIII.*

Tripoli, Libya: Wednesday 12 September

For several hours, the crowd in Green Square kept a careful watch on the sky over Tripoli airport; and when, eventually, the Libyan Tupolev could be seen, passing over the city in the clear air, the mood became ecstatic. But the waiting thousands had to wait another two hours. At the airport there were speeches of welcome, and the first of at least a dozen acts of prayer that the Arabian leader was to perform that day. At last, though, the hardiest of the watchers who had managed to keep his precarious position on the specially-erected ceremonial arch shouted down to the crowd below that the motorcade was in sight, coming towards the Square along the road by the harbour.

The word passed out across the sea of people. The noise hushed; and in spite of the pushing and craning, there was a profound silence. Then at last the open white Range-Rover carrying the exiled Arabian could be seen by the crowd in general. His slight figure, dressed in a white burnous, his head bare, was clearly visible, standing beside the Libyan leader.

At that instant, someone in the crowd called out *'Allah o Akhbar!'* – 'God is great!' – and the tension which rippled through the crowd broke into a great answering shout of *'Allah o Akhbar!'* It seemed that the entire body of people there lunged towards the Range-Rover, to touch him and see him more closely. From the black-robed women, whose position was beside the arch, there came a long, high-pitched ululating. In the fierce midday heat, the Libyan soldiers grunted and sweated as they fought to keep a narrow space around the car.

But Farouk Ismail, standing smiling a little above the shoving, adoring crowd, showed no sign of anxiety. *'Allah o Akhbar!'* he shouted, waving his clenched fist in salute; and the crowd took up the cry, and the salute, again and again. It was obvious that the motorcade could go no further through the crowd, and after a whispered conversation with the Libyan leader, Ismail abruptly fell to his knees on the platform of the Range-Rover and began the complex ritual of prayer. The crowd hushed once more, and people shuffled to make sufficient space for a sizeable number of the demonstrators to pray as well. A single voice in the motorcade behind the Arabian leader, carried feebly over the crowd as they alternately bent their heads to the ground or stood, holding their hands in front of them.

There is an animal magnetism about large crowds, which can sweep practised speakers and experienced politicians off their feet – and Ismail was neither. The soldiers cleared a path for him through the immense crowd to a makeshift platform beneath the arch itself. It took him fifteen minutes to get through, in spite of their ferocity. Finally the white-robed figure leaped energetically on to the platform. At first, his speech was commonplace enough, bringing greetings from the Arabian revolution to the Libyan one, and speaking of their common Islamic and Arabic heritage.

Soon, though, he seemed to divine the will of the crowd. His voice grew shrill.

'The revolution in Arabia is not dead,' he shouted, and the loudspeakers, relaying his voice across the demonstration, reproduced it in a hundred echoes. 'You, after much suffering, seized control of your own country back from the West. We, too, have tried. Now, our revolutions must join forces, to strike at the serpent in its own nest. The poisonous fangs can only be drawn by destroying the power that uses them to corrupt and murder us. The West hates Islam, because it can no longer dominate us. My friends, we have the power to kill the serpent. There must be no more oil from Islam for the West, until we have justice.'

For a fraction of a second there was a pause, even after the translator had finished and the echoes had died away. Then the crowd exploded into frenzy, screaming and chanting its approval, and shaking a million clenched fists in near-unison. It was minutes before he was allowed to speak again; and in that time he was able to work out a little more clearly in his own mind what words he would use.

'Your country, the Libyan Jamahiriya, has a treaty with one of the greatest powers on earth: the Soviet Union. The Soviet Union says it is the friend of Islamic countries everywhere. If it is truly our friend, it must stand by us in our hour of need. It must listen to our appeal. It must help us to stop the oil of Islam, the oil which rightfully belongs to the Islamic Republic of Arabia, from reaching the nations which have destroyed our freedom and tried to crush our revolution.'

As the crowd exploded again, almost uncontrollable with anger and joy, the Libyan leader sensed the powerful rivalry of the man beside him on the platform. And he knew, too, that he would have to ask the Russians for precisely the kind of help Ismail was demanding.

Aden: Wednesday 12 September

Once they had landed at the main airport in Aden, a little way out of the town itself, Modin found that some of his anger and bitterness had disappeared in the struggle to find a way of getting into the centre. His broken ribs still ached badly, and the fingers he had broken had still not been set; but at least he was out of danger. He had found a couple of low-ranking officers who had taken part in the coup in Riyadh, and they had forced the pilot of a Lear jet who was at the airport, preparing to escape himself, to fly to South Yemen and the security of a Soviet-supported régime. The two-hour journey had been something of a luxury for Modin: the pilot, after his initial fury, realized that he was going to need the help of someone friendly once they landed in Aden, and he had shown them the cupboard where the scotch was kept, and had handed out sandwiches. For the first time since the air-strike on the centre of Riyadh, Modin was able to take stock of his position.

The KGB resident in Riyadh had behaved badly. He had panicked at the first signs that the Americans had leant their weight to a counter-coup, and was preparing to evacuate when Modin had arrived. Worse, he had offered him no help whatever, on the grounds that they belonged to different services. He had even refused to send a message for Modin when he made his last radio contact with the KGB Residency in Aden. It offended Modin's sense of professional duty; but it also put him in a difficult position. Moscow, he knew, had wanted an almost minute-by-minute account of what was going on in Riyadh. An hour before the American air strike, Modin had sent off one message, using the resident's facilities. Moscow would scarcely be happy that they had received nothing after that one message. Serious decisions rested on such questions as whether the leadership of the revolution had survived the air strike, and no matter how good Modin's excuses were, he felt he had let Moscow down.

Once they arrived in Aden, it took them two hours to get a taxi. The temperature was dreadful, and Modin's clothes were already wet through with sweat. Every bump in the poorly-maintained airport road shot through his broken ribs and his damaged fingers. He thought about himself, at fifty-four, still performing difficult and unpleasant functions. Clearly, he thought, he wouldn't achieve the kind of eminence now that he had briefly hoped for. It was an old rule of the service: no matter how well you performed, they never promoted you for missions which ended in failure. And there was no doubt that mission had ended in a particularly bloody and chaotic failure. Modin thought of the KGB resident in Riyadh, forcing his documents into a shredder and trying to light a match to burn the strips of paper as they emerged from the machine. He thought of his own lack of success. Moscow might or might not be angry with him, but he was angry with himself.

I am getting old, he thought, and I have had a difficult time, and I have done badly. I shall stay a colonel now; they won't promote me. And there'll be no Red Star. The Party Secretary only likes winners. I shall spend my last six years doing some desk job in Moscow, or perhaps in charge of a training scheme of some kind. Vasily won't be getting treatment in Vienna. I shall have only my small apartment in Minsk, and my pension. It will be a lonely six years, and a lonely retirement. Still, if you're a failure, you're a failure: you might as well accept it.

Modin was still trying to accept it when the taxi drew up at the well-defended gate of the Embassy, and he had to start arguing with an eighteen-year-old Soviet infantryman about whether he had any right to enter the compound. His ribs and his fingers hurt more than ever by the time he finally won the contest and the taxi threw up a plume of khaki-coloured dust as it drove up the sweeping drive to the chancellery building.

Normally a tanker the size of the *Ocean Constellation* needed only one man to be on the bridge at any one time and, since everything was controlled from the bridge, there was no reason to have an engineer in the engine-room. But the Strait of Hormuz isn't a normal stretch of water. Its shoals, its shallow water, its myriad islands, its relative congestion, all mean that a cautious tanker captain will have three men on the bridge and another in the engine-room, since the delay of even a minute in transmitting an instruction can bring complete disaster.

Captain Hendricxs was a cautious man, but he was also a domesticated one; and since this was lunchtime, he was eating with his wife in his day-room immediately below the bridge while the first and second officers ate off trays. They had just started on their steak-frites, when the pitch of the engines changed, from 'half-ahead' to 'slow-ahead'. Captain Hendricxs threw down his neatly embroidered napkin, and leaped up the six steps into the chart-room in almost one movement – surprisingly fast for a man of his build. The first and second mates, both Germans, were staring through the window in the wheelhouse at a sleek grey naval ship, seven miles ahead of them.

'I've been following her on the radar,' the first officer said. 'She seems to be out to run straight into us.'

The visibility was clear in the midday heat of the Gulf: sixteen or seventeen miles. They had just rounded the tiny, uninhabited island of Sirri, little more than a shoal of sand.

'The Aldis won't be any good in this light,' he said, 'Get them on the radio and tell them to stand off.'

The second mate moved over to the radio operator's table, while the first officer called down to the radio man's cabin, to get him up to the bridge. The rule of the sea dictated that the grey shape ahead of them should have veered over to starboard to keep out of the tanker's way, since she herself had edged over to her starboard. But the *Ocean Constellation*'s change of course brought an answering move from the destroyer: she moved to port, a point or two, bringing herself directly back into the tanker's path. Hendricxs had no option but to ring 'full-astern'. Even that would take her six miles or so before she could come to a stop.

'No answer from her,' said the second officer, a little too loudly because he had his headphones on. He grinned, but Hendricxs only stroked the line of his thin blond moustache and stared out at the destroyer.

'Give them the siren,' he said.

The first officer pressed the switch, and the wild hooping noise filled the bridge and brought the last crew member out on deck below them, peering at the destroyer and looking up at them, anxiously. There was too much to do, even when the radio operator had arrived and taken the second officer's place, to consider anything but the business of keeping the *Ocean Constellation* from hitting the destroyer on the one hand, or going aground on the other. It occurred to the radio operator that he should radio to the owners to tell them what was happening; and he began to compose a message.

The third mate, a Dane, came on to the bridge. He had been asleep after finishing his watch a short time before, but the engine noise and the siren had woken him up. He stared through the window, and saw the destroyer. 'My God, what does he think he's doing?' Nobody answered him.

At that moment there was a flash from near the destroyer's bows. In the brilliant sunshine it scarcely showed, but it was followed by a plume of smoke, and there was a sudden fountain of water well away from them, on their starboard side. Hendricxs shouted out something in Flemish, then lapsed into silence. The second mate grinned again, unaware that he was doing so.

'Signal "We are stopping". Use the Aldis as well,' said Hendricxs. A great tanker, laden with an inflammable cargo, had no chance whatever of outmanoeuvring or outrunning a sleek destroyer that was prepared to use its guns. He leaped out on to the wing of the bridge, to control the tanker better from there.

Even at full astern, their speed was still 17 knots; far too fast for the destroyer to put a party aboard her.

Ten minutes passed very slowly; there was time to send off another radio message. Not even the second officer said much, as the destroyer came close enough, it seemed, for them to reach out and touch her. But Hendricxs' twenty-five years at sea, and the skill of the destroyer's captain, ensured that they stayed apart. By this time he had gathered the nationality of the destroyer, and was trying to fathom why a ship of the Soviet navy would intercept a tanker at sea. It seemed like hours later that the third mate ordered the lowering of the companion-way for the Russians to come on board. They leaped up, fifteen or sixteen men in all, with a white-uniformed officer, smartly turned out, coming up the companion-way steps three at a time, a revolver in his hand. The Dane tried to ask him something, but a Russian sailor, the next to set foot on board, pushed him brutally against the tanker's rail, arms out and legs kicked apart, and started searching him for weapons. By that time the officer had led half a dozen men up to the bridge, while the rest, under a petty officer, rounded up the crew who were mostly standing, stunned by the whole affair, in the aft part of the tanker.

The Russian sailors pushed their way on to the bridge, holding their rifles in front of them, and pointing them menacingly at the first and second officers. Another couple of sailors pulled Hendricxs in bodily from the wing of the bridge, where he had been standing filled with rage and indignation. They pushed him into the wheelhouse and stood there, with their rifles to his neck, as he sat in a chair.

Then the officer walked in.

'You are Hendricxs?' he said, in reasonable English.

'How do you know my name?'

'The Soviet Navy knows everything it is required to know. Your ship has contravened international law.'

Hendricxs felt the muzzle of a rifle in the fold of his thick neck, but not even that stopped him exploding with anger.

'You are pirates. You have no right even to talk about international law. Get out of my wheelhouse and get off my bridge.' Feeling rage taking control of him, he grabbed the barrel of one of the rifles, pushing it away from him and levering himself upright by it. 'Get out. Get out. Get out.'

He moved fast and menacingly towards the officer, oblivious of everything except his violent fury. The sailors were rattled. Each of them turned his rifle towards Hendricxs, who had started to talk in Flemish again. The officer was uncertain what to do. He had had the strictest orders that no one was to be harmed in any way; but then, it had never seemed likely that anyone would resist. As Hendricxs lurched around the chart-table, knocking against the angle-poise lamp, a slight step sounded, and the captain's wife, whom nobody had remembered, stood in the doorway.

'Joopie,' she said.

It was a ludicrous moment. Hendricxs stopped, annoyed that she should have used his pet name in front of everybody; and that brought him back to a saner sense of things.

'These men are pirates,' he said, in English so as to anger the Soviet officer.

'We have orders. We are following those orders,' said the officer.

It seemed as though everybody felt they had to explain themselves to the meek, badly dressed, middle-aged wife of an Antwerp ship's captain. Her English, unlike that of her husband, was poor.

'You must do,' she said, obscurely, and then settled herself down.

'I will send a message to my owners,' roared Hendricxs, who had had a moment to think.

'No message,' said the officer. 'You come to our ship, the *Irkutsk*, and get orders.'

'Listen.' Hendricxs felt that he was obliged to demand some respect. 'You want me to do something, you ask me. You don't tell me. You want me to go to your ship, you ask me. And you call me "sir".'

Again, the Russian looked uneasy. He said, 'Come to my ship. Sir.'

'Please.'

'Please.'

'Meyer,' said Hendricxs to the first officer, a Berliner, 'I am going aboard this pirate's ship because he has asked me. I leave the *Constellation* in your hands.' He was beginning almost to enjoy himself. 'You will be responsible for the safety of the ship, and of Mevrouw Hendricxs.' There was a ludicrous dignity about it all that made Meyer smile. Hendricxs was annoyed, and changed the mood.

'You realize,' he said to the Soviet officer, 'that you have committed an act of war? This ship is chartered by an American corporation. This could bring war between the United States and your country. And you started it.' He looked at his officers, checking that they agreed. Then he turned on the Soviet officer again.

'Don't stand there all day, man,' he said. 'If you want to be a pirate, you have to be much quicker than that.'

Chapter 7

The lovers of gambles must know that, taking into account the new balance of power existing in the world arena, the aggressors will be crushed if they unleash war. *Soviet government statement, 29 August 1961.*

Moscow: Wednesday 12 September

There was silence in the long gilded room. The Party Secretary sat at his office desk, his chin resting on his cupped hand, looking into the middle distance. In the foreground sat a number of senior officials: some restless, some apparently relaxed and confident. Beside the desk sat a younger man, pudgy faced, expensively dressed. A small table had been drawn up in front of his chair, and on it lay a pad of buff paper, several pencils, and a small silver-coloured pocket cassette recorder. In the middle of the room was a larger table, on which stood a square loudspeaker. An engineer fussed about it, and then walked over to a curtained-off area at the far end of the room. His left shoe squeaked as he walked. It was the only sound in the room.

Outside, the clock in the Spasskiy tower chimed the half-hour. Before it had reached the third note, the loudspeaker on the table came to life. The sound of clicks and mechanical groans on the specially hardened telephone line that linked Moscow with Washington showed that the line was up, precisely at the moment the Americans had proposed. Elsewhere in the building a bank of tape-recorders was registering the call for later analysis. As he waited for the President to start speaking, the Party Secretary's mind strayed a little, trying to envisage the conditions in which the Americans would be talking. Far better, he knew, than those in the Kremlin. The Americans always did these technical things superbly well. He regretted, in some ways, that they weren't using the slower, more formal telex line – the Kremlin/White House 'hot line'.

The American voice spoke for about two minutes. The translator, anxious not to make a single slip in a matter of such importance, stopped writing on the buff pad, and played back part of what the President had said on his pocket cassette recorder. The small echo reverberated round the room, now that the line with Washington had gone quiet once again. The Party Secretary tapped his fingers irritably, but the translator knew the ways of leaders, and ignored him. Finally he looked up.

'He says as follows: the action of the Soviet navy in stopping a foreign tanker in the Gulf is intolerable. It is in breach of international law and the practice of civilized nations. The danger of such a move is –' the translator paused to check his notes, and repeated with a different inflection, 'the danger of the move is that it inevitably calls for some form of retaliation from the United States. We shall be forced to take those retaliatory steps unless' – the translator looked into the Party Secretary's face – 'unless you give us an assurance that such an event will not occur again.'

'How did he sound?' The Party Secretary seemed interested in nothing else. 'You've heard him speak plenty of times; did he sound angry, or confident, or what? I couldn't tell from just listening.'

'To me he sounded nervous,' said the translator. 'He was speaking more quickly than usual, and sometimes his sentences trailed away a little at the end.' A senior official of the Party Secretary's department, an expert on Soviet-American affairs, nodded his agreement.

The Party Secretary reached out for the microphone on the stand on his desk, and clumsily pressed the button to speak.

'It is the United States which has violated the norms of international behaviour,' he said. His voice sounded almost jovial to the people listening to him in the room. 'You can't expect to move in and crush a legitimate government and then sit back and have everybody congratulate you, my friend. The days of that kind of thing are over. Our navy had information that the tanker in question was carrying an illicit cargo: it was necessary to check. That check is still continuing.'

The pause for translation lasted, it seemed, for hours. The Party Secretary sat and examined his fingernails. At last the disembodied voice filled the room again, amplified from the loudspeaker in the centre of the room. Everyone looked at the loudspeaker, as though it were doing the talking itself.

'Your attitude will lead the world to the brink of war. The US Navy must ensure that the waterways of the world are kept free, and that the oil from the Gulf countries continues to flow. You must know that we have no alternative but to ensure that.'

There was a silence again. Then the President's voice continued, 'I have to say that I feel personally betrayed by the Soviet Union's actions in this matter. The last time we used this form of communication, we talked about your military intervention in Poland. I made it clear then that, as in the past, the United States had to accept that Poland was in your own sphere of influence, your own backyard. We were appalled at what you were doing, but there was no way we would intervene. But I regard Saudi Arabia as being in much the same special relation with the US as you regard Poland. The United States has a right to ensure that its supplies of oil are protected, and you have no right to stop them.'

'My friend, you cannot dictate to the Soviet Union.' The Party Secretary's voice sounded almost gentle as he replied. 'To try to challenge our naval force in the Strait of Hormuz would precipitate a nuclear war between our countries. And since our military strength is greater than yours, we would win. To attack the *Irkutsk* and her sister ships in the Strait would be an act of suicide. I cannot believe you would be so stupid. The Soviet Union will continue to adopt a principled approach to international affairs. I have to warn you that your forces have invaded a country and imposed a puppet government on it. We, too, are obliged to respond to that.'

The President's reply was long and angry; but to the group of people sitting watching the Party Secretary, it seemed as though he was scarcely listening to the voice on the line. Before the translator had finished, the Party Secretary grasped the microphone and again spoke into it.

'This, my friend, is the way of war. There is a better way – one that does not end in incineration for all of us. I propose to you that we should jointly convene a conference which would study ways of reducing the tension between our countries. If you will agree to this conference – a European Disarmament Conference – we, for our part, will withdraw our ships from their station in the Gulf. And I undertake also to release immediately the ship we have been examining. We have made our point clear. This incident has shown how dangerous the international situation has become for world peace. It is the duty of both of us to protect that peace.'

The President's voice remained angry, as he replied. But

he was clearly trying to work out the balance of advantage and disadvantage, even as he spoke. And he wasn't prepared to turn the idea of a conference down immediately. Perhaps, too, he was thinking that the removal of Soviet warships from the Gulf could be made to seem like an American victory.

The President's voice came to an end. The two men exchanged a brief greeting, and then the Party Secretary signalled to the senior engineer that the call was over. The voice of the Moscow special operator started to say that the line to Washington was closing down. Someone leant forward to switch off the amplifier, and there was silence in the big room. The Party Secretary knew that when the American response came, it would be favourable.

Washington: Friday 14 September

Directly he walked into the State Department, Preger felt the atmosphere of suppressed excitement. It seemed to get into every conversation and infiltrate it, like tobacco smoke. People kept coming up to him and shaking him by the hand, with more enthusiasm than usual. It was as though everyone felt they had been involved in some miraculous escape from danger, and were constantly congratulating themselves, and each other.

Preger stayed out of the conversations as much as possible. He had some business with the Assistant Secretary of State for European Affairs, and had to wait around until he was free. When Preger walked in, he found the same enthusiasm, the same powerful handshake, the same air of self-congratulation.

'So we got away with it,' he said to Preger. 'We put the King back on his throne, and we got the Gulf cleared. How about that?'

Preger wasn't certain whether he should smile and join in the general mood, or whether he should point out the less pleasant side to the whole affair. But he depended too much on the Assistant Secretary of State to be able to afford to anger him over something that didn't actually represent an academic principle of some kind. The Hungarian wouldn't have turned up a chance to point out a few depressing facts, Preger knew; but he had the relationship between State and the Institute to think about, and it seemed better to go along with it all. Why not? After all, the President *had* got away with it. It just wouldn't be right, Preger thought, to call it in any sense a victory.

He had a trying lunch with a group of rather younger men, who vied with each other in praising the President's toughness. Preger started to point out the effect that the whole Saudi Arabian affair was already having on western Europe.

'Europe!' said one of the others. 'You watch, they'll come into line fast when they see they're out on their own. You don't have to worry about Europe, for God's sake.'

Preger started to argue, but for the second time that day decided it wasn't worth it. Everybody else agreed with the accepted version of events: that the United States had shown that it was capable of acting strongly in defence of its own interests. The rest of the world would take note of that. Preger joined in the conversation again, but soon saw he was boring them. He left them speculating about the possibility of forcing a show-down with the Soviets, in order to take advantage of the weakness which everyone except Preger believed Moscow had shown over the invasion of Saudi Arabia.

There was, he felt, nothing to keep him away from New York and the Institute any longer. Even if the State Department had originally wanted his services, it wouldn't be looking for them now. No one wanted to hear the kind of things he would say. He remembered the image that had come into his mind at the time of the Camp David seminar: the two superannuated gladiators, whose greatest danger lay in losing their footing. Now, he thought, we've lunged and missed; and we don't even realize that we're lying there, stretched out, with our opponent about to strike.

Brussels: Tuesday 25 September

There was a long line of black official cars to pick up the British delegation at the airport. David Wortham knew there was no point in hurrying: his would be somewhere near the back of the line. He stood outside the exit to Zaventem Airport, and looked out across the desolate car park. The rain slanted down and added a heaviness of its own to the atmosphere. Wortham didn't know Brussels well, but he associated it vaguely with great canyons of sleek office buildings, the intimate warmth of a few good restaurants, and the ever present rain. He looked about him at the bustle, and felt more than usually out of it all: a passenger, shipped off by London because they couldn't think of anything else to do with him. Almost without thinking, he put his hand into an inside pocket and felt the edges of Anyuta's absurd letter. He despised himself for his sentimentality in bringing it: it made him feel like a love-sick eighteen-year-old again. And yet somehow his relationship with Anyuta, tenuous though it now was, had become the only fixed point of his life. Everything else – his family, his career, his sense of himself, the things that kept him linked with the real world – all those had lost their ability to anchor him. He was adrift, and lacked both the energy and the desire to set himself a course.

The dull grey countryside along the motorway between the airport and the NATO headquarters stretched out on either side of the official car. He was alone, except for the driver, and the driver didn't speak. The windscreen wipers pushed the rain away, and the tyres threw up circles of water on either side of them. Wortham's sense of isolation, a kind of emotional weightlessness, increased; it had become a process of disorientation, in which nothing real and tangible had any meaning.

To shake off the sensation, he delved into his case to find the briefing documents for the NATO ministerial meeting which was to start that afternoon. It hadn't been possible, for reasons of security, to read them on the plane, and now the car journey was too short to go through the dossier with any care. It was typical of his new state of lethargy that he should have arrived so poorly briefed. He glanced through the documents: the most interesting ones were the confidential assessments from the capitals of the other NATO countries about their likely response here in Brussels to the American invasion of Saudi Arabia. But there was time only to glance through the reports from the British ambassadors in Bonn and Paris before the car turned off the motorway, and headed into the forecourt of the NATO headquarters.

The cleats banged hollowly in the wind against the steel flagpoles, and the occasional patches of grass were chewed up by tyres and the passage of feet. NATO gave him the impression of having never entirely recovered from the shock of being forced by de Gaulle to leave its old headquarters in Paris. The building had the impermanent feeling of exile about it. Officials from the different countries milled about inside, greeting each other and trying to organize bilateral meetings. Wortham knew scarcely any of them, and was uninvolved in making arrangements; he found a quiet room in the offices of the UK delegation and settled down to read the documents more carefully.

A rustle of embarrassment and stress ran round the big conference room, with its stylized NATO star decorating one wall and an equally stylized map of the world at the other. The Dutch had just followed the Danes in attacking the American move into Saudi Arabia, and it was clear that other countries were going to do the same. A senior official detached himself from the American delegation and walked swiftly over to the Secretary-General's group. Within minutes it was decided: the meeting had reached a state of such sensitivity that it would have to be continued in restricted session. The great mass of officials, Wortham included, started to gather their papers together and leave, in some disappointment at missing the crucial debate.

Even then there were at least forty people left in the room, still at the places where they had been before, but with rows of empty seats behind them. The meeting resumed. The Norwegian Foreign Minister added his complaints to those of the others: the United States had moved into Saudi Arabia almost without informing its NATO allies, and certainly without consulting them properly. It was possible, the Norwegian minister maintained, that the coup in Riyadh had been the result of genuine popular discontent; and it was certain that one of the leaders had been in touch with the Swedish Embassy in Jedda, with assurances that there was no intention of halting supplies of oil to the West.

The American Secretary of State looked angry, and started to speak; but the Assistant Secretary put a hand on his arm and whispered to him that he should deal with all the points together, at the end.

The support of the British was assured; but it was the only outright support the Americans were expecting. Even so, the attitude of the West German delegation came as a shock to the Secretary of State. The Soviet move in Poland, and the temporary closing off of West Berlin, had had a profound effect on West German opinion. For a moment it had seemed like a return to the early Sixties, when only American support could guarantee West Germany's security. But the invasion of Saudi Arabia had changed that feeling overnight.

The West German Foreign Minister shifted his portly figure in his chair, and pulled the microphone towards him. At first, like the other ministers, he emphasized his government's support for NATO and for the Atlantic alliance. But it was more of a ritual than anything else; it was clear that he had been personally angered by the American move in the Gulf.

'My country differs from just about all the others represented at this table,' he said. 'If there were to be a war in Europe – and during the past few weeks, I must confess, a war has seemed at times almost inevitable – West Germany would be one of the main battlefields; perhaps the only one. We are caught between the two superpowers in a way none of the other countries in the alliance is. We have already seen how the Soviets can put pressure on West Berlin if they choose: simply cutting off a road here and a canal there will do it. And now there is a very distinct prospect that what they did some weeks ago to West Berlin, they could do to West Germany as a whole. We will soon take thirty-five per cent of our natural gas from the Soviet Union, for instance. Now, the Russians have never in the past interfered with such supply lines for political purposes; but there's always a first time. We don't yet know how the OPEC countries will retaliate, but it is possible that my country will suffer not only the loss of a third of its natural gas, but also three-quarters of its oil supplies.' He looked across at the American Secretary of State and waved his finger aggressively at him. 'In my opinion the action you, as the senior partner in NATO, decided to take in Saudi Arabia has brought all these possibilities dangerously close. If my country is to be beggared by the loss of its energy supplies or, even worse, if it is to become a battlefield for the superpowers, it should at least be in a good cause. Invading Saudi Arabia wasn't a good cause; and all of us look like suffering as a result.'

Directly the red light on his microphone went on, the Secretary of State launched into a powerful defence of the American action in Saudi Arabia. The Secretary of State had done a great deal to ensure that the Administration in Washington had been nowhere near as radical as many western countries had feared. But he wasn't a good speaker;

and even if it had been possible to sway the delegations which were anxious and angry about American policy, he wouldn't have been the man to do it. He argued that by securing the Saudi throne the West was assured of supplies of oil from the world's biggest oil producer. He assured everyone that the only way of dealing with an aggressive opponent like the Soviet Union was to show what he called 'firmness under fire'.

'If we split up and go our own ways now,' he said, and there was something of a plea in the way he said it, 'then any idea of real security goes right out of the window.'

He stopped speaking, and the red light went off. The Secretary-General spoke briefly, urging a spirit of compromise and give and take.

Most of the foreign ministers at the table were already starting to work out what they would tell their governments back home.

David Wortham stirred his coffee at a quiet table in a restaurant in the southern suburb of Uccle. Opposite him was a West German diplomat whom he had known at the beginning of his tour of duty in Moscow. Nowadays the German worked in Brussels, at his government's NATO delegation.

'I must say, David,' he said as they sat drinking their coffee and watching the charcoal fire where their steaks had been cooked, 'it all worries me a great deal. You talk about a new feeling in Britain, but I can tell you that things have changed in Bonn, too, over the past few months. I mean, we've always had the far left, and there's always been a bit of noise about pulling out of NATO. But it has come from the JuSos, and the rest of those leftist groups. Now it's starting to come from right inside the Social Democrats, not just the' – he paused, almost more for effect than because he couldn't quite remember the exact phrase in his near-faultless English – 'the lunatic fringe. Sometimes, I promise you, it doesn't seem like the old Germany I've grown up in and worked for. We're starting to lose our bearings as a country.'

Wortham grunted sympathetically. That sounds, he thought, like me.

Part Three

Vienna Fall

Chapter 1

A people elated by pride, or soured by discontent, is seldom qualified to form a just estimate of their situation. The subjects of Constantine were incapable of discerning the decline of genius and manly virtue, which so far degraded them below the dignity of their ancestors; but they could feel and lament the rage of tyranny, the relaxation of discipline, and the increase of taxes. *Edward Gibbon, 'The Decline and Fall of the Roman Empire'.*

Baltimore, Maryland: Monday 1 October

Beside the road north from Washington, D.C., close to the port of Baltimore, lies one of the biggest graveyards of old, smashed cars in the world: perhaps the biggest. It is a Hissarlik of the auto industry, an artificial mountain of twisted, rusting steel which has thrown out spurs and smaller ranges on each side. Laid down in strata, each year's crop discarded and heaped on the previous year's, it is tended by a small gang of wreckers who perform a kind of archaeological function, stripping off the upper layers but never able to reach down to the lowest of all. There at the bottom lie the earliest autos to be junked: the victims of smashes that occurred in the early Fifties. Those layers never see the light of day. The cars there lie in the last stages of rust, the massy chrome of their bumpers oxydized beyond recognition, their rockets and tail-fins impacted, their eau-de-nil and lilac and primrose bodywork flaked and discoloured. The years of the gas-guzzler were the years of America's unquestioned dominance of the world. American power and the ten-mile-to-the-gallon auto declined together, in the Seventies; but it wasn't until the start of the Eighties that the final decay of political power became as obvious as that of the great wasteful automobile.

The President of the United States of America flew over the automobile graveyard by helicopter, using fewer gallons per mile even than the wrecks below them had once done. His eye took it in, as he looked out of the helicopter's window, but he made no comment. The idea that there might be some analogy between it and his administration's position in the world was not one that would have occurred to him, even if his mind hadn't been on the speaking engagement he was flying to in Baltimore. Instead, he switched his gaze to the far neater and more attractive sight of the port, beyond the *memento mori* of the scrap-heap.

'WELCOME TO THE AMERICAN LEGION AND THE PRESIDENT OF THE UNITED STATES OF AMERICA!!!' The President looked up at the banner which hung across the hotel lobby, and smiled. The staff, neatly drawn up behind the reception desk, applauded him enthusiastically. The manager stepped forward to shake hands, and then showed the way deferentially to the Louis XIV banqueting suite, at the far end of the lobby. A couple of polite questions from the President elicited the facts that President Nixon had addressed a fund-raising dinner of $1000 a plate in 1971 in the same banqueting suite, which had then been called the Egyptian Room, and that four hundred people could be seated there at a time. $400,000, the President thought to himself, and speculated briefly on the uses the money would have been put to. The secret servicemen fanned out ahead of them as they walked, forming a vector of security. The waiters had lined up along the walls, which were decorated with what someone imagined Versailles must have looked like in 1680.

The President passed the waiters, and the frescoed wigs and gowns, with scarcely a glance. He was preparing himself for his entry to the banqueting suite, and the manager fell obligingly silent.

Inside, people were already on their feet, waiting for him. A spotlight played on the teak double doors, ready for the moment when they would open. In a bay, on one side of the Louis XIV suite, the Bert Schultz Three sat, ready to break into *Hail to the Chief* on the electric organ, the electric double bass and the drums. The mood was one of mellow anticipation. The doors duly swung open, operated by two waiters in powdered wigs. The spotlight shone on the President in his midnight blue dinner jacket. The anthem to the President was played. The legionnaires stood stiffly to attention. The President walked slowly, easily, down the room.

Then the slight tension of the moment evaporated. The band began to play selections from *South Pacific*, the conversation became general, and the President shook hands with the senior officers of the Legion before sitting down beside them at the top table. Cigar smoke billowed into the air, coffee cups clinked in their saucers, and the President, after eating a light dinner, settled back in his seat to listen to a long-winded introduction. Television cameramen stood by in the centre of the big square formed by the tables, and for the last time checked the light and focus on the small lectern from which the President would make his speech. The President shuffled the square pieces of yellow card which contained his notes. He was anxious not to get them mixed up, as he had once done during the election campaign.

When he finally stood up, he talked for a little about the

traditions of the American Legion, and the wars that people around the room had fought in. He mentioned, in the most modest terms, his own record. There was occasional applause. But then he struck a new vein. Drawing on the frustration aroused by the attitudes in western Europe to the American success in Saudi Arabia, he began talking about the sacrifices Americans had made for freedom over the years.

'There must come a limit to the amount of help any country can give to any other country. There must come a day when the American people are entitled to say to their President, "Think of us first." I do not say that day has yet arrived. But American patience is not limited, neither are American resources. This country has grown great by believing that self-help is the best help. And the day may be coming when the best advice we as Americans can give to our friends abroad, who've been happy – let's be a little frank about this, my friends – happy to leave everything to us, is to say to them, "First you must help yourselves; you must show us that you are willing to fight your own battles; and then we shall be prepared to help you all the more willingly." '

The hall exploded with the thunderous applause of the legionnaires, who thumped heavy, liver-spotted hands on to the white table-cloths, and one by one and row by row stood up to applaud him, many raising their arms and clapping the hot, smoky air above their heads. The President sat down, minutes later, glowing with the pleasure of the moment. He had touched a nerve: the resentment of people who feel that they have been betrayed by their friends.

The President's speechwriters would not have gone that far, and the Secretary of State wouldn't have wanted the topic to be raised in the first place. But now that it had been, and now that it had been broadcast throughout the United States and beyond that, throughout the western world, there was no calling back the words. And there was so much support for them at home that there could be no question of recalling them. In the months to come, the beginning of American isolationism would be dated to that warm evening in Baltimore.

Moscow: Tuesday 2 October

The queue shuffled forward slowly in the half-light. No one spoke. The counter, with the dehydrating samples of food on display behind it, was lighted by hanging lamps, heavily shaded, which left customers and servers alike out in the gloom. The food wasn't altogether bad; better, certainly, than in any of the ministry buildings round about. Modin, moving forward with the others, and pushing his grey plastic tray along absent-mindedly, examined the cooked meals which were there as a form of advertisement, and rejected all of them. He paid for a portion of beef soup and a cake with cream cheese inside, and collected a ticket for them, before queuing again for the food itself. For a man who had lounged beside the swimming-pool of the InterContinental Hotel, Riyadh, and ordered sirloin steak, it seemed an inefficient and unsatisfying system. Still, he thought, it's our system; at least I feel more comfortable here than I ever did in the West. Criticizing is easy; what we need are people who will support the system, but try to change it from within. One day, we will become as efficient as the West, and it will be through our own hard work. For a moment, he almost felt that he believed it.

Coming back to Moscow hadn't been easy. Perhaps other people didn't feel he had been humiliated; he wasn't sure. But he thought it himself. He had assumed that after the mission to Saudi Arabia he would simply be sent back to his post in East Berlin. Instead, he had been brought back to Moscow with a half-rank promotion, and given a desk job which hadn't existed before. His place in East Berlin had been taken by an obsequious ferret of a man whom he had known briefly during a tour of duty in Beirut: a man who wouldn't make any mistakes, who'd keep his nose clean and fill in all the necessary reports on time, but who wouldn't have a milligram of flair or sensitivity. Imagine Kuznetsov breaking up Dr. Gartner's little system, or hijacking a Lear jet to Aden. You need guts to do that, thought Modin; and you need to have the killer instinct. When it comes down to it, you've got to shoulder everyone else aside and pick the apples off the tree. No one else will do it for you. Still, he thought, the only qualities I need now are good eyesight and strong writing muscles.

To be deputy director of covert operations in western Europe meant in practice that he had charge of the dossiers of the less senior GRU officers: those who held posts in Soviet trade and governmental organizations abroad. The senior officers worked at Soviet embassies as military attachés. In his first disappointment, Modin had asked the general in overall command of his department if he might occasionally be allowed to take charge of an individual operation as case officer. The general had agreed in principle; but nothing had happened.

The old woman behind the counter tapped on Modin's plate irritably and leaned into the light.

'Come along, come along, we've got other people to serve, you know.' She looked meaningfully at another old woman beside her in the gloom. Obediently, the deputy director of covert operations picked his plate up and moved across with it to an empty table lighted by another hanging lamp. He had never been a gregarious man. Partly it was the need for security which made him keep to himself; chit-chat always made for loose talk, he had been taught as a cadet at training-school. But he felt an outsider, here at GRU headquarters. And the idea of eating his lunches with the other senior officers, in their restaurant at the top of the building, where the food was served by army stewards, held little attraction for him. I'm a soldier, not a politician, he thought, as he drank his soup slowly and noisily. Gossiping with senior officers might be good enough for the likes of Kuznetsov, but for me, with only a few years to go before retirement, there's no point in crawling round people who wouldn't know a covert operation if they found one lying on their desk.

It was while he was finishing his soup that he started worrying again about whether Kuznetsov might go through the accounts he had left for his time at the Berlin station. It seemed almost certain; and Kuznetsov was just the kind to use it against him. It wasn't even as though he'd made a great deal of money with the System; not enough, certainly, for Vasily's operation. Modin had always intended to protect himself against trouble by doctoring the files at the Berlin office, as he had doctored the files in Beirut and Lusaka, but there hadn't been the time, and he had never quite believed it to be necessary. When he first came back to Moscow he thought that the First Party Secretary's favour would help him, but as the weeks went past it became obvious that the Party Secretary had forgotten all about him since his unsuccessful mission to Riyadh. He was, as always, on his own; and he had left his back unguarded.

A dead-end job, and the fear of being sacked from it; an ironic combination Modin thought. He bought himself a glass of tea to round off his frugal meal, and as he sat at his table he thought about the alternative prospect which presented itself to him, each time he considered the problem. Pochinkov, a kindly and jovial man in charge of training some years back, had got word from a friend that he was about to be charged with selling off old equipment illegally. For some reason the authorities had wanted to get rid of Pochinkov. A few days before he was due to be arrested, he had managed to get himself on to a duty visit to Belgrade, and from there had crossed the border into Greece. Everyone knew that friends of his had helped him, but there was never any evidence, and no one had lost his job over it.

But Modin wasn't a popular man like Pochinkov. He found it hard to make friends and to keep himself from speaking his mind about people he disliked. He had no patrons in the service, and no network of allies who owed him a favour. No one at the East Berlin station would let him know if Kuznetsov really was planning to pull some trick. Probably he wasn't, Modin thought; but on the other hand there was no security, no assurance about it. He was vulnerable, and the slightest touch would bring him down. He thought of the years he had left in the service, the flat he occupied with his dowdy wife in Moscow, the pension he would depend on, Vasily's chances of a career. He had to live, and he didn't want to be humiliated.

He finished his tea, staring absently at the stained and pitted surface of the table. He tried to keep himself from thinking about the way Pochinkov had escaped from a similar predicament. Modin was a deeply loyal man, and he had no wish to be a traitor. He would live with his fears and his disappointments, obediently blowing the dust off other men's files, and supporting other men's operations. He stood up, and took his cup and plates over to the hatch where the cleaners collected them.

Outside in the corridor there was light from the windows, as the sun shone in. It was only dark in the restaurant itself, he thought; how simple it was, just to walk out and feel the sun on your face.

London: Tuesday 2 October

Apart from brief duty visits, Wortham hadn't spent any long periods of time in London for eight years. But it had changed greatly for the worse. Even Janet, who had complained endlessly about Moscow, now seemed to be looking back with a certain amount of nostalgia. Things had gone badly wrong in London, and the places they had known and liked from the time they were first married seemed somehow spoiled and decayed. Even in the most expensive shopping areas – Bond Street, Knightsbridge, Sloane Street – there were empty and vandalized shops.

Wortham walked from the house they were renting to Parson's Green underground station. 'Kill traitors' said one spray-paint slogan, in the place where an advertisement had been ripped down. A crudely stylized Union Jack had been painted beside it. Farther down, another slogan pledged allegiance to Chelsea Football Club. On the station platform, someone had sprayed 'General Strike Now' on the windows and door of the waiting-room. And when the train came in, shambling, noisy and late, Wortham found that several of the seats in his carriage had been ripped open, and then inexpertly sewn up again with coarse binding thread, as though they had been the subjects of an autopsy, and the looks of the body were never going to matter again.

So much violence, Wortham thought; so much aggression feeding on itself. Perhaps it was simply part of a recurrent pattern: the systole and diastole of a society. Over a period of time, the theory went, a society purged itself first of its aggressions, and then of the aggressors themselves. It was even said that only a basically healthy society could afford to express its inner tensions: look at Italy, at Jamaica, at the United States. Wortham looked instead at the message of the spray-paint. 'Commie Filth', 'MUFC Kickers', 'Nigger scum'. Even the more personal statements had a ferocity to them, more like a defensive alliance than a love affair: 'RJ + DH of Acton'.

Nowadays he had been told, it was unsafe to be on a tube-train after eight o'clock at night, and even in the daytime it wasn't always a good idea. One friend of his had been held up and robbed in the tube at lunch-time; another had been attacked by a group of young boys with a knife, and had had some of her hair cut off. His evening newspaper screamed at him about the murder of a judge; elsewhere the children of a well-known actor had been kidnapped. Wortham thought of Montaigne, retreating from the Wars of Religion to write his essays in a tower in the Gironde. Nowadays, it seemed, you couldn't be entirely secure even in your tower; the papers reported that the murdered judge had been found at his country cottage in Norfolk.

Wortham changed trains, pushing through the crowd like the rest. Then he waited on an uncomfortably full platform for a connecting train. The antique sign-board was broken. When the train did come, it was as ramshackle as the previous one, and filled with the refuse which other passengers had dropped.

From Westminster underground station he walked down Bridge Street. The pavement was blotched and stained, and there was rubbish on every corner. He guessed that the subway passage across Whitehall would probably stink of urine, and he walked across the road instead. Nowadays there were fewer cars than there had once been. He walked along the side of the Treasury, and looked across to the vandalized statues in Parliament Square. It was dark, and he was late. Already he could hear the shouts from the demonstrators outside Central Hall, and the ragged singing. And there was another, more sinister sound, which he couldn't identify until he was much closer.

He turned the corner, near the north face of Westminster Abbey, and saw the tail of the hostile crowd. Youths and girls, wearing the nightmarish face-paint and hair styles of their cultural sub-group, had their hands on the shoulders of the people in front, and were stamping their feet menacingly, in unison. It was the quiet shuffling beat of the rubber soles that Wortham had heard, a hundred yards away. From time to time the chanting became a roar: 'Commies out! Commies out! Commies out! Out! Out!' The police, mostly in riot gear, held the crowd back by organization and physical strength, rather than weight of numbers. Wortham pushed his way through the crowd, but eventually he had to break through into the empty space beyond the front row of the demonstrators and the line of policemen; and when he did, a shout rose up, and several things were thrown at him as he hurried through the main doors of Central Hall.

Inside, the meeting was well under way. All the seats were taken and the aisles crammed with people standing, and trying to peer over the shoulders of those in front. On the platform was a long line of people sitting at a long trestle table. Wortham recognized the faces of many of them from the newspapers and from television: elder statesmen of the Left, and from the unions, leading members of anti-nuclear groups, and of pacifist causes. Above their heads floated a white banner proclaiming in green letters the unexceptionable slogan 'INDEPENDENCE, PEACE, CO-OPERATION'. Wortham, who had only come to the meeting because he found it impossible to make up his mind on the issues, looked down at the leaflets he'd been handed as he came in: *Arguments for a Nuclear-free Britain*; *Why we should Leave NATO Now*; *US Imperialism in the Middle East*; *Solidarity with the Struggle of the Peoples of Southern Africa*. It was a measure of his feeling of emotional and political weightlessness, he thought, that he should be here at all; there wouldn't be many other Foreign Office people in the hall.

'Already,' said a voice from the platform, 'the race is on for the weapons which will threaten our children, and even our children's children. What kind of government is it, which encourages that sort of race with all the resources of the State? How can anybody seriously believe that by getting rid of these obscene weapons from our soil, we will be endangering our safety?' Behind him, the chairman of the meeting gently tapped a glass with his pen. The speaker took the hint. 'In conclusion, then, I believe our country should renounce its geriatric nuclear weapons, which can kill just as surely as the newer and more advanced weapons of the superpowers, and that Britain must be included in the zone of peace which must and will open up on the continent of Europe.'

After him came a well-known union figure, slightly greyer now than he had been in his most fiery days, but still able to bring people cheering to their feet with his rhetoric.

'There's nothing we've heard tonight which I wouldn't agree with. The trouble is, if you say these things, you're automatically accused of being in favour of the Soviet Union. No one can say I'm in favour of the Soviet Union. My opposition to it may not be the same as you'll read every day in the Tory press, but I dislike it just the same. But you can't hope to get a peaceful government in this country, which gets rid of nuclear weapons and pulls out of NATO, unless you have a different *kind* of government. A people's government, which isn't afraid to take those steps. I promise you, the Russians would never recover from the shock.'

There were cheers for that; though as the meeting dragged on, the tone became sharper, and the different factions of the Left began to savage each other from the platform and the floor over their concentration on one or other aspect of the movement. Wortham walked out, more uncertain than ever. But, he thought, we may find that there won't be anything much to debate soon, if NATO really does begin to fall apart.

Outside the evening was cool and quiet. The ground was

littered with the traces of the demonstration: leaflets with union jacks on them, the occasional crowd barrier which no one had bothered to pick up. A few policemen were still around, but none in riot gear. Nevertheless, the police had parked a large van directly opposite the main doors to the hall. Wortham walked past it with scarcely a glance. Inside, the sweating photographers took his picture, as they'd taken all the others.

Chapter 2

Article One: High Treason High treason, that is an act committed deliberately by a citizen of the USSR to the detriment of the state independence, territorial integrity or military might of the USSR: defection to the side of the enemy, espionage, handing over a state or military secret to a foreign state, fleeing abroad or refusal to return to the USSR from abroad...is punished by deprivation of freedom for a period of ten to fifteen years with confiscation of property or by death with confiscation of property. *The Criminal Code of the USSR 1958.*

Moscow: Tuesday 2 October

Ivan Feodorov, the first Russian printer of books, looked down in preoccupied fashion from his statue in the small patch of green. There weren't very many people there at that time, but everyone had a shopping bag or a brief-case. One man even had a small suitcase. Sometimes two people would talk earnestly for a short while, then one of them would reach into his bag and pull out a book or a sheaf of typed paper, money would change hands discreetly, and the buyer would walk away, hastily shoving what he'd bought into his own bag. Suitably enough, the first printer overlooks the scene of Moscow's biggest black market in books and *samizdat* literature. Modin was close enough to one small group of people to hear that one of them had a copy of Tolstoy's *Kreutzer Sonata* for sale: not by any means underground literature, simply unobtainable outside a library. No doubt, thought Modin, there would be completely illegal things for sale here: novels by Solzhenitsyn, essays by Sakharov, works by western writers. He disapproved of that kind of thing, and found it hard to understand why his friend Vinogradov should have chosen this, of all places, for them to meet. He strolled around the small park, staring censoriously at the black marketeers.

He had called Vinogradov within half an hour of getting a report that morning. It had in fact been sent to the head of the department, but he was away, and the report had been marked urgent. It was from a GRU major, who worked as a desk officer at one of the Aeroflot offices in London. The GRU had a number of posts among Aeroflot staff in Britain and elsewhere in the West, and controlling them was one of the chief jobs of Modin's department. The Major had recently been back in Moscow on leave: Modin had met him there, and been impressed with his efficiency and air of sharpness. His report described how he had been asked by the wife of an extremely high official in the Kremlin to carry a letter to a middle-ranking British diplomat based in London. The woman was tactfully left anonymous, but the report gave David Wortham's name, and enclosed a photostat of Anyuta's letter which the Aeroflot major had carefully opened before delivering. It also described the brief interview the Aeroflot man had had with Wortham in the street near the Foreign Office. Modin thought about it for a long time. It was almost inconceivable, he thought, that the KGB wouldn't know about this case, and somehow be running it themselves; and yet it was possible, as the Aeroflot man maintained, that the woman in question was simply acting on impulse in handing the letter to a GRU agent. The Aeroflot man admitted knowing Anyuta, though not her husband. It could, Modin reflected, be an extremely useful contact. Some carefully organized rendezvous between the woman and Wortham might well result in a much-needed success for the GRU. The KGB still hadn't recovered from the change which had brought the new Party Secretary to power; but the GRU had been unable to show any particularly impressive results since Modin's own success in Berlin. It would also, he thought, help to cement his own position, if there should be any trouble over his handling of funds in the Berlin station.

Nevertheless, Modin was a careful man. There could be difficulties if the case were already in the hands of the KGB, and the man from Aeroflot had somehow walked into the middle of it. It was not completely impossible either, Modin thought, that a GRU major who worked for Aeroflot was also working in some way for the KGB as well. Such things had happened before. There was only one person he could easily turn to for advice, if he wanted to keep some kind of personal control over the case – Vinogradov, who had been a close friend of his during their time in Beirut, and had since gone on to bigger and better things at the KGB's administrative headquarters in Dzerzhinsky Square. A case involving the wife of a senior Soviet official and a foreign diplomat was precisely the kind of thing Vinogradov in his new role would be likely to know about.

Modin took another turn round the little park, and glared once again at the hawkers. Some of them, seeing him there, had already packed up and left. One, more daring than the rest, had actually tried to sell him something; not a western book, but Turgenev's hunting sketches; and because Modin was a hunting man, as much as because he wanted to maintain some semblance of cover while he was waiting, he agreed to pay the twelve roubles the man was asking. He was just putting the book into his pocket when Vinogradov's voice made him turn suddenly.

'My dear Nikolai Federovich, if it's dirty books from the West you want, why didn't you come to me? I could have saved you a great deal of money.'

Modin laughed, ruefully, and felt obliged to show him that the book was perfectly respectable. Vinogradov was a friend, and a good one, but Modin preferred that even friends should know that he was an honourable man. They walked over to a bench, and watched the unofficial traders at their business.

'Amazing, isn't it? We have the most advanced society in the world, and own all the means of production. And still you can't seem to satisfy everybody.'

Modin looked at him carefully. Vinogradov had once been well known for his outspokenness about Soviet society and the Party; now, Modin couldn't be altogether sure whether he was being ironic, or whether he meant it. High office, Modin knew, could make the most heretical people orthodox. In reply, he simply laughed. It seemed the safest thing to do.

They went through the necessary small-talk for a while, as Modin tested out the strength of the relationship that still existed between them. The incident over the books had slightly worried him, but it gradually became clear that Vinogradov was still as ironic as ever, under the covering which the necessary instinct of self-preservation had created for him. It wasn't often, in their line of business, that a real friendship could spring up between two men from different services. People were normally too wary to commit themselves, and often too competitive as well. But, during their time in Beirut, Modin had done Vinogradov several good turns; one of which, indeed, had helped him make his sudden rise in the system. There was a silence, and they sat side by side. Vinogradov waited for Modin to tell him why he had asked for the meeting.

Modin went carefully through the facts – not too precisely, in case the KGB wasn't aware of the whole thing.

He couldn't count on Vinogradov's friendship to the point where he could ask him to stay out of a case as good as this. At the end he paused for a moment before asking, 'Does any of this ring a bell?'

Vinogradov sat looking straight ahead, trying to work out how to reply. Finally he turned and looked at Modin. 'Thanks for telling me. If you want my advice, you should be very careful about all this.'

'But do you know about it? Has the KGB got an interest in the case?'

Vinogradov seemed irritated at the way Modin said the name of his organization out loud. Although no one could have heard, he looked around them in an exaggerated way before saying anything more. And when he did reply, it was along the same lines as before. 'Listen. Any case has got to be handled carefully, but something like the one you've been telling me about has to be handled as though it was an unexploded bomb.'

'You still haven't said whether or not you've got an interest in it.'

Vinogradov laughed, and stood up. He moved away a few paces, then came back and stood over Modin.

'I've got no right to tell you this,' he said, with the familiar half-smile on his face that Modin remembered from the days in Beirut. 'But you ought to know. Watch your step, Nikolai Fedorovich. People are looking for a scapegoat. It could be you. I can't say anything more than that.' He walked away, without saying goodbye.

Modin sat on the bench without moving, watching him. The sellers and buyers of books parted to let him go, and the pigeons fluttered up from around his feet as he walked out of the park.

Modin stayed where he was. There were several interpretations to be put on what Vinogradov had said. It still seemed to be an open question whether the KGB really was running the case. What was far more worrying was the warning. Modin thought carefully. Vinogradov, like himself, had had close links with East Berlin. Could it be that he had heard of some move by the GRU, or perhaps even the KGB, to use the issue of currency smuggling against him? The KGB had reason to be angry about Modin's earlier success and perhaps they were trying to bring him down over that. Or perhaps his successor had brought certain irregularities to Moscow's attention.

Modin had always found that the best decisions were the instinctive ones. Now, as he sat on the wooden bench close to Ivan Feodorov's statue, it came to him that there was only one clear solution to all his difficulties: he must defect, and he must use the case of the British diplomat and his Soviet girlfriend to do it. And once the unthinkable had been accepted, Modin felt a great deal easier. He knew that it might not work or that he might be found out before the whole thing came to fruition. But staying on in Moscow, without trying to make a break for it, was sheer defeatism. Now, too, he could see other advantages: the Americans or the British – he wasn't yet sure whom to choose – would pay him handsomely. Vasily would certainly have his operation, though he would have to leave Moscow somehow. And Modin would be respected. He would be treated properly, instead of working out his remaining years at a desk at GRU headquarters. Loyalty meant a great deal to him, but loyalty was a two-way street; an organization which failed to stay loyal to you no longer deserved your loyalty. There was a time when Modin would have rejected arguments like that as self serving and cheap. Now, with Vinogradov's warning still in his ears, he saw that self-preservation was a more powerful force than an outworn faithfulness to an unheeding master.

He would, he thought, take personal charge of the Wortham case. It would be his ticket to the West. It might well be a race with the KGB, but there was no helping that. You couldn't jump over the wall without taking a risk or two. But if it were a race, then the faster he moved, the better. He stood up, feeling more energetic than he had for weeks. A black marketeer, seeing his face, came over and offered him a copy of Mayakovsky's poems for fifty roubles. Modin smiled at him, and shook his head politely. How I have changed already, he thought, as he walked out of the little park.

Hamburg: Tuesday 2 October

The café was glaringly lit by white fluorescent tubes. People who eat cheaply in Hamburg prefer to know what it is they're eating. The seven people round the table said very little until they had ordered. The café was a safe place and it was empty apart from them. But they had to keep a watch on the door in case of a police raid.

The orders given, they all started talking at once, and the conversation fragmented as it became clear that the group as a whole wasn't going to discuss the events of the day. There was no real leader among them. They were known as the co-ordinating group of seven. There had been a certain amount of quarrelling over the weeks, but they had achieved a good deal in bringing together the different K-groups which represented the often minutely differentiated factions on the far left. And this evening they had totally justified their existence.

It had been the biggest demonstration anyone could remember in Hamburg. The police, who habitually underplayed the significance and size of left-wing manifestations, said there were 120,000. The organizers themselves made it 250,000. But the precise numbers were unimportant. It was the overall effect and feeling of the demonstration which counted. They had surprised themselves by becoming a major force: no longer the leaderless 'Spontis', who could only get into battles with the police and disrupt the flow of traffic, but a significant political grouping which, for the time being at least, represented the wishes of a sizeable number of people. The Federal Government in Bonn might now be forced to crush them or to come to terms with them – but it couldn't any longer pretend they weren't there.

The entire meal was taken up with an argument about what the group of seven should do to capitalize on the day's success. The two JuSos, a man and a woman from the

Young Socialist group, wanted to wait for a little, to allow the full extent of their success to sink in, before staging another mass demonstration.

'The reason why we did so well,' said the girl, making prodding movements with her knife to back up her point, 'was that we got the workers to come in with us. We have to continue to show them that we're on the same track: that calling for a nuclear-free Germany and a withdrawal from NATO is a part of the same struggle as their demand for a higher wage. These are men who want to work, who've got jobs to go to during the day. They aren't going to want to join in weekday demos. And from now on, the bigger the numbers we can produce, the more significance we as a movement will have; and the fewer we produce, the easier it will be for the capitalist press to say we're falling apart. And that means the workers won't turn out in such numbers.'

There was a babble of voices, and those round the table who disagreed argued confusedly for a little, contradicting each other on points of analysis. Eventually, though, it was the sheer impossibility of arranging the posters and contacting the necessary figures among the dockworkers in anything less than four or five days which dictated the decision. But even while they talked and ate their poorly-cooked food, the aftermath of the demonstration continued as groups of protesters ranged through the city.

Their faces lit by the shifting light from the screen, where a group of six girls thrashed in an unenthusiastic frenzy, the early evening customers sat in comfortable plush seats, many of them holding drinks. Some were serious about it; others, often foreigners, were there in groups, and felt obliged to laugh and make jokes. Of the hundred or so people in the cinema, only two – apart from the topless hostesses with the drinks – were women. One sat staring seriously at the complicated writhings on the screen, holding hands with the older man beside her. The other woman was with a man near the back of the cinema; they didn't seem to need much in the way of lessons from the performers.

The figures on the screen changed their tempo; the hostesses moved as unobtrusively as any woman in a lilac-spangled leotard with silver tassels swinging from her nipples can, and refilled some of the glasses. The couple at the back began moving more urgently.

And then the lights went on. It was a moment or two before anyone in the cinema quite realized what was going on. But in the transition from quiet darkness to sudden bright light, there came the noise of chanting and fighting from the foyer of the cinema. And a second later, a group of fifty or so women who had been part of the earlier demonstration burst in, and began beating people as they sat there, using as weapons their banners protesting about rape and the sexual murder of women. For the most part, they only hit the men, and they pushed the hostesses out of a side door. No one was particulary badly hurt, and the protesters scarcely reached the men sitting in the middle of the block of seats. The whole incident took about four minutes, from beginning to end, though there were sounds from the projection room which made it obvious that a small group of women had gone there to smash up the equipment and destroy the film. By that time, most of the audience had disappeared.

Then the police arrived. Cramming through the narrow doorway of the cinema, they blocked the exit for most of the women. There was total panic, as the police wielded their night-sticks left and right at any of the demonstrators they found. One woman with long red hair was pulled to the ground by it, and kicked as she lay there. The face of another streamed blood from a smashed nose, but she couldn't do anything about it because her hands were jerked behind her back and plastic handcuffs snapped into place. The noise and the fear reached a crescendo, and one women tried to break through the cinema screen to escape from a couple of policemen, one of whom was swinging his radio transceiver as a weapon. And then everything went quiet again, and the only sounds were those of an occasional sob, or the laugh of a policeman.

Moscow: Tuesday 2 October

When the grey-haired man walked in, Anyuta was sitting in an ungainly fashion on top of a desk in the front row of the empty class-room. She was swinging her legs, and whistling tunelessly to herself, almost below her breath. On the blackboard was a quotation from Pushkin. The last class of the day had finished five minutes before.

Anyuta looked at the man thoughtfully before saying anything to him. If she was suddenly struck by nervousness, she didn't show it. She glanced down at her fingernails, and then up at him again.

'Is it me you want?' The man, who was susceptible to attractive young women, found her voice too low for his taste. He said nothing, but walked over to Anyuta's own desk, and sat at it. A woman in Anyuta's position was not used to being treated like that; most people were respectful to the wife of one senior Kremlin official and the daughter of another. The man's attitude can only be explained one way, she thought. He knows what's happened. She felt no particular fear, and to show it, she went on whistling. But she stopped when he started speaking.

'It's a pleasure to meet you. I've been hearing about you from some strange people.'

She looked at him, in as disapproving a way as she could manage, and got down off the desk.

'I've no idea who you are. If you have a request to make about your son or daughter, you should make it to the Dean's office.'

The man was nettled, but he laughed. 'You have been writing letters to people you shouldn't.'

Anyuta was astonished to find that she was experiencing no sign of nerves whatever. It was as though this were happening to someone quite different: the condition that enabled you to observe your unconscious body and the friends gathered round it. 'I think you had better explain yourself, before I get someone to throw you out.'

Modin stood up. 'I am a colonel in the *Glavnoye Razvedyvatelnoye Upravleniye*,' he said. 'One of the men under my command has intercepted a letter written by you to a man in London: a British diplomat. You have been extremely stupid. You have also committed a criminal act. Fortunately, it may not be necessary to arrest you. All you need to do is to co-operate with us in the best interests of your country, and perhaps the damage can be set right.'

'Co-operate,' said Anyuta, thoughtfully. She swung her shoe in front of her, and examined it from a distance.

'It'll mean writing another letter. It may mean going to the West to see him.'

'That's helping you, and helping my father and my husband?' Her voice was sarcastic.

Modin pulled a piece of paper from his inside pocket. 'To be the wife of a slave, and a slave yourself, is a kind of death. It is a death ...'

'Shut up, you bastard – give that to me.' Anyuta lunged across at him, and Modin allowed her to snatch the flimsy piece of typescript from his hands. For a moment he thought she was going to attack him, but she looked at the copy of her letter instead, and started weeping, uncontrollably, as she stood in front of him. He watched her distastefully for a few moments, as the tears covered her face, and ran unchecked into the sides of her mouth.

It was a good minute before either of them spoke.

'I'm not asking you for your co-operation, I'm ordering you to give it to me. I have brought you a copy of the letter I want you to write to your friend in London. It will inform him that you will be accompanying your husband to the international conference in Vienna next month, and it asks him to be there too. Your husband will not be told why you are allowed to go with him; you can rely upon me for that. The letter will also ask your friend to write back to you, and to make arrangements for you to meet him in Vienna. As long as you leave the arrangements clear, as they are in the copy I give you, you can change the wording in any way you choose. I have left blank the place where you must ask some friend of Mr Wortham's at the British Embassy to deliver the answer to you.'

'You're wasting your breath. I won't be writing it.'

'In that case, my dear, here is another letter – a copy of it – which I shall be sending to your husband.' Anyuta glanced at it. It was filled with lies about their relationship, she noticed, but it had with it a photocopy of her letter to Wortham. She felt calm again.

'Did my letter get to him?'

'I made sure of that myself.'

'You know, I suppose, that this is the second time I've been mixed up in this despicable kind of game you're playing? Once is enough, I can assure you.'

For the first time, Modin looked uncertain. 'The second?'

She told him a little about the circumstances which had led to Wortham's expulsion. Modin had known about that, but it had never occurred to him, in the water-tight world of Soviet security, that Anyuta might have been linked with the case.

'Was that done through the KGB?' he asked, quietly.

'Frankly, one of your loathesome organizations is exactly the same as any other to me.'

'And have you had any contact with the KGB since then?'

'None at all, I'm glad to say. I felt like bathing in disinfectant the last time.'

Modin seemed reassured; but he realized now that time was short.

'Write the letter out for me, like I ask. I can promise you that no harm will come to your friend, or to yourself. As I said, you will at least see him again in Vienna.'

Anyuta had been thinking about it now for a couple of minutes. She had damaged Wortham once before, she thought. This time, she would warn him. She would die rather than let him in for a trap again. But she would at least see him if she wrote the letter – and, surely, she had the intelligence to outwit idiots like this man. Why should she not be able to stay in the West, once she got to Vienna? Stay with David Wortham. That way, none of the conspiracies of these reptiles – she glared briefly at Modin – would come to anything.

As she hesitated, Modin began to threaten her again, but she cut across his words quickly. 'For God's sake, don't start again. I'll write it, if I have to.' Even under these circumstances, the thought of filling up a piece of paper which Wortham would read was a sufficient pleasure. Once she stopped and looked at Modin.

'I suppose that animal Polyakov was the one who gave you the letter.' She had half expected that he would betray her. Modin smiled. For some reason it infuriated Anyuta. 'That's it,' she said. 'I'm not writing anything else for you if you aren't going to be straight with me about the past.'

She snatched up the piece of writing paper, as if she would tear it in half. Modin, anxious that the whole thing shouldn't begin to collapse over a point of detail, said quickly, 'Yes, it was Polyakov.'

Anyuta felt she had won a mild victory. She rearranged the paper, and started writing again with a smile.

Chapter 3

It is an unavoidable necessity for Germany to take into account the presence of Russia to the east of us. It is a geographical and political fact that we have to come to terms with. *W. Rathenau, German Foreign Minister, on the Rapallo Pact with the Soviet Union, 1922.*

Paris: Thursday 4 October

Without warning, the tapestry curtains at the head of the chamber were flicked open and there, theatrically revealed, stood the President of France and the Chancellor of West Germany, talking to each other in an ante-chamber. They seemed as startled as the onlookers for a moment, and then they walked forward to the table which had been prepared for their press conference. The officials who had opened the curtains pushed gilded armchairs into place, and as they did so the silver chains they wore round their necks clinked in near unison on the wooden backs of the chairs. The President waited for the Chancellor to sit down, then sank carefully down himself.

Ever since 1958, presidential press conferences in France had been held in the same grand manner. They were intended to show French government policies in the light of grandeur, of distant effectiveness. They were invariably performances; and the hall in the Elysée was essentially theatrical, with its gilded columns, its allegorical tapestries of time, art and nobility, its massive chandeliers depending from a ceiling crowded with life-sized figures in gold plaster. The sunlight, shining in through the upper windows on so much art imitating nature, seemed pale and limp by comparison. It gleamed faintly on the spindly, tapestried chairs of the journalists, and glinted on the carefully groomed hair of several dark, elegant men in their early forties who stood together under a tapestry of a naked old man with a scythe. They belonged to the President's *cabinet*, his private office: men whose job it was to advise, and fix, and stage-manage.

The President absent-mindedly fingered the discreet red ribbon in the buttonhole of his immaculate pin-striped suit, and arranged the microphone on the table in front of him to suit some unconscious notion of neatness and pattern. He flexed his fingers, and began to make his opening statement about the two days of talks he and the West German Chancellor had just had. The arc-lights shone on the Chancellor's glasses and made their colourless frames shine momentarily, as he turned to acknowledge the implied compliment in the President's tone. Then he made a short statement of his own, in French with a good accent. The waiting journalists wrote it down, wrestling with the opaque prose, trying to spot the code-words that would reveal to them the true meaning of the meeting. The stills cameramen fired off round after round of identical poses. The ENG cameramen strained and grunted with the effort of the recording, and tried to use their shoulders to brush away the sweat that ran down the sides of their faces.

A stout, bearded French correspondent stood up. 'Monsieur le Président, what position will France adopt at the forthcoming conference on disarmament in Europe?'

The President fenced a little. France would work for a Europe which was free, and able to protect itself, and act in harmony with nations outside its immediate compass. The Chancellor gave his answer, also couched in abstractions. An American stood up, and asked what effect the warning of the American President about the need for more self-reliance in Europe would have on the Atlantic relationship. The French President made chopping movements with his hands, dividing up the semantic value of each word as he used it, but failed to answer the question. Then the Chancellor broke in with his own reaction to the question.

'In many ways the American attitude is understandable; especially at a time when the economy of the United States is undergoing such difficulty. But it must give allies of the United States, and especially the Federal Republic of Germany, grounds for great anxiety. It leaves us,' he said, almost as an afterthought, 'in a very difficult and –' he searched for the right word in French, 'a very exposed position.'

There was an immediate rush to follow that up; but the President, sitting beside him, was careful in choosing which journalist should ask the next question. For a time he was successful. Then, just before it became obvious that the President was about to declare the conference over, a correspondent from *Le Matin*, stood up. The President was irritated, but felt unable to prevent the question from being heard.

'In the last few months, Mr Chancellor, you have observed the United States fail to keep the roads open to West Berlin, and fail to bring its influence to bear to prevent the Russians sending their troops to Warsaw. Now the Americans are seemingly trying to warn you that you must look after yourself more. There are people in your own party who say that West Germany should become neutral. What conclusion do you draw from all these different facts?'

Long questions rarely receive long answers from political leaders. The Chancellor, in his slow, accurate French, showed a flash of irritability.

'The conclusion I draw,' he said, 'is that the old world order is in the process of changing. My country, like any other, has to look after its own interests.'

The President brought the press conference to an end, and the tapestries closed again over the two figures who had given it. In spite of the careful stage management, the Elysée press conference had produced a *coup de théâtre*.

The Chancellor could sense the hostile atmosphere in the cabin of the small jet, even though he deliberately stared out of the window at the ragged streaks of cloud as they climbed to their cruising altitude back to Bonn. Then he switched his gaze to the face of the Foreign Minister, sitting opposite him. 'I take it you want to talk about the press conference,' he said.

'You went much farther than we had agreed. It sounded as though you wanted us to pull out of NATO.'

'Did I say that?' The Chancellor turned to his political adviser, who dutifully shook his head. 'All I said was that the Federal Republic, like any other country, had to look after its own interests. I suppose you think I should have said we ought to look after everyone else's instead?' His effort to remain unflappable was forgotten, and his old irritability showed itself. He regretted it immediately.

'Look,' he said. 'We aren't living in the old days any more. The Americans are losing interest in us. The Russians are getting stronger every day. No one else can help us. We're on our own and we've got to look after ourselves.'

For a minute or so no one spoke. Then the Minister of Finance said, 'My father was a socialist by conviction,' he said, looking at the window straight in front of him, and through it at the thick layer of white cloud that underlay them. 'But in 1933 he took part in the Gleichschaltung, just as everyone else he knew did: they all queued up to join the

Nazi Party. Not because they believed in Hitler, or had suddenly been converted, but simply because it seemed a sensible thing to do. The safe thing. It meant you could be sure of holding on to your job. No one announced that jobs would be limited to Party members, or anything like it. It was just a type of insurance, that was all. And if my father and the millions like him hadn't all joined the Nazis, maybe things wouldn't have turned out as they did.

'I know you haven't really said that we'll split off from the Americans, Chancellor,' he added, turning for the first time and looking at the Chancellor's profile as he sat beside him, 'but that's what plenty of people within the party, and the country, are going to think. All I can tell you is that my father never forgave himself afterwards for what he did in 1933, and I'd hate to see you getting us into the same position.'

After that there was a much longer silence. As the plane taxied across to the terminal, they could see the television cameramen lining up. Inside the building would be another group of journalists, with the same questions to ask. The Chancellor was famous for his ability to deal with journalists, but this time even he thought over what he was going to tell them with special care.

Chapter 4

The sense of danger must not disappear:
The way is certainly both short and steep,
However gradual it looks from here;
Look if you like, but you will have to leap.
W. H. Auden, *Leap Before you Look.*

Moscow: Thursday 4 October

It was snowing lightly as Margaret Addison stepped out of the bright light around the open doors of the Bolshoi and into the slush and the cold outside the crowded porch. Her husband followed slowly after her, with the Ambassador's private secretary and his wife in tow. There were no signs of the British Embassy Rolls yet. Behind them, the crowd spilled out as people pushed downstairs from the upper galleries. As the four of them stood by the side of the kerb, they were engulfed by the wave of people. Margaret Addison stood talking to the other woman about the ballet. Like many Western women in Moscow, she had devoted herself to the subject in a way she wouldn't have believed possible before she came. She turned to her husband for confirmation of a point. But he wasn't there. A man had pushed between them, and she felt a sharp blow from his fist on her side. For an instant she thought he had stolen her handbag, but before she could call out, he had shouldered his way through the crowd and run across the street to the small park opposite. The headlights of the Rolls-Royce picked him out briefly, before the snow and the dispersing crowd hid him.

'Extraordinary.' Margaret Addison shifted her handbag on to her other arm. 'People are so rude here.' She felt the place where he had hit her. In the pocket of her coat on that side, was something that hadn't been there before: an envelope folded in half. Her ungloved hand pulled it out. It was addressed to her husband, in English. She handed it to him, amazed, and started to say something about it, until he shook his head meaningfully.

It was only when they got home that he opened the letter, and even then he didn't read out the contents of it. Military attachés from western countries have more reason than most foreigners in Moscow to imagine that their apartments are bugged. But he felt his wife was entitled to see what it said. He relied completely on her discretion.

'I am senior officer (Colonel) in Red Army, and wish to live in Britain. I shall be attending the top meeting in Vienna next month. If you can help me, please leave me a letter which will say where I can meet you in Vienna. The spot where to leave it is on top of cupboard in upper floor of empty house, Oryzheniy Pereulok 16, near Peking Hotel. The house is to be destroyed on Monday. Leave letter on Saturday night. I want US $45,000 and asylum for myself also my son.'

Colonel Modin was preparing his escape route from Moscow carefully.

London: Monday 8 October

Once, David Wortham almost decided to tell Janet about the position he was in. But there was a look on her face over dinner which seemed to announce that she wanted no confidences. Much better not, he thought, remembering how he had decided against saying anything to Horwood, as they drove to Sheremetyevo Airport. He went to bed that night still undecided. But as he lay there, listening to Janet's even breathing, he was afflicted by high-flown thoughts of duty and honour. He felt at his most vulnerable, so close to sleep, and notions which at other times might have been brushed aside by the instinct for self-preservation settled on him and wouldn't leave. He decided to tell the head of his department; though, when he woke in the morning, he realized he was wrong, that he would be making use of an unsuitable confessional.

As the underground train lurched its way to Westminster station, the certainty hardened. The man to talk to was the unpleasant character from security who'd been at his interview with the head of the Eastern European Department. Having decided that, Wortham felt a great deal easier in his mind. He might be damaging his career, but the idea that he'd laid himself open to blackmail was unbearable. That had to be settled, no matter what the cost.

It wasn't easy to trace Gregory Stallard. He wasn't listed in the Foreign Office internal telephone directory: a clear indication that he worked for DI6, the Secret Intelligence Service. Eventually, Wortham went down the corridor to a public telephone booth, and rang the Foreign Office number. The operator who answered put him through, after a short pause.

Stallard stood up, courteously enough, when Wortham came into his office an hour later. He even smiled.

'You've saved me a great deal of work, Mr Wortham – or may I call you David? You see, if you hadn't come to see me, I should have had to come to see you; and that would have been a great deal more difficult and awkward. Coffee?' Stallard busied himself with a complicated percolating machine at a table in the corner. He said over his shoulder, 'I do hope, by the way, that I'm not jumping to conclusions. You came to see me because ...?'

'I thought I ought to tell you about something that happened to me the other day.'

'Exactly. Our friend, the Major. The GRU Major – the man who spoke to you in Cannon Row the other night.' Wortham said nothing. 'These goons, you know, sitting in their wretched cars and waiting hour upon hour for people.'

There was another silence. Wortham looked round at the bleak office, with its unadorned walls and its high window. How would this have gone if I hadn't got here first, he wondered.

'My dear David, I have to confess to you that I wasn't altogether happy about the answers you gave us when we interviewed you, even though the others were. I'm afraid I had you followed, especially when you went to that wretched meeting at Central Hall. Why on earth did you go there, by the way? I assure you, it was all I could do to stop Five picking you up there and then. Would have caused immense upset with the old lefties inside, I suppose.'

The thought of being arrested by DI5 outside Central Hall was appalling. Wortham sat there, stirring his coffee and thinking about it.

'I went because I was interested, I suppose.'

'I knew it was something like that. But they're as stupid as any Russian, you know, the Five boys. Anything to the left of Winston Churchill should be picked up and charged on the spot, in their opinion. Winston Churchill junior,' Stallard added, as though it was a point that needed making.

They sat there looking at each other for a few seconds. Wortham felt he didn't like the look of Stallard any more now that he was making coffee and calling him David, than he had at the interview. The brown eyes were too close, the chin too long, the hands which played with the inevitable pencil too brutal. Wortham noticed that the ends of Stallard's fingers were nervously picked at; Stallard caught the look, and covered his finger-ends with practised carelessness in the sleeve of his jacket.

'Have you got the letter with you?' he asked, smoothly.

'Letter?' Wortham had been thinking about the previous meeting, and answered stupidly. Stallard's whole manner changed in an instant, much as Wortham had suspected it might.

'We aren't going to have any difficulties, are we? The letter your friend in Moscow wrote to you.'

'Oh, I'm sorry, I thought I was going to have to explain all that.' Stallard was appeased and went back to fiddling with the percolator. 'I've been wondering what to do with it for some time. It's been burning a hole in my pocket ever since it got here.'

Wortham put the absurd green paper on the desk. Stallard showed no sign of having heard. He turned round, finally, with a refilled cup.

'Were you having it off with this girl?'

The brutality of the question inflamed Wortham immediately. 'I don't think that's any of your damned business.'

'Listen, sonny. My business is getting you out of a hole. If I ask you a question, it's not because I'm practising to be a marriage guidance counsellor. Were you having it off with this girl?'

'Yes.'

'But she was involved in the meeting, the night you were photographed, and Belov was her husband?'

'Yes.'

'Well, my dear old fruit, you certainly seem to pick them. Are you still keen on her?' Wortham shrugged. 'I asked you a question. Again. Perhaps this time you'd just answer it for me.'

'I suppose I am.'

'Good. That'll mean that when you write back to her, you'll mean it.'

'But I told the Russian I wouldn't write back.'

'Well, you've just changed your mind. Look here. This thing, as they say in the women's magazines, is bigger than both of us. I work for Century House, and I just keep an office here for convenience. Century House is extremely interested in this whole business. It's not every day that they get British civil servants writing to the wives of people as close to the leadership as Belov is. I'm sure you feel it's an entirely private business. What I'm telling you is that Century House wants to sit in, as well. Look on us as a kind of Cupid, helping the arrows of love along a little. I do hope, David, you won't deny us that. Who knows, we may even get the lady out for you in the end, if you're nice to us.'

Wortham was still thinking about that when Stallard reached into a drawer and rustled around in it. 'Somewhere in here,' he said, 'I've got something for you.' He pulled out a white envelope. 'This arrived yesterday at the Foreign Office. I'm afraid we took a look at it first. Recognize the handwriting?'

There was no mistaking the scrawl, as the white letter lay beside the green one on the desk in front of Wortham. He tried to avoid the appearance of snatching at it. Inside, the scrawl told him that Anyuta loved him, that she was going to Vienna and hoped to see him there. Modin's dictated phrases were noticeably more coherent than Anyuta's own.

'Better write back to her, sonny boy. Doesn't do to keep these eager ladies waiting, you know.' Stallard let the pencil drop off his balancing finger. Then he looked at Wortham again.

'You don't have to like me, you know. You just have to co-operate with me. I'll let you know tomorrow what you're going to write to the little lady.'

Chapter 5

The people of the Union of Soviet Socialist Republics send their fraternal greetings and heartfelt declarations of friendship to the people of the Democratic Republic of Germany, on the occasion of their glorious National Day. Glory to the people of the Democratic Republic of Germany! Glory to the principles of Marxism-Leninism which hold the Socialist peoples of the world in fraternal unity! *Soviet government message to the government of the GDR October 1979.*

East Berlin: Monday 8 October

The bands blared out marching music, there were choirs performing patriotic and socialist anthems over the loudspeakers, helicopters hovered overhead in contravention of the agreement with the three western powers, and file after file of East German soldiers goose-stepped past the podium in their grey uniforms and grey helmets.

The Soviet Party Secretary had always disliked coming to East Berlin for the anniversary of the founding of the German Democratic Republic, but he found it was even worse when he was the figure whom the soldiers were saluting. Their helmets were a little modified from the ones worn by Hitler's forces in the battle for Moscow; he could visualize these men, or some very like them, marching in victory across Red Square. He remembered the cold, and the privations, and the awful sacrifices, and the leg which had been injured in the battle ached suddenly, in sympathy. Tanks, rocket-launchers, tank transports, mobile guns, armoured cars rolled past, leaving the street stinking with the fumes of their exhaust. How essential it is to make sure that this part of Germany, at least, is kept under some kind of control, the Soviet Party Secretary thought. He glanced sideways at the Party Secretary of the GDR: an ageing, grey-haired man with an unpleasantly insinuating manner. He had never liked him. The Soviet Party Secretary remembered the time when, as a partly discredited Defence Minister, he had listened to the complaints of the GDR leader who had berated him about the inadequacy of some Soviet reserves. It had been an awkward moment. Now, this same man is obliged to fawn on me and flatter me, thought the Soviet Party Secretary; and I have to rely on him, because the Party in East Germany is in such difficulties that to force him out would endanger the whole structure. The Soviet Party Secretary had had exhaustive reports on the other leaders in East Berlin, and it had been unfortunately clear to him that no one else in that group of nonentities was capable of exercising power. So, much as he would have liked a change of leadership, he was stuck with what he'd got. He looked again at the GDR Party Secretary, and this time the GDR Party Secretary noticed the movement of his head, and turned himself, smiling deferentially. The government photographer who was posted on the platform for precisely such fraternal moments snapped the pair of them. The Soviet leader felt obliged to give a chilly smile in return. But he thought, 'You arse-licker.' He turned away, and watched more glum lines of soldiers marching past.

After this, I must tell him a few home truths, the Soviet Party Secretary thought to himself. He and his aides had already gone over the thing fairly clearly: the need for greater discipline in East Germany, the danger of following what had happened in Poland, the danger of leftist as well as fascist contamination from West Germany. The most dangerous thing, as far as the Soviet Union was concerned, was the possibility of some kind of link-up between West Germany and the GDR. He would warn the East German leader to restrict the links as best he could. Everyone had told him there was nothing that could be done about people watching West German television. What about the days when Young Communists had swarmed up ladders to turn people's television aerials away from the West? Apparently that was no longer possible: the Soviet Party Secretary wasn't entirely sure why, but the experts told him so. Jamming was out of the question too. Well, one way or another, they would have to cut the links; it was a matter for them, they were a sovereign government. He smiled sourly at his own joke.

Yet the fact was that the GDR was becoming independent. He recognized it, everybody recognized it. The only people who didn't, and who couldn't afford to, were the people in the GDR leadership. Their only hope was to continue the Soviet link, and the Soviet Union's only hope was to continue with the present leadership.

Automatically, the Soviet Party Secretary returned the salute of a GDR general, who careered up and down in a big open Zil, organizing the parade. All over Eastern Europe we've been in trouble, the Party Secretary thought, as he watched the Zil head for the far end of the parade. In Poland it needed firm action, and that brought them to heel. It won't last, but it's done the trick for the time being. Czechoslovakia seems completely quiet; no one there wants a repetition of 1968. Hungary could be difficult, still: too much money, too efficient, too many links with the West, again. But the Hungarians won't start anything, they'll only follow someone else's lead. No question whose lead, either:

the GDR's. Thinking it over the night before, the Soviet Party Secretary had been inclined to give the East German leader a warning about putting his house in order, and leave it at that. Now, as he watched him fawning and grinning in his expensive overcoat, the Soviet Party Secretary felt inclined to go farther. A purge of the Party in the GDR: nothing else would do.

There remained the problem of West Germany. In some ways, the Soviet Party Secretary found himself wishing that the old days of clear divisions between the power blocs were back again; at least everyone knew where they stood. Now, West Germany seemed to be tilting towards neutrality; and neutrality would be a half-way house to a reunited Germany. The grey helmets and the marching bands seemed endless, as the Party Secretary watched them and gave the occasional obligatory wave. Imagine these men united with the West German army again, he thought. Still, there was nothing for it: the disarmament conference must go ahead, the neutralization of West Germany must be encouraged, and we must hope that our little Party Secretary here, smirking away for his discredited Party newspaper and his discredited television service, will have the strength and the wit to make sure that he isn't swept away by the tide from the West.

At last the parade was over. The Soviet Party Secretary inclined his head slightly to the East German leader, and congratulated him sourly on the show. Then he said, 'You must set a little time apart for a talk after our dinner tonight, comrade. I've got a lot of things to talk to you about.' The East German leader's face became set and anxious. That's the way I like to see you, thought the Soviet Party Secretary. Tonight I'll give you something else to worry about. Then he turned, and walked painfully down the steep wooden steps to the ground. Overhead, the flags snapped in the cold wind, and the smell of the tanks was starting to blow away.

London: Tuesday 9 October

Gregory Stallard had insisted that they walk from the Foreign Office across the river, and all the way down the Westminster Bridge Road to the undistinguished block of glass and concrete where the road divides and becomes St. George's Road. Stallard walked fast, and talked all the time; it gave David Wortham the chance to think about what he would say at the interview he knew was coming. As they passed Lambeth North underground station, Wortham felt that he couldn't keep up the pace any more, and he had to pretend to do up his shoe-lace, while Stallard stood, making an irritable whistling noise through his pursed lips, and tapping the side of his leg with his rolled-up newspaper.

The unexceptional block of glass and concrete called Century House was built – like the KGB headquarters in Dzerzhinsky Square – as an insurance company's headquarters. It has instead become the home of an intelligence organization: the Secret Intelligence Service or DI6. Nothing much distinguishes it from the outside; there is a Mobil petrol station at the side of the forecourt. The only external signs that something other than insurance is dealt with at Century House are the unusually-shaped aerials on the roof and the fact that the windows on the ground floor are all protected from the inside by extendable steel barriers.

Stallard opened the buttons of his British Warm overcoat, and felt in his pocket for the necessary passes. The enquiries desk, manned by five men who had all been sergeant-majors in the army, took some time to negotiate; even though Stallard himself had an office in the building. Finally, after the passes had been written out, the searches finished, and both men had gone through an electronic scanner, Stallard and Wortham, accompanied by one of the sergeant-majors, got into the lift and made their way up to the eighteenth floor. Stallard's office was at the end of the corridor, and was reached through an ante-chamber where a pleasant-faced girl of well-to-do appearance was sitting at a typewriter. On the wall were postcards people had sent her from their holiday resorts, and a photocopied notice that said 'Bugger Work'. Otherwise the room seemed to be inhabited only by grey filing-cabinets.

'Bit better than my hutch at the FO,' said Stallard, complacently, as Wortham looked round him at the Graham Sutherland etchings, on loan from the Department of the Environment, which supplies such things to senior civil servants. There was an ugly portrait by Duncan Grant on the wall opposite Stallard's desk. He particularly liked it. Behind him was a framed Victorian text with the words 'Father Forgive Them' embroidered on it in faded silk. A replica of his Foreign Office coffee percolator stood on a side-table, by the desk. Next to it was a glass-fronted bookcase, filled with copies of White Papers and elderly editions of *Britain*. On top of the bookcase was a broken-backed Victorian novel which needed rebinding, and a gun-metal bust of Lenin. Someone had fixed a made-up bow tie round Lenin's neck.

'Yes,' said Wortham.

Stallard started making some coffee, and while they drank it, Wortham looked out of the window towards the Elephant and Castle, across the expanse of building land which no one had yet started to build on. Sitting where he was, he could see only a corner pub, propped up by wooden posts, the sole survivor of an entire block of houses which had been destroyed. Wortham speculated about the motives of companies which destroyed houses and left an isolated pub on crutches to await the needs of office-workers from the security services.

The aristocratic girl came in. 'H.S.T.D. is on his way now, Mr Stallard.' Accustomed to the uses of bureaucracy, Wortham tried to work out the title the initials stood for; but he gave up on the 'T.' When H.S.T.D. appeared, and the long silence was eventually broken, he proved to be a tall, mild, balding man, who bore a vague resemblance to the bust of Lenin on Stallard's bookcase, except that his bow tie was green and blue, while Lenin's went with a dinner jacket.

'Glad you could come,' said H.S.T.D., looking at him in an almost deferential way.

'Wortham's giving us his complete co-operation now', said Stallard, pointedly.

H.S.T.D. nodded, seriously. 'Good of you,' he said. There was another brief silence, which was only broken when H.S.T.D. looked at them brightly, and rubbed his hands together. 'Well, time to get writing,' he said. He pulled a couple of pieces of foolscap paper from a manilla file he had brought with him.

Wortham wrote as he was told. Occasionally he objected to a phrase, and once they had an argument about a point of Russian grammar, but they allowed him to fill up the second sheet with personal things that they didn't interfere with. It was embarrassing, Wortham thought: like kissing your wife in front of a prison warder. Everything he wrote seemed unnatural and stilted, even in Russian; it breathed a peculiarly English self-consciousness. The other two read it when he had finished, in spite of his brief protest. H.S.T.D. was apologetic, but Stallard simply said, 'Well, that seems to be more or less all right, then. I'll get this to your friend Horwood at the Embassy through the diplomatic bag, and he can pass it on to her through there.'

'This is all pretty cheap stuff, Stallard,' said Wortham, as he sat looking out at the pub in the waste ground.

'Nonsense, my dear chap.' Stallard was in one of his expansive moods. 'Everyone will get what they want, you see. Anyway, you shouldn't complain, you're going to get the best deal of all.' He turned and fiddled with his coffee machine, while H.S.T.D. pretended to re-read the letter.

Wortham stood up. 'You've obliged me to write all this,'

he said, picking his words as carefully and as accurately as possible. 'I must say, all my experience has shown me that the less people like me have to do with people like you, the better.'

Stallard laughed indulgently, his back to Wortham still. H.S.T.D. rubbed his hand over his bald pate. He seemed to want to show he was disclaiming any involvement in the less pleasant side of it all.

Suddenly Stallard turned round again. Something in Wortham's voice had activated his anger. 'Listen, sonny,' he said, his face mottled, 'you're in a spot. Your little girlfriend's in a spot. Who do you think dictated her letter for her? She just signed at the bottom of the page. Now we're doing the same for you, except that we've given you a bit more space to write the things you wanted. Perhaps that's the only difference, but even if it is, you should be damned well grateful.'

Wortham got up to go. Neither of the other men took any notice. He didn't feel there was any point in saying more. The only thing that counted was the letter, and he'd written that. He opened the door into the secretary's office, and started to walk out. The girl looked up, surprised, and as she did so, Stallard's voice came mockingly from the other room. 'You can't get away from the system as easily as all that, my dear chap. We have to get someone to come and let you out.'

Wortham stood and waited in the secretary's office, looking at the postcards from Crete and North Africa, until one of the sergeant-majors came to escort him downstairs. As he left, he heard Stallard's voice talking in a serious monotone to the other man in the room. They had already dismissed Anyuta as a topic of conversation. It was Colonel Modin who interested them now – and they hadn't shown Wortham that letter.

2500 miles away, Modin sat at his tidy desk in Moscow and worried about the whole situation. Was it all going a little too smoothly – the permission for him to go to Vienna on the case, the permission for Anyuta to go, the permission even for Vasily to enter the clinic in Vienna? He could hear Vinogradov's voice telling him to be careful. But then he would, after all, be in the West with the only person who mattered to him – his son. If he couldn't get to safety there, he might as well give up right now. The prizes were too tempting, he thought, as he reached out a hand to tidy an already orderly pile of grey cardboard files.

London: Tuesday 15 November

There was an indefinable charge in the atmosphere. The Chamber of the House of Commons was filling up: there was no longer any room on the green leather benches, and MPs were beginning to crowd the area by the Bar of the House: a white line across a grey carpet. Others were already heading for the seats in the members' galleries. The public gallery, at the far end, was full; so was the press gallery, above and behind the Speaker's chair.

The debate hadn't, so far, been particularly good. The outcome was in doubt, with the Government's majority so small, but disarmament and the question of nuclear deployment was something people judged by sentiment and emotion, not on the basis of knowledge. For five and a half hours, since 3.30, those MPs who foresaw nothing but disaster and holocaust argued for the immediate abandonment of nuclear weapons, and the adoption of a neutralist approach at the forthcoming Vienna conference. Those who foresaw Soviet domination of Europe, east and west, were loud in their demands that the newly-installed Cruise missiles should remain on British soil until the

Russians withdrew their ss-20s and Backfire bombers from Europe. There were few uncommitted people in the House.

Members of the Cabinet began crowding on to the bench on the right of the Speaker. A row of cared-for black shoes shone in the light as their owners rested their feet on the table of the House. The last backbencher ground on, glad to have such an audience, though everything he was saying had been said before.

There was a rustle of appreciation as the shadow minister stood to wind up for his side. He was a pleasant-looking, paunchy Welshman with thinning hair and a freckled face: a wit, and a powerful speaker, but a man who, it was always said, would never quite make it because he lacked the necessary ferocity.

'There is a clear slide towards war,' he intoned, leaning over the brass framing on the despatch box, and tracing the lines of the filigree as he spoke. His voice was becoming more strident, but he was determined to leave the emotional thrust to the end. 'We have seen it in the Gulf, we have seen it in the build-up of armaments on both sides – yes,' he said, as Conservatives started to call out 'What about the Russians?', 'yes, I accept that it's on both sides. The necessity is to break out of the futile cycle, whereby one power uses the threat from the other as a reason, or an excuse, to build up its stocks of these horrific weapons. Cruise and the ss-20 were only the beginning of it. Now we have the prospect, not just of a neutron bomb race, but of a chemical and biological race as well. There can be only one answer, Mr Speaker: these things must be kept out of Europe or there will be nothing but a desert between the Urals and the Atlantic.'

His front bench colleagues leant accross to congratulate him when he set down, and he scarcely heard the Minister's opening remarks. The Minister was in his late fifties, prematurely white haired, and radiated a geniality which disguised a shrewd tactical mind. It was fear of the Soviet

Union, rather than of nuclear destruction, which he evoked. The Government was going to the Vienna conference in a spirit of compromise, but it was essential that the West should not give way to what was nothing short of blackmail by the Soviet Union. The SS-20s and Backfire bombers which were trained on targets in western Europe must be withdrawn or dismantled, before the Cruise missiles stationed in Britain could be withdrawn in their turn. His style was flat, but persuasive – if there had been anyone left to persuade. The danger of unilateral disarmament was that western countries which could no longer defend themselves effectively would inevitably slip into the Soviet sphere of domination. It wouldn't be necessary for Soviet troops to be stationed in Britain, he said, any more than it was for them to be stationed in Finland. But we would be just as effectively neutralized. And the United States would withdraw behind its own national defences.

There had been no new ideas, and few new arguments. The ritual was as fixed as that which followed: the Speaker calling 'Ayes to the right, noes to the left', the policemen on duty in the Members' Lobby calling out 'division' down the corridors, and fixing open the doors; and the division bells ringing in restaurants and some private houses within a quarter-mile radius of the House. The vote was one which the Government couldn't afford to lose, nor the Opposition to give away. The lines stretched out on either side of the Chamber, as people queued to register their vote in the division lobbies. The tellers checked each name on their lists, agreed the total, and then, with the MPs settled in their seats, stood in a line, four abreast, in front of the Speaker. The ritual took its course: the four bowed their heads, stepped another pace forward, and bowed again.

The left-hand teller looked down at the piece of paper he was carrying. 'The Ayes to the Right, two hundred and ninety-six; the Noes to the Left, two hundred and ninety-four.' The noise, suddenly, was deafening. The Government had a majority of two. The cheering and shouting went on, even while the galleries slowly emptied and the Whips got down to the business of working out who had voted in which way. The logic of the system meant that the two MPs who had decided to register their votes in one lobby rather than another had decided the issue. The Government was strengthened in its determination to go to Vienna and demand the withdrawal of Soviet missiles before it would agree to the parallel withdrawal of NATO missiles from British soil.

Chapter 6

The hand that signed the paper felled a city;
Five sovereign fingers taxed the breath,
Doubled the globe of dead and halved a country;
These five kings did a king to death.
Dylan Thomas, *The Hand that Signed the Paper.*

Vienna: Monday 19 November

Just when the officials were starting to get restless, the ornate doors opened, and the leaders and foreign ministers of the countries represented at the European Disarmament Conference trooped in, stiffly and formally. It was a big conference in terms of countries represented: fifteen on the NATO side, and seven on the Warsaw Pact side. Spain and the neutral countries of Europe – Sweden, Finland, Switzerland, Austria and Yugoslavia – were there as observers. But everyone knew there were only three delegations which really counted: the Soviet Union, the United States and West Germany. The rest would have to go along with whatever the three of them decided.

There was the usual confusion, as twenty-eight delegations threaded their way through the room, to find their places at the vast carved cherrywood table, which looked as though it might have done duty at the Congress of Vienna which shaped nineteenth-century Europe, but had, more prosaically, been made for meetings of the customs and tax officials of the Austro-Hungarian Empire; and since even that wasn't large enough to seat the new Congress of Vienna, extra tables had been brought in and placed at either end of the main one. It was ten minutes before everyone was properly seated, and all the necessary adjuncts, from blotters to trays of soft drinks, had been correctly bestowed. Flunkeys in evening dress with gold medallions on heavy chains moved forward to the right shoulder of each of the heads of government at the table, offering them a selection of things rather as the waiters had offered them the flavourless veal at the State banquet somewhere else in the Hofburg palace the evening before. Another flunkey leant over each man's left shoulder, offering him an inkwell as though it were sauce for the veal.

The Soviet Party Secretary disliked these formalities, and was anxious to get through with them. He looked at the American President on the other side of the cherrywood table from him; a careful Austrian secretariat had juggled with the alphabet so as to leave two of the principals face to face. The American President glanced briefly back at him, but there was no answering smile on the President's face. It occurred momentarily to the Soviet Party Secretary that the Americans might have got wind of what he was planning to do; but he dismissed the thought quickly. It had been far too carefully disguised.

The Party Secretary looked along the line beside him: the sombre faces of his Warsaw Pact allies, anxious, many of them, to know what the conference might mean for them, and for their continued running of their countries. Not a man of them, the Party Secretary thought, would survive an uncontrolled election, and in most cases he felt he wouldn't blame the people who threw them out. He, on the other hand, felt himself to be genuinely popular in the Soviet Union; though such things were difficult to judge, he knew, and he was fully aware of the workings of the state's flattery machine. Nobody on the other side of the table looked much more enthusiastic either, he decided; not many of them would have much to hope for from this conference, and scarcely any had confidence in the American President's leadership of them. How much easier, it all was, the Soviet Party Secretary thought, when we knew, each of us, that our side was right, and that we were winning. It's the habit of doubting the ends that causes us to have second thoughts about the means; both we and the West would happily go back to the days of Stalin and Truman, when the lines were clearly drawn. Or am I just feeling my age, and regretting the days when I had real energy?

The cameramen came in, with an explosion of confused noise. Almost immediately, the harassed officials lost control of them, as they darted round the long H-shaped arrangement of tables, each looking for the best shots of his own country's head of government, and of the Soviet and American leaders as well. There was a good deal of pushing and shoving. A Chinese camera team, which had somehow been accredited, created more noise and ill-feeling by shining monstrous portable arc-lamps into everyone else's lens. The stills cameras got in the way of the television ones, and vice versa. And in the middle of the confusion, the Soviet Party Secretary suddenly stood up, and started to walk slowly and purposefully round the table. At first the Austrian officials tried to hustle the cameramen out of the room, but the prospect of a more interesting kind of shot than was usually available at a formal photo-call encouraged most of them to stand their ground. The Party Secretary ignored the cameras, walking right past them, until he reached the far side of the table from his own seat. Then he stopped, beside the chair of the American President. For a second, even the cameramen were quiet.

'We should begin our meeting by showing that we are friends,' he said, in a strongly-accented English. The President glanced round, startled by what was happening.

He looked quickly at the Secretary of State beside him, whose blank look was instantly captured by the cameras. Then the President slowly stood up, and turned to face the Soviet Party leader. He was not a man who liked to give away the initiative quite so easily, but it was clearly impossible for him to do anything else. He took the Soviet Party Secretary's outstretched hand and shook it; and then he found himself gripped by the other man's free arm, and forced into a powerful bear hug. From all around the room, there was a sudden outbreak of applause at the theatrical gesture. Even some of the cameramen called out, enthusiastically.

But if they had had the leisure to turn their cameras away from the President and the Party Secretary, and towards one or two of the other leaders sitting round the table, they would have had a clear picture of their feelings as well. The West German Chancellor seemed delighted, and joined enthusiastically in the clapping. But the French President didn't. And not far from him, both the British Prime Minister and the British Foreign Secretary looked worried, and the Prime Minister leant across and whispered something in the Foreign Secretary's ear.

Vienna: Monday 19 November

From the moment Anyuta set eyes on Mrs Gribanova, she knew that she belonged to the type she most despised and disliked – the New Class, the grasping, corrupt élite who used their opportunity for contact with the West to feather their nests at the State's expense. Anyuta had little time for her own husband, having dismissed him in her sweeping, irreparable, cruel way as nothing more than a slave of the bureaucracy. At least he wasn't corrupt in the same way. He enjoyed the chance to get things from the West, but there was none of the calculating lustfulness about him that marked out people like Gribanova; he reserved that, she thought ruefully, for his pursuit of advancement within the structure. There was nothing he wouldn't do, no moral line he wasn't prepared to cross, to further his career. But at least it was his career he was pursuing; not some new electronic gadget to go with the television, which might not work in the Soviet Union, and was intended solely to impress other members of the New Class.

Anyuta stared hard into the window of a jeweller's shop, to avoid having to speak to Gribanova about what they were going to do next. Anyuta had been outside the Soviet Union twice before, once to Cuba to accompany her husband, and once to Romania for a holiday with her parents. She had never seen shops like the ones here in the Mariahilferstrasse, and there were moments when she was prepared almost to understand the desires of a Gribanova. The little group of Soviet wives moved on slowly, and their chatter became more and more intolerable for Anyuta. As she tried experimentally to think herself into the mind of a westerner, they sounded so provincial. She remembered how David Wortham had once accused her of being a metropolitan snob, and although it had annoyed her at the time, she now accepted that there was some truth in it. She could imagine the picture they must all be presenting to outsiders: vulgar, wondering, impressed, dowdy. She was wearing an expensive fur jacket, but in the gentle drizzle that was starting to fall she realized that not even that looked particularly smart. She felt deeply envious of the passers-by she saw: people to whom all of this was an ordinary part of life, people who didn't feel drawn to every shop window as if the things on display were museum-pieces.

Gribanova called out a peremptory little warning to Anyuta not to hang back. She was the group leader, the one among them who knew all about living in the West. Her husband was counsellor at the Soviet Embassy in Vienna; all the other women in the party of six were visitors from Moscow. Obediently, they gathered round her, Anyuta hanging at the back.

'We shall now go into that department store,' she said, pointing to a long row of glittering windows on the other side of the road: the Herzmansky Kaufhaus. The eyes of the six, Anyuta included, followed her assertive wave. 'For me, at least, it's the best Vienna has to offer. You'll find the prices outrageous, after Moscow, but at least the quality is reasonable.' Anyuta thought there were so many points being scored there that she could scarcely keep up with the final total.

'Do they charge us to go in?' she asked, mischievously. Gribanova started to answer, then decided that Anyuta was deliberately trying to needle her.

'Yes, do they?' asked Mrs Morozova, a gentle, stout woman with a permanently anxious expression.

'Vera Grigorevna, I can assure you that I have never had to pay to go into any store in the West. Once or twice in Paris the shop people tried to ask for it, but I personally never gave them anything.'

'Perhaps they just wanted a deposit,' said Anyuta. She could see that Gribanova's patronizing ways were getting on the nerves of some of the other women as well. Gribanova shepherded them across the road.

Anyuta found herself growing more and more tense. She knew that if she were to get away from Gribanova, it would have to be done at Herzmansky's. She had assumed that they would at some stage tour the department stores as well as the small shops around the Stephansdom, and she had worked out in her own mind that it would be far easier to escape among the crowds indoors than in the open street. The letter from Wortham had left it entirely up to her, as to when and how she should escape. All he had said was that he would meet her in Room III at the Albertina Gallery at eleven; and if she weren't there, he would wait for her until she arrived, even if it meant sleeping in the gallery for a week. She smiled at the thought; and then the anxiety about getting away crowded in on her again. It was such a final act, leaving her husband and her country and her politics; and simply walking away from a small group of badly-dressed Soviet women would achieve it.

As they walked into the store, and the hot air which acted as a door enveloped her and made her clothes billow around her, she thought briefly of the damage she would do to her husband. Did she hate him that much? she wondered. Still, those who live by politics and intrigue must face the prospect of dying by them, she thought. Such a thing had never happened in her husband's circle before, as far as she knew, but if it had, and there had been a centimetre of advantage for him in it, he would have used the occasion with complete ruthlessness. She thought of him for the last time: poor Kostya, he's just about to discover what it's like to be on the messy side of a scandal. Then she dismissed him from her mind, and turned to the business of making her own way in the world.

She had seen nothing like the store in her life. She often went to the Beriozka stores in Moscow to spend the certificate roubles her husband received as part of his salary. The choice was reasonable; a great deal better, certainly, than ordinary Soviet citizens even dreamt about. But it was mostly manufactured in one or other of the socialist countries, and apart from fur coats like the one she was wearing, and a certain amount of jewellery, Anyuta thought the only thing worth buying was the vodka. Herzmansky's was a completely different experience. The atmosphere of ordered calm, of affluence, of service, the faint awareness of perfume in the air, all worked on her powerfully.

People seemed to be almost as rude as in Moscow, she thought, but at least they weren't pushing because they thought the supply might run out before they reached the head of the queue. In the crowd, the obedient group of Soviet women was gradually forced to separate. Anyuta saw Gribanova's self-indulgent figure a little way ahead of her, and she thought it would be sensible if she stuck with her for a little. It would make Gribanova less suspicious when the time came for making the break; though she had detected no sign whatever of suspicion. Gribanova had simply been given orders to make sure that the group was protectively steered around the shops; she wasn't there as their gaoler. Regretfully, Anyuta decided that Gribanova probably wouldn't even get into trouble when it became known that one of her charges had defected.

Now that the moment was getting nearer, Anyuta found it hard to make up her mind precisely what she should do. A boyfriend of hers had once escaped from the militia in Moscow by dodging into GUM and crouching down in one of the small shops that make up the store, until the militiamen had passed; he had pretended that he'd hurt his ankle, but that would scarcely work here. She listened for a little to Gribanova's voice telling her patronizingly about buying silk scarves. For once in her life, she had to forego the opportunity to deflate mindless pomposity and greed. She murmured an occasional 'Yes' or 'Really?', which kept Gribanova happy. She even asked her advice about what colours to look for. And when Mrs Morozova got into difficulties because she wanted to buy something for her daughter, and couldn't make the assistant understand, it was Anyuta who noticed that she was missing, and who guided Gribanova back to rescue her.

The moment came, among the kitchen gadgets in the basement. The crowd was certainly thinner, but Anyuta noticed a ladies' lavatory nearby, and all the others in the party, including Gribanova, were interested in a West German food-blender which was being demonstrated at one of the counters. Anyuta held back as the others crowded round for a better look, and then walked purposefully across to the lavatory. A quick look showed her that no one in the Soviet group had noticed that she had gone. She made her way quickly into one of the booths, and sat down on the seat to think things over. She was still not finally committed. If they found her there, she could easily make a convincing excuse. All the same, she would have to stay in the lavatory for a good long time to be really safe. It occurred to her now that it would have been much more sensible if she had shown a particular interest in something on a different floor, so that Gribanova might assume she had gone back there.

As she sat and waited, a more practical idea came to her. It would, she decided, be better if she unlocked the door. Nothing was more suspicious than a locked lavatory door and complete silence. The thought made her giggle, but she undid the lock, leaving the door almost shut. A second later, the outer door to the ladies' opened, and Gribanova's voice suggested loudly that she might be in there. Anyuta sat, very still, as Gribanova and whoever was with her called her name.

Then she heard the footsteps going to the end of the block of a dozen or so cubicles, and it flashed through Anyuta's mind that Gribanova was going to look underneath the line of cubicle walls for the tell-tale sign of feet. Sitting on the lavatory, she held her legs out straight in front of her, hoping that the inspection wouldn't last too long. Almost as she did so, she heard Gribanova grunt, some way away, and pictured her kneeling painfully on the floor, her corset cutting into her ample stomach, looking for a couple of Muscovite legs in a Viennese lavatory. Anyuta had already begun to fashion it into a story that would make David Wortham crease up with laughter. She could see his face as she told him.

The grunting stopped, and Gribanova suggested they try upstairs. Anyuta had at least half an hour to wait, she thought. The time went very slowly; and now that she had begun to allow herself to think about being with Wortham again, the time seemed to pass slower still. It was already gone eleven; suppose he couldn't wait for her, and she found herself alone in the city? Then she remembered the letter. 'I don't care how long I have to wait for you.' It was a promise. She thought briefly about the promises he had once made to his wife, and was now breaking. Still, Anyuta had made promises of her own.

She hadn't always played fair with Wortham, she thought; but she had used the system – the KGB and all the rest of them – and bent it to her own will. She had seemed to be going along with what they wanted, while making them help her do what she wanted. Only the final result in a deal shows who has made the profit, she thought; and the profit was going to be hers.

She looked at her watch. It was eleven-thirty-five. She came cautiously out of the cubicle, washed her hands, and then walked boldly through the door and into the store itself. There was no sign of Gribanova or any of the others. Anyuta made her way quickly to the emergency exit in the far corner of the basement. It might be difficult, she thought, to find her way back to the main street, the Mariahilferstrasse, which would lead her to the Albertina and her appointment with Wortham.

It had never occurred to her to watch out for the stocky, grey-haired figure of Colonel Modin, who with the utmost patience had been examining machines for cutting carrots and peeling potatoes for the whole time Anyuta had spent in the lavatory. Nearby, one of his men was comparing the prices of pressure-cookers. Modin felt completely at ease. This was the kind of operation he understood. He was confident that the plan would go smoothly. Experience had taught him that you worked for your luck, and he had put a great deal of work into the plan. He had obtained permission to bring his son Vasily with him to Vienna, and his office had allowed him to head the operation against David Wortham. That meant the KGB could know nothing of the affair; Vinogradov must have kept quiet out of friendship for him. The difficult part was getting to Vienna in the first place. From now on, it was going to be like any other operation he had carried out; except that at the end of it he would be staying in the West. And so would Vasily.

He and the man who had been examining the pressure-cookers followed Anyuta at a careful distance up the emergency stairs, and through the door into the open street. Anyuta's tall, slim figure was clearly visible a couple of dozen metres ahead. They settled into the familiar pattern of street-shadowing, without needing to say anything to one another.

Vienna: Monday 19 November

The tables in the open area in the centre of the ground floor of the Vienna Hilton were filled with American journalists who were waiting for the first briefing of the morning, on the opening ceremony a mile or so away at the Hofburg. Others had been out with the President's wife, on her trip to look at the Stephansdom; their pooled reports were available within half an hour of her return: what she wore, who presented her with what, how she had reacted.

It was at 11.30, ninety minutes after the Hofburg conference had opened, that the pleasant Viennese English of the hotel's telephone announcer broke into the quiet atmosphere to announce that the Soviet press delegate had arrived to give a briefing about the Warsaw Pact's position on the conference. Even the best-served journalists in the world are a prey to curiosity; and soon only a very few men and women were left at the tables to wait for the possible early arrival of the President's press secretary. The rest pushed their way into the conference room which the White House had booked for the use of the journalists, and the few people who were already working away at early stories politely stopped typing so that the sleek, rather podgy man who stood on the platform at the far end of the room could be heard. Not far from him stood two younger versions of himself – well dressed, well fed, well educated. In their arms they carried large piles of typed documents.

'First, before we talk any further,' said the man on the platform, 'my colleagues here will pass around copies of the initiative which the Soviet Union has this morning put before the Conference on Disarmament. You might prefer to look at it, before asking me any questions. Oh, by the way,' he said, with well-rehearsed carelessness, 'I should have introduced myself. I am, like yourselves, a journalist; my name is Mikhailov, Ilya Mikhailov, and I work for the Novosti Press Agency.'

His English was flawless, and his accent superb. But in the front of the conference room, at least, no one was paying any attention to him. There were gasps and whistles of amazement from the journalists there who had got their copies of the hand-out and were reading it. Hearing the noise, the journalists at the back started to push forward to get copies of their own. Already some of the Americans, particularly the ones who worked for news agencies, were running out to file the details of the initiative. From his platform, Mikhailov looked down with amusement. He was a man who enjoyed creating an effect.

The questions began.

'Are you, in Moscow, really offering to demilitarize Cuba?'

'The Soviets are calling for an American withdrawal from continental Europe, is that right?'

'What happens to the two Germanies? Will they be free to unite together, if they want?'

'Gentleman, gentlemen,' said Mikhailov, laughing, 'I'm

sorry to say that I cannot take in all your questions at once, let alone answer them. Perhaps it would be easier if I first summarized the Soviet *démarche*, and then answered your questions one at a time after that.' There was a general mutter of approval.

'Following the danger to the future of the entire world, created by the extremely rash decision of the United States to invade Saudi Arabia after its people had risen to overthrow the reactionary régime there, the Soviet Union felt it was a matter of great urgency to devise some way to defuse the situation. This conference is the result.' Mikhailov waved aside the interruptions and went on. 'But it is not enough to meet. We must have some constructive suggestions to make as well. As a result the Soviet Union and her allies have come forward with the most far-reaching plan for world peace which has been proposed since the war.'

At this point Mikhailov, aware that the slightest deviation from the official text could cause difficulties, pulled out a pair of glasses which his vanity had prevented him from displaying before, and started to read from the prepared notes he had brought.

'The Soviet Union and its allies propose that both the German Democratic Republic and the Federal Republic of Germany should cease to be members of their respective military alliances, and that both parts of Germany should become a nuclear-free zone. American and Soviet nuclear weapons should be withdrawn to their respective national territories. The Soviet Union further proposes that United States conventional forces should be withdrawn from other countries in continental Europe; and that Soviet military forces should be withdrawn from the Republic of Cuba: all withdrawals to be staged over three years, commencing January 1st next year.'

Mikhailov finished reading. He appreciated the slickness of the public relations operation which, for once, the Soviet

Union had organized. The proposals would be on all the morning news bulletins on the East Coast long before Washington could get together even a satisfactory holding reply, he thought complacently. We'll achieve a tactical lead which with luck the American administration won't match. The clincher is the offer over Cuba; they'll never reject that. He looked around at the faces of the journalists, as they stopped writing and stared up at him.

'Now, do you by any chance have any questions?'

Chapter 7

About suffering they were never wrong,
The Old Masters: how well they understood
Its human position; how it takes place
While someone else is eating or opening a window or just waking
dully along.

W. H. Auden, *Musée des Beaux Arts.*

Vienna: Monday 19 November

They had been over it all so many times that Wortham felt obliged, eventually, to break away and go and look at the Rembrandt etchings in the room where they had told Anyuta to come. Wortham disliked his ally in the arrangement intensely. James Dudley was a supercilious man, slightly younger than himself, whose striking good looks were just starting to fade. He was the SIS resident in Vienna, and the case-officer supplied by London. Wortham would have preferred Stallard, but so far he had done his best to put up with Dudley, without showing the resentment and irritation he felt. Now he couldn't bear to be patronized any longer. He hoped to dissipate the pressure by immersing himself for a little in the atmosphere created by Rembrandt's silent, gentle, melancholy etchings.

It didn't work: Dudley's braying voice, as he chatted to

Black, the ex-SAS corporal who had come with them as escort, broke in continually. The thoughtful interiors, the outlandish Biblical scenes, the studies of Saskia and Titus and old men in turbans, couldn't compete, and Wortham found himself listening to Dudley and the corporal, as they chatted desultorily about skiing. Black was a strong, saturnine man, with dark hair and heavy eyebrows over bright blue eyes. His conversation was filled with people who had been forced, eventually, to bend themselves to his will, or his views. Dudley's conversation was mostly scathing. From time to time other people would walk into the room, and Black would examine them tensely while Dudley pretended to look at the pictures on the wall. They had long ceased to take any notice of the old attendant, who sat on a gilded chair in the corner. There seemed to be none of the stratified relationship between the two of them which normally marks ex-soldiers and ex-officers in Britain; working for a secret organization seemed to have created a familiarity between them, as if they belonged to a rugby club. How intolerable, Wortham thought, that even matters of security should be treated by the British as though they were some form of sport, complete with rules and opposing teams. He bent closely to look at a tiny nativity, where a peasant girl cradled a baby, and local tradesmen gathered round as if they were welcoming a civic dignitary.

Anyuta had been sent a photocopy of a map of the old quarter of Vienna by Wortham and she had committed to memory such extra detail as she had been able to extract from an elderly *Michelin* guide in German which someone had bought for the Soviet Embassy. She was reasonably clear what would happen when the Mariahilferstrasse turned into the Babenbergerstrasse, and then ran at right-angles into the Burgring. In the thickening drizzle it was hard to see too far ahead, but she guessed that the elaborate grey nineteenth-century building that lay in front and to the right must be the Neue Hofburg, and that if she struck out across the Burggarten she would reach the end of the Albertina building, where she would find the entrance.

Her face was thoroughly wet now, and her clothes were being soaked layer by layer, in the fine drifting rain. Her feet sent out little half-circles of rain with each step she took. She felt entirely free; the freedom of someone who has gone too far for recall. An occasional shaft of panic would cut through her, but she knew that there could be no acceptable explanations now. There was nothing for it but to go on through the rain. A cyclist went past her in bright yellow oilskins as she waited to cross the Burgring, the rain forming a dew-drop at the end of his nose, which caught the light for an instant and then fell away with the wind and the motion of pedalling; a driver jerkily wiped the condensation from the inside of his windscreen with the back of his hand. She waited obediently for the pedestrian lights to go green, and crossed the road, bringing with her the two powerfully built figures who had followed her from the Mariahilferstrasse: men who looked almost like brothers as they walked one behind her and the other parallel with her on the other side of the road. Modin knew where they were going; but he was anxious that Anyuta should arrive at the Albertina a moment or two before him.

Wortham made his way around the room. By now he could scarcely take in the details of any more etchings. He looked at his watch. It was past 11.30. Dudley and Black were standing idly together near the doorway into the next room of the exhibition, where the drawings by Rubens were displayed. It seemed absurd to Wortham that they should all three be clustered together in the same room, and he went across to Dudley and broke into the conversation to tell him so. Dudley seemed annoyed. He pushed back the cuff of his shirt with a finger to see what the time was. The elephant-hair bracelet he wore round his wrist tangled with the watchstrap.

'No harm in sending Bob down to the main staircase if you want, I suppose,' he said. 'No need to panic, though. Everything's in hand.' Bob took that for an order, and walked out in the direction of the entrance. There was something about his bearing, Wortham thought, that inspired precisely the kind of confidence that Dudley somehow undermined. 'Don't worry, chum,' whispered Dudley. 'I've done dozens of these jobs. Simple as pie. You've just been reading too many spy-novels. It's not like that at all, you know.'

Wortham turned away and said nothing. The room started to fill up a little with tourists for whom one etching was much like another. The advantage was that they kept moving. Only Dudley and Wortham stood there, in the middle of the room, watching the others. Dudley undid his tweed overcoat and complained about the heat. It was the first sign of strain Wortham had detected in him.

Anyuta stamped her feet as she walked up the stone steps of the Albertina, almost as if she were trying to get rid of the snow of Moscow on them. The violent excitement which had flared up in her more than once since the escape from the Soviet group had now given way to a deep pessimism: a certainty that somehow it was all just a mistake, a misunderstanding, that she was now adrift, without friends or covering, that she had committed herself too strongly and would pay the penalty. In these last moments she scarcely even thought of Wortham; for a moment, indeed, she wondered whether he existed. To keep herself calm, as she came to the end of the passage where the exhibition began, she stopped briefly and flicked through the posters which were on display in big wooden racks. Then she paid her ten schillings and walked into the first room of the exhibition, swallowing nervously to try to dispel the dryness of her throat.

Behind her, Colonel Modin had reached the top of the echoing stairs, and was walking fast to catch up with her. He had sent the man who had shadowed Anyuta to one possible exit, and the other two GRU men who had been waiting for them at the entrance to the Albertina to another. He had brought them with him because to have come alone might have aroused suspicion. Now all three would be out of the way. Modin checked his watch: Vasily should be entering the clinic in the south of Vienna in thirty minutes.

Wortham for his part had stopped believing that Anyuta would come, some time before. Perhaps tomorrow at eleven, he thought; that had been London's arrangement, prepare for a rendezvous between eleven and one each day of the conference; though he would stay all day if necessary. Perhaps she never will come; I have no guarantee that she's even in Vienna, he thought. For the sake of doing something, he walked over to where Dudley was standing, glowering at the tourists and sweating in the brown overcoat he refused to take off. Wortham started to say something, when Dudley interrupted him. 'Looks like your little piece of fluff has just walked in, old boy.'

It seemed to take Wortham a long time to turn. As he did so, he heard Anyuta shout out to him from the doorway. The attendant, scandalized, stood up and began to call in a strained old voice for silence. Wortham found himself pushing through the latest group of sightseers, trying to reach her, while another couple of attendants crowded in to see who was doing the shouting.

'Over here, Dudley,' Wortham started to say, but he saw

as he turned that Dudley wasn't looking at Anyuta at all, but at the stocky, grey-haired man in his fifties who was standing in the doorway. Anyuta, too, turned to stare at Modin. She felt she should have been surprised to see him there, but there was a certain inevitability in his appearance.

'Have you got anything to prove to me who you are?' asked Dudley. The four of them were clustered together near the doorway of the exhibition room. Behind them, Black was talking soothingly to the chief attendant. Anyuta thought Dudley was speaking to her, but it quickly became clear to her, as it had to Wortham a few seconds earlier, that Dudley's only interest was in Colonel Modin.

Modin's voice came huskily out of his heavy chest as he pulled a plastic card from his wallet. 'I have an identification.' It was said in a whisper. The noise from the other people in the room covered the sounds they were making. No one noticed that Anyuta and Wortham were standing, simply looking at each other and smiling. In the outer room, Black had established friendly relations with the chief attendant, and was clapping him on the shoulder.

'Good lad,' he said, in English.

'Well,' said Dudley, in a satisfied voice, speaking for once at his normal level. 'That seems to be that. We've all got what we were after. Especially you, old boy,' he added, as he looked appraisingly at Anyuta.

Vienna: Monday 19 November

The conference had broken up in confusion directly the Soviet Party Secretary announced his initiative. The Americans, in particular, were anxious to formulate their own views on the Soviet offer at top speed. The Secretary of State was in a hurry to get off to his Embassy, not far away, but he felt obliged to have a word with the only man he counted as a personal friend in any of the other western delegations – the British Foreign Secretary.

The two men stood near the window of a small ante-chamber which had been assigned to the British as part of their suite at the Hofburg Palace. The room was cold, and the Secretary of State had his overcoat on.

'So what do you think?' The British Foreign Secretary poured out two generous glasses of malt whisky. The Secretary of State swirled the liquid around in his glass for a moment, as though it was going to make a pattern that he could read.

'Jim, I just can't say. But you must recognize that it's got its attractive side.'

The Foreign Secretary looked up at the ceiling and saw, without thinking about it, that the nineteenth-century moulding ran round only three sides of the room. On the fourth side the moulding ran into a partition wall. As he thought about the Soviet offer, the Foreign Secretary also tried to work out what size the original room would have been, before it was converted.

'You'd really agree to pull out of places like Belgium?'

'Sure we would. Why ever not? Most of those guys have to pay their cops overtime every weekend just to keep the crowds out of the US Embassy. It'd be the most popular thing since Marshall Aid. Jim, I don't know, really I don't. It's up to the President. But what I would say is that it runs very much along the kind of lines his own thinking does, especially since Saudi. My guess is, he'll haggle over it and agree to a cut-down version. With Cuba included. That's a powerful plus for any US President, you know, to clear the Russians out of Cuba. John Kennedy never made it.' There was a silence which the Foreign Secretary only broke because he wanted to keep the Secretary of State from leaving.

'And us?'

'Listen, Jim, this isn't a good time for being sentimental. Britain, as far as we're concerned, is washed up. Nice place, Stratford-on-Avon, Speakers' Corner, all that crap. But there aren't any English votes in the States. The President knows that whatever happens, you've got to hang in there with us.'

'And what happens if the pressures inside Britain – the social and the political pressures, you know – get so bad that we just have to tell you to get out? That could happen?'

'Well, you know my feelings. I'm just telling you what the President's going to say when I put the same things to him. What does he care? Believe me, when you've got the troubles he's got, the idea of feeding someone else into the grinder – someone nice and small and quiet like Britain – isn't going to bother him any. It'll bother me, it'll bother a lot of other people. But not enough to show up in any opinion polls.'

The Secretary of State stood up and shifted the coat on his shoulders to make it sit better. 'Thanks for the malt,' he said.

'Thanks for the comfort.'

When the Secretary of State went out, the Foreign Secretary stayed where he was, staring out of the window at the park outside. It looked very cold. A plane tree stood on the edge of the park nearest to the window, its bark flaked away, its branches denuded of leaves. That's going to be us soon, the Foreign Secretary thought: dead and alone.

Vienna: Monday 19 November

Wortham found it impossible to say anything, either to Anyuta or to Dudley. He realized he hadn't said a word since she'd appeared. He could scarcely believe that, after all, the ramshackle plan had worked. It was obvious now to him that there had been more in the deal than he had known: the handsome, formidable-looking Russian was plainly the prize Dudley had been after, and in some way Anyuta had brought him with her. Well, he thought, so be it; as long as she stays.

'And what does your wife say about all this?' Anyuta's question, the first words she had addressed to him, was typically cool and sardonic.

'I'll have to break it to her,' he said, heavily.

'And one day you'll have to give the same news to me, I suppose.' Wortham knew there was only one way to deal with Anyuta when she was in that mood. He searched briefly for something funny to say.

Just as he opened his mouth to say it, there was a sudden movement behind him. He turned, and saw that several of the sightseers who had somehow managed to ignore what had been happening, were moving away in fright from a man standing near the far corner of the room. He had brought out a machine-pistol, and was angrily motioning everybody to one side, so that he could have a clear field of fire towards Wortham and the others. It happened too quickly for any of them, even Modin and Dudley, who were trained for such things, to do anything about it. Another man with a machine-pistol was also standing nearer to the middle of the room; Wortham hadn't noticed either of them before. The attendant started to say something, then stopped in mid-syllable. In the stillness footsteps could be heard coming in from the farther room. As the man walked in, Modin had the feeling that he had known all along who it would be; though it was, perhaps, a trick of the mind. The man walked across the room, ignoring the two groups of tourists and the gunmen who had frozen them with their command. He stopped, a little way from Modin.

'My dear friend,' said Vinogradov, 'I did try to warn you that they were looking for a scapegoat, and you didn't take any notice. You're an idiot, Nikolai Fedorovich, and it gives me no pleasure at all to tell you so.'

Once again, there was silence. Then Dudley, with remarkable self-possession, said, 'You might tell me what it is you're saying.'

Vinogradov's English was nearly perfect. 'I apologize, Mr – Dudley, is it? We work for complementary organizations, Nikolai Fedorovich and I, and I'm afraid I shall have to borrow him back from you.'

Dudley said, 'None of us have guns. I really think you're causing an unnecessary scene by having your two friends there pointing those things at us. People here don't like that kind of thing, you know: it gets noticed.'

Vinogradov laughed, but didn't do anything about the guns.

'Well,' said Dudley, rather more loudly, 'I think you and I might as well get out of their line of fire for a moment and talk it over.'

Vinogradov smiled, and started to say something. At that moment, Black appeared at the doorway, a .45 revolver in his clasped hands. He steadied his arm for a fraction of a second, then fired at one of the KGB gunmen. The silencer, which made the gun absurdly long, reduced the sound of the discharge to a hollow slapping sound. The KGB man was thrown back against the wall, his throat welling blood.

The second gunman began to swing round towards Black, standing in the doorway, but fractionally too slowly. His alarmed face still registered the first shock, and he was unsighted by two of the tourists. A woman let out a low moan of fear and an attendant in the next room called out to ask if there was any trouble. No one had the time to answer him. Wortham grabbed hold of Anyuta, and pushed in front of her, so that he faced the KGB man. Anyuta put her arms round him and held him fast.

Dudley laughed. 'Looks as though we've got as far as we reasonably can,' he said. Vinogradov, whose face had not registered any sign of emotion, nodded. Modin simply stood where he had been standing all along. The two gunmen, one on one side of the group of tourists, the other on the other, searched for an advantage and couldn't find one.

'I suggest,' said Vinogradov, in a casual enough voice, 'that we each ask our colleague with the gun to put it in his pocket.'

'Perhaps you might like to do it first?' said Dudley.

Vinogradov smiled. 'Or at the same time,' he said.

Each of them spoke, and the guns disappeared. Immediately people started talking, and the woman who had moaned slipped down on to the floor in a faint, and lay there in an untidy heap of coat and handbag and camera straps. Black started moving everyone tactfully into the next room, taking care to keep someone between him and the KGB man the whole time and ignoring the woman on the floor.

Vinogradov and Dudley moved over to one corner of the room, and stood there talking under a pen and wash drawing of Saskia.

'There's no reason really why we shouldn't both get what we want,' said Vinogradov smoothly. 'I am here mostly for the girl. She is the wife of a very senior officical – we can't let her go, there would be a scandal. But as for Modin, I don't really care. He's GRU, as you know. My only orders are to make sure the GRU is thoroughly discredited, which will allow my service to resume its normal dominance over it. The GRU will be just as discredited if he goes off with you, as if he comes back with us. You're welcome to squeeze anything you like out of him about the GRU – tomorrow I don't suppose such a service will exist. But we must take the girl.'

Dudley was confident. 'If that's the bargain you want, you can have it, with pleasure. I don't give a toss about the girl any more; she's simply been the hook to catch old Modin there. Very successful it was, too.'

'My congratulations, then, Mr Dudley. It's been great

doing business with you; or would you prefer I expressed myself in more English English?' Dudley grinned. They walked side by side to where the others were standing. None of them had moved. Dudley spoke first. 'The girl goes with the Russians. The man stays with us. Let's go.'

Wortham felt Anyuta's arms tighten round him, and he held tightly on to her with his own arms. 'Anyone who tries,' he began to say. But Black, at a wave from Dudley, pulled her away, towards the KGB man, who had finally come across the room. He grabbed her arms, and pushed her out of the room before Wortham or Anyuta could say or do anything. Anyuta started to call out something, but her words were cut short.

Wortham stood watching stupidly. He felt as though the whole thing were happening at the end of a long tunnel or in only two dimensions. He looked round him at the shocked faces and then back at the wall, at the small drawing of a peasant nativity which another man had examined closely in another life, a long time ago. It seemed a lot more real than his own experience.

Vinogradov started to walk out of the gallery, following his men and Anyuta. As he reached the doorway, he turned and looked at Modin.

'I did try to warn you, you know,' he said. His hands were hidden. There was a sharp explosion from his right pocket and Modin fell to the floor, his face and head a bloody ruin.

Before Black could get to his .45, Vinogradov fired an arc of bullets through the air, burning out the front of his overcoat, and punching neat holes through several of the etchings on the wall. There was screaming as the glass tinkled to the ground, and Vinogradov ran out and down the corridor that led to the main stairs. Black started to follow, but Dudley called him back. It was Wortham who ran out after Vinogradov, dodging once as the Russian fired a short burst from the machine-pistol which had killed Modin. Wortham reached the top of the stairs as

Vinogradov got to the main door, colliding with a group of people who were just starting to come in. The delay cut Vinogradov's lead to a mere five yards, and then Wortham was in among the group, pushing them violently out of his way as they squealed and protested.

Now they were out in the open, Vinogradov was less willing to use his gun. In the narrow roadway stood a large black Mercedes, with its engine running and the nearside rear door open. Anyuta and the other KGB man were already inside. Vinogradov leaped in, and the car began to pick up speed; but Wortham had moved across the pavement at an angle and flung himself across the front of the car as it roared away.

Momentarily, the driver was blinded by Wortham's body, spread out against the windscreen, but he swung the car from side to side and then slammed on the brakes. Wortham's hold, precarious anyway, slipped completely, and he fell off to the side of the car, following the direction of its lurch. He heard Anyuta's voice scream something at him through the open window, and he had time as the driver turned the key violently to start the stalled engine to get to his feet. The Mercedes picked up speed as it headed towards the Opera House, but for fifty yards or so Wortham kept up with it, running behind, with other cars hooting at him as they swerved. Anyuta's face, ugly and white, stared out at him, her mouth wide open in a shout, as he began to fall back, his heart and lungs weakening under the strain, his chest heaving, his legs unable to carry him any more. The Mercedes pulled away from him and he was left, an isolated figure, out of his element, in the middle of the traffic, slowing to a walk, careless of whether he was knocked down or not. People shouted warnings at him as he walked along the road following the same direction as the Mercedes which was now a quarter of a mile away. Once a car nearly hit him, and went shrieking off, its horn blaring.

Ahead of him he saw a park. He walked dully over to it and sprawled out on a bench, exhausted and drained of emotion. His sense of the whole affair was reduced to a few images, each imposed on the other: Modin's wheeling body, Vinogradov's tense crouch as he fired, Anyuta's white face, trying to scream some message to him. And the etching, of a peasant nativity, shredded by the bullets.

Wortham sat slumped on the bench for a long time. Finally, without any clear idea why, he got up, his mind empty of thoughts, and walked slowly back through the park, past the empty bandstand. As he went the rooks called out harshly in the wet, bare branches of the trees.